.32

Return to Embthwaite Farm

Return to Embthwaite Farm

A Mowbray Sisters Romance

Kate Hewitt

TULE
PUBLISHING

Return to Embthwaite Farm

Tule Publishing First Printing, September 2023

The Tule Publishing, Inc.

First Publication by Tule Publishing 2023

Cover design by Rhian

ISBN: 978-1-961544-02-4

Dedication

To all the lovely readers in my Kate's Reads Facebook group.
You are such a wonderful community and encouragement!

Chapter One

THE UNKNOWN NUMBER making her mobile buzz insistently had the area code from home. Rachel Mowbray squinted in the hard glare of the bright Ibiza sunlight as she glanced down at the unfamiliar number and wondered whether she should answer it. Did she really want to hear from anyone in the 01653 dialling code? The truth was, not particularly.

She switched her phone to silent and slipped it into the oversize straw bag leaning against her sun lounger. This was the first proper holiday she'd had in several years, and it was only her second day of it. The knots between her shoulders had yet to loosen, and last night she'd been too exhausted to hang out by the beach bar as she'd intended and so she'd gone to bed at ten-thirty after a single mojito. Hardly the knees-up, hair-down scenario she'd been hoping for herself, but that would come in time. She had five more days here in the sun, after all.

In her bag her phone buzzed again, quietly, like a trapped wasp. Rachel closed her eyes and leaned her head back against the plastic slats of her lounger. The sunlight shimmered on her closed lids, and she could hear the gentle lapping of the sea, the distant laughter of some children playing on the beach…and the buzz of her phone.

For heaven's *sake.*

She took a deep breath and opened her eyes, the dazzle of the sun on the water blinding her for a second. Her phone was still ringing. Whoever was trying to call her was being annoyingly persistent. A flicker of worry licked at her insides, and she immediately squashed it. If it was anything important, she would recognise the number, and really, the only person who would be calling her from Yorkshire was her sister Harriet, and they hadn't spoken in months, maybe years. It was probably just the library chasing up a book she'd taken out twenty years ago, or maybe the local surgery reminding her she was due for a cervical smear. She might not have lived in Mathering, North Yorkshire, for over a decade, but locals liked to forget that. Just as an outsider could never be fully accepted into their exalted ranks, an insider could never leave. Not truly. Not even if you did your best never to go back.

Her phone thankfully, finally, fell silent. Rachel let out her breath in a gust and leaned once more against her lounger. Time, at last, to relax…

Buzz. Buzz. Buzz.

"Damn it!" The words exploded out of her, earning her a censorious look from a woman on the lounger a few metres away, who had a toddler by her feet, building a sandcastle with a bucket and spade. The little girl looked up at her, wide blue eyes blinking slowly.

Rachel spared the mother a fleeting, only semi-apologetic glance before she snatched up her phone. "*Yes?*" she demanded, not able or even willing to hide her surly impatience.

"Hello, Rachel."

The voice, low and smooth and assured, with a generous hint of Yorkshire accent, had the same effect as a fist slamming into her solar plexus. For a second Rachel was breathless, blinking in the bright sunlight, her mind spinning uselessly as she did her utmost to keep any memories at bay.

"Are you there?" Ben Mackey asked.

Her breath came out in something alarmingly like a gasp before she said shortly, "Yes. Obviously. Why are you ringing me?" *How did you get my number*, was what she really wanted to ask. She hadn't talked to Ben Mackey, not properly anyway, in twelve years. And not at all in at least about five. The last time she'd been home she'd seen him on a tractor in the distance, his stony gaze moving right over her as if she were invisible. Well, so what? It wasn't like they were *friends*. Not anymore.

"I'm ringing," Ben told her in that slow, careful drawl he had, like he was never going to rush about anything, "about your dad."

"My dad—" Rachel heard the panic in her voice and strove to moderate it. If it was something serious, Harriet would have called, she reminded herself. She would have called about six times.

"He's all right," Ben said in that same slow way, "but you need to come home."

"What? Why?" She couldn't get her head around what he seemed to be implying. "What do you mean? What's going on?"

"I can't go into it on the phone," Ben said. "At least, I shouldn't. Harriet can tell you more. But you need to come home."

There was an implacable note in his voice that Rachel instinctively bristled against, even as she felt a deep, sudden shaft of fear slice right through her. Who was her neighbour, whom she hadn't talked to in donkey's years, to tell her what to do about her own father? If he'd ever had that kind of prerogative, he'd lost it a *long* time ago. "Well," she said, unable to keep from sounding just that little bit snarky, "that's a little difficult because I'm on holiday right now, in Ibiza."

A short silence greeted this pronouncement before Ben remarked neutrally, far too neutrally, "Ibiza, eh?"

So what? Rachel wanted to snap. *I'm allowed to go to Ibiza. I'm allowed a holiday, the first one I've taken in years, as well as a life away from the farm and all that it is. I am!* Of course, no one back home was likely to agree with that, even as they'd tell her that of course she was. Rachel still felt their judgement, had felt it for twelve years, since she'd taken up her place at the University of Exeter, which was about as far as she'd been able to get away from the North Yorkshire Moors without actually leaving the country.

"Well," Ben continued when Rachel had not said anything because her jaw was clenched too tight, "can you get an earlier flight home?"

"Is it that serious?" She heard the thin needling of fear prick holes in her snarky tone. "Why can't you tell me what's going on?"

"It's important, Rachel."

Ben's voice was gentle, and Rachel's stomach dipped unpleasantly. "Is my dad ill?" she asked abruptly, and she was greeted with another one of Ben's meaningful silences. The things the man didn't say outweighed, by far, the things that he did. He'd always been that way, so had his father, and her own, for that matter. Yorkshire farmers were sparing with their words—and their feelings.

"He needs to go in for some tests," Ben said at last. "Not that he'd admit it. But he's been forgetting some things. It's starting to worry us."

Us. The word was like a hedge surrounding him, Harriet, everyone Rachel had left behind. Us definitely did not include her. Everyone back home had always made that abundantly clear. "All right." She breathed out evenly, focused on keeping calm. Controlled. It was a strategy that worked in her high-stress job in finance, and it would work with this—even if the memories were already rising in a dark tide.

You want to go? Fine. Go. Like I care. Don't bother coming back.

And as for Ben, back then? Ringing silence. He hadn't said a single word. She'd stood in the Mackeys' barn while he'd mucked out a stable and waited for him to say something. Anything. He hadn't even turned around.

Okay, breathe. In. Out. Rachel opened her eyes, having not realised she'd closed them until she was met with the sun's glare once again. "So he needs some tests," she stated, knowing the silence had gone on too long, but relieved to hear how calm she sounded. "Why do I need to rush home for that?"

"Because he's refusing to go in for them," Ben replied. "He's got an appointment at a memory clinic the day after tomorrow and Harriet can't convince him to go."

Of course not. Her sister Harriet's strong suit was *not* convincing anyone of anything. Or doing anything remotely proactive. She was more in the huffing and hand-wringing line. "And you think I can?" Rachel asked, trying to scoff.

"You know you can." Ben did not make it sound like a compliment.

Rachel stared out at the aquamarine sea, shining like a jewel, the white sand beach stretching out, so soft and inviting. She'd barely unpacked her suitcase; she hadn't even tried on her new bikini yet. She'd signed up for a Zumba class that afternoon. She wanted another mojito.

"You owe this to Harriet," Ben said quietly, and Rachel's fingers clenched so hard on her phone that her knuckles ached.

"I don't actually owe anyone anything," she replied curtly, "as it happens." Ben let out a small sigh that communicated as clearly as if he'd said that he expected no less of her, to say something like that, because his expectations of her were so very, very low. "I really don't," Rachel insisted, even though, with a weary resignation, she already knew she was going to go. It felt inevitable, like an undertow she was slowly, inexorably being pulled into, or maybe like quicksand. Sucked down, down, down, into the depths, and there was absolutely nothing she could do about it. This was her family, and even if she'd been avoiding them for ten years—and they'd been avoiding her, in their own way—she was still going to go home when she was asked to.

And Ben must have known that, as well, because he asked calmly, "When can we expect you?"

"I'll get a flight tonight," Rachel snapped, "and drive up tomorrow." And then she disconnected the call, because she could not bear to hear the smugness in his voice when he told her, so patronisingly and yet still managing to seem so unimpressed, that she was doing the right thing.

With a growl of frustration Rachel hurled her phone into her bag, earning yet another reproving look from the toddler's mum.

IT WAS RAINING in Yorkshire. It was *always* raining in Yorkshire, Rachel thought with a sigh, as she drove her rental car up the A1(M). With a reluctant sigh, she acknowledged that this sentiment was at least a little bit unfair; for the *very* few days a year when it wasn't raining up here, it was utterly beautiful. And as if God Himself were trying to score a point just then, the dank grey clouds cleared away as she turned off the motorway for the A-road that led to Mathering, the market town on whose outskirts she'd spent the first eighteen years of her life. The sky turned a fragile, ethereal blue and sunlight poured over the rolling moors, touched with the first autumn colour, like liquid gold. Stone barns and farmhouses peeked out from where they were nestled in gentle valleys, their windows glinting diamond-bright in the sunshine. A few sheep, cows, and horses dotted various slopes and fields like they'd been placed there as props; the whole thing was absurdly and perfectly pastoral, a postcard brought to life, an oil painting turned to reality. Yorkshire was called God's Own Country, and you could see why on a day like this. Never mind that for Rachel going home felt far more like going to hell.

All right, that was a *bit* extreme, she told herself, determined to get out of her funk, at least a little. She still smelled of sun cream and she'd had a morose mojito in the airport back in Ibiza, her holiday fast-tracked to forty-eight hours. Going home wasn't like going to *hell*, but it definitely had some purgatory-like vibes. Walking down the high street felt like going back in a time machine. Stepping into her family's farmhouse felt like becoming a child again, with all its ensuing, unhappy memories, not to mention the chilly silence from her sister, the utter indifference from her father. Was it any wonder she'd wanted to leave?

She followed the road up hill and down, past sleepy farms and cheerful bed and breakfasts; the area near the motorway was semi-gentrified, thanks to tourism's benevolent effect, with one farm offering glamping yurts, another an organic farm shop. It was another thirty-five minutes to Mathering, which tourism had not touched with quite the same generous hand.

At least it hadn't the last time Rachel had, reluctantly, been there, for her father's seventieth birthday. There had been no notable celebrations, but Harriet had acted as if she'd be the most heartless daughter alive if she didn't come home for the big day. And, Rachel knew, she'd semi-hoped her father would have been happy to have her there. She had, unsurprisingly, been disappointed on both counts. No matter what she did—or didn't do—it was never enough for Harriet, and her dad never even seemed to notice.

And so, three years ago, she'd driven back to London

determined not to bother again, or at least for a very long while. Why torture herself? It wasn't as if Harriet or her dad enjoyed her company, either, so why torture them, for that matter?

So why was she here for yet more punishment for all three of them? Oh, right. Tests. A memory clinic. Rachel had spent several hours on her laptop last night researching memory clinics and the seemingly inevitable dementia diagnoses going to one indicated. Back in her tiny flat in Putney she'd printed out several relevant documents, an array of literature to give to her sister to equip her for dealing with their dad, if that's what it came to. And if it did, she supposed she'd have to make the drive from London to Mathering as often as she could, to help out. The thought made everything in her clench and cringe. Harriet would not appreciate her help—that much she knew—even as she would be sulky that Rachel wasn't doing more. It had been a lose-lose proposition for Rachel for a long time.

But maybe, she told herself, this was all the typical tempest in a teapot. Maybe their dad was becoming a little absent-minded; he was seventy-three, after all. It didn't mean he had *Alzheimer's*, for heaven's sake, but that's where Harriet's mind would have immediately gone, even if she hadn't bothered to mention any of it to Rachel. Why had *Ben*, of all people, called her? Had Harriet asked him to?

For a second she let herself picture Ben—his weathered face, shock of brown hair that stood up at all angles, eyes the colour of acorns, a glinting golden-brown. That slow, lazy smile. That broad chest.

She decided to stop that train of thought. She and Ben

might have shared a couple of kisses in their teens—or something like that—but those days were long, long gone.

Anyway, Rachel told herself, this might be an easy fix. She could hope, anyway. She was giving it three days, which was the rest of her holiday time, plus a day to get back to London. After that, well, she supposed they would have to see, but she wasn't going to let Harriet guilt her into staying any longer than that, because her sister thought she *owed* her.

Even if she did.

EMBTHWAITE FARM LOOKED exactly the same as it always did, which was both comforting and depressing. Same Georgian-era square, squat farmhouse of grey Yorkshire stone, same dusty curtains at the living room windows, the best room of the house and hardly ever used, except for when her father read the newspaper after tea, as regular as clockwork.

A wisp of smoke curled up from the chimney into the pale blue sky, and sunlight glinted on the rain puddles in the farmyard. It would have been a lovely sight, if it hadn't been home.

Rachel pulled her car into the drive, wincing as the wheels hit the deep ruts. She turned the car off and sat there for a few seconds, her hands resting on the steering wheel, trying to steel herself for whatever lay ahead. She could pretty much predict it, unfortunately—Harriet's bristling hostility and covert-yet-constant suspicious looks; her father's continued silent, brutal indifference. Her self-confidence took a battering every time she stepped across the threshold, even if she did her best not to show as much, not to be the girl she'd been here growing up—frightened, angry, hiding her hurt, trying to protect the sister who now couldn't stand her.

She let out a gust of breath and then squared her shoulders and got out of the car. She took her one small suitcase out of the back, along with her work bag, and then headed for the front door.

It creaked as she opened it and the smell of home hit her, with all its accompanying memories—must, dust, dog, woodsmoke, a hint of cooking grease and coffee. The dog in question heaved his arthritic form from his usual place in the hall, by the welly boot rack, and came trotting faithfully towards her, lying down at her feet, his plumed tail beating a determined staccato on the floor as he looked up at her with cataract-clouded eyes.

Quite suddenly, tears stung Rachel's eyes and she blinked them back, crouching down to stroke the dog's silky brown ears. "Hey there, Fred." He had to be thirteen years old now, she realised. Ben had given him to her from his own spaniel's litter, back when they'd been friendly. He'd asked what she was going to call him, and she'd said she didn't like all those cutesy dog names—Fido, Lucky, Spark. "I'm going to call him Fred," she'd declared, and Ben had let out a sudden huff of laughter. The man rarely cracked so much as a smile, but when he laughed, even in a small way, it was a sound of genuine joy.

Rachel gave Fred one more pat on the head before she rose, bracing herself for whatever lay ahead. No one, of course, had come out to greet her. Fred trotted back to his spot and flung himself down on the bit of battered old carpet that served as his dog bed. The last time she'd been here, Rachel had bought a top-of-the-line dog bed, leather lined in fleece, thinking Fred deserved it for his old bones, but he'd turned up his nose at it, just as Harriet had.

Even the dog beds you buy are fancy.

In Yorkshire, that was definitely not a compliment.

Slowly Rachel walked down the hall, the floor's flagstones worn down in some places to match the tread of farmers' footsteps through the centuries. The house was two hundred years old, bought by her great-great-great-great-grandfather after he'd worked as manager for the big manor house on the other side of Mathering. It had been a proud day when the Mowbrays had become landowners, her father had liked to say, as if he'd been alive in 1819, or whenever Albert Mowbray had taken up residence here. There was a needlepoint sampler hanging over the hall table that had been made by his wife, Jane—the alphabet laid out in neat stitches, with a Bible verse beneath: *In His hands are the deep places of the earth; the strength of the hills is His also.* Psalm 95, verse four. Rachel had read it every time she'd put on her shoes.

She continued past it to the doorway at the back of the hall that led to the kitchen, the true heart of the house, if this house even had a heart. There had been times when Rachel had wondered.

The room, large and square, was empty now, and the same as it ever was. The ancient, rattling Rayburn taking up one wall, the deep farmhouse sink and the countertop another, a Welsh dresser on the third, filled with dusty bits of china no one ever used. A big rectangular table of scarred oak in the middle, where she'd eaten every meal as a child. A memory came, sudden and sharp, of her mother flinging a pan of toad-in-the-hole onto the centre of the table, where it had clanged and bounced, both Rachel and Harriet drawing away in fearful surprise.

"I can't do this anymore," her mother had said, bent over the kitchen sink, her head in her hands, her body shaking with sobs. The emotion Rachel remembered feeling the most had been annoyance, underlaid by a terrible fear she hadn't wanted to acknowledge. *Mums aren't meant to do that,* she recalled thinking, and it had felt like the world had tilted on its axis, because you were meant to rely on your mum, but she knew in that moment that she hadn't been.

She hadn't said anything, though. She'd just taken the oven mitt her mother had hurled onto the floor and righted their supper. Then she'd cut large slices of toad-in-the-hole and put them on her and Harriet's plates. While she'd begun to eat in silent defiance, Harriet had run to their mother and wrapped her arms around her waist.

"Don't cry, Mummy, don't cry," she'd pleaded.

While their mother had put her arms around her youngest daughter, Rachel had stolidly eaten her way through a large helping of toad-in-the-hole, and then taken a second, simply to make a point, although in retrospect she wasn't even sure what that point had been. She didn't think her mother had even noticed, anyway.

Letting out a weary sigh, she leaned over the table to inspect it; yes, the scorch mark from that sorry episode was still there, faded but visible. How old had she been then? Ten, maybe? It had been another seven years before her mother had finally left, but in retrospect Rachel had realised she'd been working up to it the whole time.

She straightened just as the back door opened and Harriet came clomping in, wearing a pair of muddy boots and holding a basket of eggs. Her eyes widened in surprise for a second; Rachel realised she hadn't actually told her sister she was coming, so taken up had she been with her dad's potential illness. She supposed she'd assumed Ben would have, but he clearly hadn't.

"Hi, Harriet—" she began, only to have her sister cut across her flatly.

"So, you're back." She deposited the basket of eggs on the counter next to the sink, not looking at her. The tentative smile that had been curling the edges of Rachel's mouth flickered and died like old ash.

"Yes," she agreed, just as flatly. "I'm back."

Chapter Two

WELL, THIS WAS fun. And typical. Harriet stared at Rachel without speaking and Rachel stared back. Yay for family bonding times. Then Harriet broke the silence.

"What are you doing here?"

What a welcome, as usual. "I'm here," she replied evenly, "because I was asked to come."

Harriet's dark brows snapped together. She and Rachel shared the same colouring—hair and eyes like dark chocolate, olive skin, the same as their mother's. But that, Rachel thought, was where the resemblance ended. Harriet's hair was a frizzy halo, her face scattered with golden freckles, her figure curvy and generous. Rachel, on the other hand, had stick-straight hair, a lanky body without any real womanly curves, and no freckles. With only fifteen months between them in age, their mother had used to call them the twins-that-aren't.

They certainly *weren't* now.

"Who asked you?" Harriet demanded, sounding sceptical. "Dad?"

As if. Rachel couldn't remember the last time she'd exchanged more than three words with her father. "Ben," she replied, and Harriet scowled.

"He had no right."

"Dad has an appointment tomorrow?" Rachel cut across her futile fuming. When it came to her family, it was better to stick to basics, get to the point, and then hopefully move on.

"There's one scheduled, but he doesn't want to go."

"Which I suppose," Rachel filled in, trying not to sound reasonable and not sarcastic, "was why Ben rang me."

"Because you can bully Dad into it?" Harriet retorted, her hands on her hips. "Rachel, he's a grown man. He can make his own medical decisions."

"Can he? Because the fact that he has an appointment at a memory clinic suggests otherwise." She turned away, knowing there was no point in talking about it any longer because they would just argue. Her sister never wanted her to come home, but then seemed mad when she didn't. She could never win, and so she'd stopped trying a long time ago. Except it seemed she hadn't, because here she was. "Where is he, anyway?"

"Out in the barn."

Where as far as Rachel could tell, their father spent most of his life. She'd seen him in there many times, sitting on a milking stool, reading the paper, happy as Larry to be on his own. When they'd been little, he often wouldn't have come back into the house until after she and Harriet were in bed.

"All right," she said. "I'll put my bags in my room and then I'll go see him."

"You didn't tell me you were coming, so I didn't clean your room," Harriet replied, an accusation.

"I can clean it myself," Rachel told her, deciding not to

remind her sister that she never cleaned her room for her arrival. The last time she'd come home, the sheets on her bed had smelled of mildew and there had been mouse droppings on the *pillow*. But it was fine; she could make her own bed.

"Fine," Harriet gritted between her teeth. "You know where the sheets are?"

"I did live here for eighteen years," Rachel replied as lightly as she could, "even if you like to act as if I never did." And without waiting for a reply, she walked out of the kitchen.

The front stairs creaked under her footsteps as she climbed them to the first floor, standing for a moment in the square hallway at the top of the stairs, the four bedroom doors leading off it—her room, Harriet's room, her parents' room, the guest room. The air smelled faintly musty, as it always did; the same faded antique runner was on the stairs, the same pictures on the walls—a muddy oil painting of the moors, a black-and-white wedding photo of her grandparents. Not one thing about this place had changed since she'd left, she thought, which was what she always thought when she came back. Not one blessed thing.

How did her sister stand it? It was no wonder she was so irritable, Rachel supposed. Heaven knew she would be if she had to live here, but then she didn't, and neither did Harriet, even if she liked to act as if she did, as if someone had hogtied her to the house, for heaven's sake. No one ever had, not remotely.

That was a point, one of many, on which they had never been able to see eye to eye, not that they'd ever truly battled it out. But Harriet had always blamed Rachel for leaving, even though she'd had the exact same opportunity. Yet no matter how much Rachel reminded herself of that salient fact, she still struggled with a vague sense of guilt about how it had all happened, and that irritated her as much as her sister's attitude.

Well, never mind. She'd sort her dad out and scarper after three days. Harriet would probably be glad to see the back of her, and she'd return in a month or so, if she needed to. Harriet would insist that she didn't, but then act aggrieved if she stayed away. Never mind. She could handle it. Rachel walked into her old bedroom, dumping her bag on the bed.

To say the room hadn't been cleaned was something of an understatement. Boxes of old papers were stacked halfway to the ceiling, filling a good third of the room. The bed had been stripped of sheets, and it looked like a mouse had been nesting in the mattress. Tattered, faded lace curtains hung limply at the window, and a bookshelf of Rachel's old schoolbooks was the only reminder that this had once been her bedroom.

A sigh escaped her in a long gust, and then she set to work. She'd tidy things up and then she'd go find her father.

It didn't take too long to dust the room, clean the mattress—a mouse *had* nested in it, but was thankfully long gone—and make the bed. Rachel glanced at a paper lying on top of one of the boxes and saw it was from the bank, about a mortgage application.

Rachel frowned as she scanned the brief correspondence. There had never been a mortgage on this place; it had been in their family, free and clear, for hundreds of years. What mortgage? Something she'd have to ask Harriet about, although Rachel doubted her sister would know. She'd never bothered too much about financial matters; when they'd been children, she'd given their pocket money away with a sort of blithe carelessness while Rachel had hoarded her precious pound coins and fifty-pence coins, dumping them out of her piggy bank and counting them up like a happy miser.

Yet another way in which they'd always been different.

Still frowning, Rachel returned the paper to its box and headed downstairs. No reason to put off the happy reunion a second longer, she thought with a sigh. Because of course that was just how it was going to go.

Harriet had disappeared as Rachel came into the kitchen, which made things a little easier. She filled the kettle and plonked it on to the Rayburn, deciding a cuppa might help the conversation with her father go more smoothly. As she waited for it to boil, Rachel looked slowly around the kitchen with its usual clutter—muddy boots by the back door, a tottering pile of papers on the dresser. The complimentary calendar that they were sent every year from the local feed store was tacked up by the fridge.

The memory clinic appointment wasn't even written on it, although several other dates were, in Harriet's writing: *4pm Delivery, Wainwright. 9am, The Old Bakery.* What was that all about? Rachel wondered. As far as she knew, her sister didn't have a proper job and never had. She'd done a few part-time things locally—worked in the aforementioned bakery, been a dog walker, helped out at a nursery. But they'd never been full-time and they'd never seemed to last, which was part of the reason why, Rachel supposed, her sister had never left home. She simply couldn't afford it.

The kettle boiled and Rachel made two cups of tea—black for her, and strong but milky with two sugars for her dad. Then, taking a deep breath, she hefted the mugs and headed outside.

The Mowbray farm had always been something of a hodgepodge of interests—historically, they'd raised sheep and dairy cows along with chickens and vegetables for the family, but sometime in the last hundred years, Rachel couldn't remember when, they'd had to sell off some of their acreage and they'd got rid of the sheep. In her lifetime, it had only been dairy cows, but as her father had got older, the pace of the farming life had become challenging—up at four a.m. for milking, arranging the local deliveries, never having a day off. Now there were only a couple dozen cows and he kept the deliveries local, hiring Ray, a grizzled, amicable guy in his forties, to drive the truck—at least that was how it had been three years ago.

But as she came into the barn, breathing in the strong, sweetish smell of cow that reminded her so much of her childhood, she realised things must have changed, because half the stalls were empty.

Her father was at the far end of the milking parlour, doing the second milking of the day. A few years ago, he'd finally modernised to a mechanised milking method; in her childhood, it had all been done by hand, taking hours. She watched him for a moment as he carefully cleaned the cow's teats with iodine before attaching the suction cups. He looked exactly the same, she thought, as the last time she'd seen him—thick white hair, a bit mussed at the back, a craggy face and gnarled hands. He wore a holey fisherman knit jumper underneath his milking overalls, rubber boots and gloves that went up to his elbows.

"Hey, Dad," she said quietly as she walked down the centre aisle, past cows patiently waiting for their turn, big, velvet eyes watching her progress. Her dad didn't even turn his head, so Rachel wasn't sure he'd heard her.

Then, gruffly, without looking at her: "What are you doing here?"

The exact same thing her sister had said. Rachel held in her sigh as she passed him a mug, which he took without a word.

"I thought I'd come visit."

"You could have rung."

"I suppose I could have." She wasn't going to be nettled, she told herself, before she found herself adding, "Thanks for the warm welcome." So much for that.

Her father's mouth tightened, and he took a sip of tea. He still hadn't actually *looked* at her.

"Usually someone says when they're coming, that's all."

"Yes, well, I'm sorry I didn't." Now the sigh escaped her. "I came because Ben Mackey rang me, actually. He says there's an appointment you need to go to tomorrow, and I thought I might take you to it."

Ire flashed in her father's eyes as he finally looked at her. She knew it would annoy him, to realise other people had got up in his business; it was why she'd told him. The only way she thought she could get him to go to the thing was if he was goaded into it. "No need for him to get involved," he said tersely.

"Well, I suppose he was concerned." She realised she didn't know how or why Ben had got involved; she made it her business not to know anything about him anymore, although the neighbouring farms, sharing the same lane, had always been friendly over the years, helping each other out the way farmers often did. Ben's dad had died from cancer about four or five years ago, and Ben had taken over from him; his mother, Diana, as far as Rachel knew, still helped out. She knew all that from Harriet, but not much more.

"No need." Her father had turned back to the cow he was milking, adjusting the suction cup even though Rachel doubted it needed it. She pulled a milking stool towards her and sat down on it.

"Why don't you want to go, Dad?" she asked quietly.

"Don't need to."

"Are you sure about that? How did the appointment come about, anyway?"

"Harriet made it," he said gruffly. "Shouldn't have done. I'm fine."

"Well, it can't hurt to check, can it?" Rachel persisted. "Prove everyone just how fine you are."

"I don't need to prove a damned thing, missy." He turned to her, his eyes flashing, his mouth tight.

She took a sip of tea, saying nothing. She'd learned to wait her father out when she needed to. The cow was finished, and her father spent the following few minutes setting up the next one while Rachel watched and waited.

Finally, when the next cow was being milked, he sat back on his stool and said tersely, "It's just headaches I've been having. Everyone gets those."

You didn't go to a memory clinic just for headaches, Rachel thought. There had to be something more. "So go and find out if there's a reason why you're getting them," she said with a shrug, like it didn't matter to her at all, like she hadn't cut short her holiday in *Ibiza* to run up here and chivvy her father along because no one else could manage it.

"Don't need to know the reason."

"There might be some treatment they can offer—"

"For headaches?" he scoffed, but Rachel heard a bleakness under those words that made her feel a sudden shaft of sympathy. He was afraid, she realised, and then thought, *of course he is.* Afraid and proud, a lethal combination. How could she possibly tackle it?

"All right, fine." She stood up from where she'd been sitting and turned towards the door. "Don't go. But you know how this place is. Everyone in Mathering will know you didn't go, and they'll feel sorry for you, because they'll think you're afraid to go to a silly doctor's appointment."

Her father snorted. "Don't try that psychology bollocks on me, my girl. It won't work."

She almost smiled then. Sometimes she forgot, in her own hurt about the past, how surprisingly *fun* her dad could be, at least when you got used to him and his taciturn ways. "You still know it's true."

"They're already talking," he said after a moment, his head bent. "The damned nurse in the GP must have told someone, to have all this palaver. I didn't ask for it."

"You know how news always gets around here. I remember Ben said the vet knew his dad had cancer before he did."

Why had she mentioned Ben? She didn't want to think about him. Not now, not ever. And in any case, it was Harriet who had told her that, not Ben himself, which somewhat proved her point.

Her father let out a huff of something that could, if you were being generous, be called laughter. "Maybe so."

"So you'll go?" Rachel replied briskly. "I did come all the way from London to take you, after all. You wouldn't want to disappoint me, would you?"

He turned to give her a glare. "You didn't have to come."

Rachel met his glare with a measured look of her own. "I know."

A long silence, the only sound the hiss and swish of the milking machine. "Fine," her father said, shrugging in twitchy dismissal. "I'll go. And then that'll be the end of it." Spoken like a warning, as if he could be in control of such a thing.

"All right," Rachel replied, as if in agreement, although she had a feeling that wouldn't be the end of it at all. It would just be the beginning.

Chapter Three

BACK IN THE farmhouse, Rachel realised she was starving—she'd skipped lunch during the drive up and all she'd had for breakfast was a cappuccino and a protein bar. Taking three eggs from the dozen or so Harriet had collected earlier, she cracked them into a pan on the Rayburn.

The kitchen felt surprisingly peaceful. Fred came in at the smell of the eggs frying and plopped himself down right at her feet in front of the Rayburn, so she had to step over him every time she moved. She didn't mind. She cut a thick slice from the homemade loaf resting on the table, under a dish cloth—Harriet had, she acknowledged, always been a very good baker—and put it in the toaster. As she moved around the kitchen, her gaze took in a few things she didn't recognise—a bright red mixing bowl, a framed watercolour of the River Derwent. It was a pretty thing, its banks bursting with flowers, the water burbling by.

Upstairs she'd assumed nothing had changed in this house, but it stood to reason that Harriet might have bought a few new things over the years. Her father wouldn't, Rachel knew. He preferred to spend as little money as he could, wearing out his clothes until they were nothing but holes and worn patches.

Still, it was a little bit disconcerting, to see new things in a place she'd freeze-framed in her mind. She'd assumed in some way, without ever realising she'd done it, that nothing ever changed in the old farmhouse. Her sister and father were here, day in and day out, exactly as they'd always been, but clearly that wasn't the case. Her sister had bought a mixing bowl and a painting; had she changed in other, significant ways? Rachel realised, somewhat uncomfortably, that she didn't have the first clue.

As if summoned by her thoughts, Harriet rounded the doorway, humming under her breath, coming to a stop and a scowl as she caught sight of Rachel sitting at the table, eating scrambled eggs on toast. Harriet's gaze flashed to the basket, and then the loaf of the bread, and the scowl deepened.

"Did you use some of the eggs?"

"Yes, just three," Rachel said, keeping her voice mild. "I thought it would be all right."

"And the bread?" Harriet whipped the cloth off the loaf that had a single slice cut from it; Rachel hadn't thought much about it but now she wondered if Harriet had been saving it—but for what?

"Yes, just one slice," she said, meaning to sound conciliatory and not quite managing it. "I'm sorry, I was hungry."

"You could have asked," Harriet replied, her mouth tight as she covered the bread with the cloth. "Or did that not occur to you?"

No, it hadn't, because even if she'd been away a long time, this was still home. "I'm sorry, it didn't," she admitted. She knew she didn't sound very sorry, but that was because Harriet was so *hostile*. "I suppose I assumed the food in the kitchen was for family consumption." Was she not considered family anymore? "Were you saving them for something?"

"As it happens, I was," Harriet snapped. "But never mind."

Rachel wasn't sure whether to believe her; there was something decidedly cagey about her tone, but she decided she would be the bigger person and apologise, anyway, properly. "In that case, I really am sorry I used them. If you need more eggs, I can run into Mathering and buy some." Even though there were at least nine still left in the basket. "Or a loaf of bread," she added. "From the bakery?"

"Thanks but no thanks," Harriet replied, and now she sounded weary. "That's not the point."

Then what, Rachel wondered, was the point? Or had Harriet just wanted to pick a fight, as she always seemed to?

"I spoke to Dad," she said. "He's willing to go to the memory clinic tomorrow."

"Oh, well done," Harriet said, her voice full of sarcasm, and Rachel blinked.

"Sorry, but that is why I came?" she retorted, an edge to her voice.

"I don't recall asking you to," Harriet shot back.

"I don't recall you being able to make him go," Rachel returned with just as much force. She'd actually forgotten just how much they could bicker. "Look," she cut off her sister's furious reply, "I don't actually want to argue with you. I just want to hear about what's been happening. Dad said you made the appointment with the memory clinic—why? What kind of things were you noticing?"

Harriet looked like she still wanted to fly at Rachel, but she closed her mouth and gave a shrug, and when she spoke again, her voice was more measured. "A couple of things. He was complaining about headaches, and you know how he is with pain."

Yes, Rachel knew. Her father had once sliced off the top of his thumb and he'd said, mildly, that it 'stung a bit'.

"But more than that," Harriet continued, "he was forgetting things. Little things, but it felt strange."

"What kind of little things?"

"Words, mostly. He'd be in the middle of a sentence, and he'd suddenly forget a word, like, a really basic word. But bigger things too—he went into the barn and couldn't remember why he was there." Harriet regarded her unhappily. "And the cows needed milking. He came back into the kitchen after about five minutes, and I had to remind him what he was supposed to be doing."

"Okay," Rachel said, absorbing this, unsure how alarming it all was. "How long has it been going on?"

"A couple of months. He's pretty good at masking it, so it might have been longer. After the episode with the cows, I finally decided to call the clinic. That was about three weeks ago, and tomorrow was the first appointment they had available."

"Do you think it's Alzheimer's?" Rachel asked bluntly. Their father's mother had had it, and she'd died in a nursing home when they'd both been small. Rachel barely remembered her—just a wispy-haired, vacant-eyed figure in a bed they'd had to visit every other Sunday.

Harriet shrugged. "I don't know. That's why I booked

the appointment."

"But you weren't even going to make him go," Rachel pointed out, an edge entering her voice that she hadn't meant to be there. "And you didn't even call me to let me know about any of it."

"Why would I have called you?" Harriet asked, like it was a genuine question. She looked almost confused by Rachel mentioning it.

"Because he's my father, maybe?" Rachel suggested. Definite edge to her voice now, serrating it, slicing like a blade, but come on. She had come home a few times over the years, for important things. Birthdays, when Harriet had had pneumonia and her dad had needed help with the farm, the anniversary of their mother's leaving, when Harriet had seemed low. She hadn't been completely out of the picture, even if Harriet acted as if she had. Even if she'd wondered, on more than one occasion, if it would be better for both of them if she was.

"Oh, is he?" Harriet replied in a parody of surprise, smacking her forehead with her hand. "Because I must have forgot, the way you forget ninety-nine per cent of the time."

Aaand...now they were back to bickering. Of course. "All I'm saying is," Rachel replied evenly, "I would have liked to have known what was going on."

"Oh, and am I supposed to be a mind reader, now?" Harriet snapped back. "Because the last time I called you about Dad, for his birthday, you acted as if it was a *major* inconvenience to your oh so important life to so much as buy him a card. So, forgive me if I thought you wouldn't be interested now."

She didn't think she'd acted that reluctant, had she? Even if she had been, because she dreaded coming home. Rachel decided not to go into all that. "Harriet, this is different," she protested, keeping her voice quiet in a vain hope to avoid an all-out argument. "This is serious."

"It might not be," Harriet replied. "You can't know for sure."

"Come on—"

"I mean it." She sounded fierce. "It could be anything. And I still think it's Dad's decision if he wants to go to a memory clinic or not. He's not that out of it, you know, Rachel. He's still perfectly competent to make his own medical decisions, and he knows what Alzheimer's looks like. Maybe he doesn't want to know if he actually has it."

"To what purpose? There are medications you can take now—"

"Actually, there aren't." At Rachel's look of blatant scepticism, Harriet continued acerbically, "I did some research too, you know. I'm sure you came with a whole folder file of stuff you're going to lecture me on, but contrary to your belief, I am *not* an idiot. The medications that may slow cognitive decline are still in the clinical trial stage. The medications that *can* be prescribed only deal with a couple of symptoms—anxiety, aggression, that kind of stuff. And he doesn't seem particularly anxious to me."

"What about aggressive?" Rachel asked, and a tiny smile twitched her sister's mouth.

"No more than usual."

Rachel smiled back, sort of, and for a second it seemed they'd called a truce, which was such a blessed *relief*. When was the last time they'd had a civil conversation, never mind actually shared a moment of solidarity? Before she'd left for university, certainly. This brief moment of shared humour reminded her of how close they used to be, as children. Two peas in a pod, their dad had said sometimes, except they'd never been that, not really. Rachel had been fiercely protective of Harriet, and in return Harriet had adored her. A symbiotic yin and yang that had worked until Rachel had chosen to step away.

"Well." She heaved a sigh. "I guess we'll find out what's going on tomorrow. But if it is Alzheimer's..."

"Let me guess. You'll move up here and work remotely so you can help out with the farm, take Dad to appointments, just generally be around."

Rachel stared at her, unsure how to reply, and Harriet let out a dry, humourless laugh. "Relax, I'm joking. Let me guess for real this time—you're going by the end of the week, so I'll have to manage as best as I can but maybe you'll send money, come by every six months or so, and meanwhile you've got some information you got off the internet that you think I should read. Is that more or less the gist of it?"

Rachel felt herself flush. That was *exactly* the gist of it, and she didn't like how wearily knowing her sister sounded. How callous she made her seem. She was actually trying. Sort of. "I can't really work remotely," she said stiffly, and Harriet laughed again.

"Like that was ever seriously on the table."

Nettled, Rachel replied, "If I could—"

Harriet arched an eyebrow. "You would?" she finished, when Rachel hadn't said anything more. "You would *what*, exactly?"

She was backing herself into a corner, Rachel knew, and no good could come of it. She'd made her choices, and so had Harriet. "If Dad has Alzheimer's," she said evenly, "we'll have to work out some kind of plan."

"*We* will?" Harriet shook her head. "The last think I need, Rachel, is for you to swan in here and tell me what to do before you swan out again. I'm the one who lives here, who deals with Dad, day in and day out, so maybe you'll just let me get on with it, yeah?" With one last fulminating glare, her sister whirled around to stalk out of the kitchen. At the doorway she stopped to throw over her shoulder, "And, as it happens, I'm going to have to make an entire new loaf of bread because that one actually *was* for something, you know? I have a life even if you don't think I do."

Before Rachel could reply to *that*, Harriet was gone, marching down the hallway and outside, the front door slamming behind her. She'd half-risen from her chair when her sister had started shouting at her, and now Rachel sat back down in it with a thud. She'd always known her sister had resented her for leaving—how could she not know, when Harriet had made it so very clear—but she couldn't remember the last time her sister had been that vocal or vicious about it. Rachel had become used to the passive-aggressive techniques her sister liked to employ—martyred looks, gusty sighs, telling silences—but not out-and-out accusations, flung at her like handfuls of mud, making her feel guilty, *dirty*, when she had nothing to feel guilty about.

Well, nothing *much*.

Harriet had been just as free to leave as she was, Rachel

reminded herself as she tidied up; damned if she'd let her sister rake her over the coals for leaving a dirty plate in the sink. She was determined not to give Harriet a single reason to lambast her again.

But back then, twelve years ago? Harriet had been in her last year of secondary school when Rachel had gone to university, applying to universities herself, desperate to get away just as Rachel had been. The fact that she'd chickened out was *not* Rachel's fault. If anything, it was their mother's, who had left their father—left them—just before Christmas that year. Harriet had had three uni offers, good ones. She could have gone, started over the way Rachel had, left Mathering and all its memories far, far behind, if she'd really wanted to.

She could have, but she hadn't, and she'd been blaming Rachel for it ever since.

Rachel turned from the sink, determined to put such useless thoughts behind her. She was here now, and she had to make the best of it—and so did Harriet. They would have to do their best to survive the next three days without trying to kill each other. Not a high bar, admittedly, but one that was at least achievable. Hopefully. After that…well, somehow they would have to figure it out.

AT TWO O'CLOCK the next afternoon Rachel was sitting with her father in the outpatient waiting room of Mathering's tiny cottage hospital. The last time she'd been there had been when she was ten, and she'd broken her arm falling out of a tree. Ben had dared her to climb higher, and Rachel had never been able to resist a dare—or Ben. She'd had a crush on him since she'd been about six, although she would have furiously denied it to everyone and anyone, especially Ben himself. They'd always been in fierce competition—who could race to the end of their shared lane faster; who could climb the highest tree; who could pick the most blackberries in five minutes; who could do a handstand for the longest. Anything and everything had been something to win, until—

No. Best not to think of that.

Rachel turned to her dad, who had, predictably, not said a single word on the ten-minute journey into town, or in the fifteen minutes they'd been waiting for their appointment. He hadn't spoken a word last night, either; they'd eaten the casserole Harriet had made in near-total silence, which was fairly typical for their family but still put Rachel on edge. She'd thought about at least engaging her sister in conversation, but considering the insults and accusations that had been flying between them so far, had decided against it. Maybe silence was better.

"Not long now, Dad," she said in a pseudo-cheerful voice that people seemed to reserve for hospitals and small children. Her father did not so much as grunt a reply. Rachel leaned back in her chair, her arms crossed, one foot jiggling. She knew they wouldn't get a diagnosis today; at best, there would most likely be a referral for a neurologist, and then that appointment might not be for months. If that was the case, what would she do? Come back to make sure her father attended it? Stay away the way Harriet seemed to want her to?

As much as Rachel dreaded coming up here, the thought of just leaving her dad to get on with the business of having Alzheimer's seemed callously cruel, and wasn't something she was willing to do. Her father might not have been all that much of a hands-on dad, but he'd visited his mother in her nursing home every week, as far as Rachel could remember, bringing her and Harriet to every other visit. Strange, she hadn't really thought about that, about what it meant, before. She just remembered the boring Sunday afternoons, her scratchy dress, the nursing home's smell of medicine and old age that she hadn't liked.

If her father could do that for his mother, she could certainly do it for her dad. But maybe it wouldn't come to that…

"Peter Mowbray?"

The nurse's kindly voice had Rachel looking up and her father stiffening, his wide-eyed gaze trained on the nurse.

"Come on, Dad," Rachel said gently; seeing the frozen look of fear on her father's face had made a sudden, surprising tenderness rush through her. Then his expression returned to its usual implacable lines, and he shook off the hand she'd put on his arm to walk slowly towards the nurse by himself, in his stiff-legged, old man's gait.

The so-called 'memory clinic' was actually an appointment with a specialist, a chirpy young woman with curly blonde hair and a wide, ready smile. She had a set of items on her desk that looked like they belonged in a preschool—some building blocks, a clock face with large plastic hands, the kind of thick pencil used in younger years classes, and some wide-lined paper.

Her father looked down at this assortment of objects, his mouth twisted in something like a sneer.

"I won't be needing all that," he said, with a nod to it, his tone dismissive, final.

"Oh, but I will," the doctor replied in a voice that was gratingly cheerful, like she was a teacher, and her dad was a toddler. "My name's Rebecca. Do you know why you're here today, Mr Mowbray?"

Her father looked at this young woman—all of maybe twenty-five—with obvious disdain and Rachel tensed. This was so not going to go well.

"I'm here because my daughter thought I needed to be," he replied, "but I bloody well don't."

Rebecca, to her credit, was unfazed. "Well, since you're here," she replied, her cheerful tone dimming not one iota, "shall we get on with it? You strike me as a man who doesn't like to waste time."

To Rachel's relief the corner of her father's mouth twitched in what could almost, *almost* be called a smile. A very tiny one. Maybe this wouldn't be so bad, after all, she thought. She could have given the consultant more credit. "You're right about that."

"Good. Then shall we get started?" She put the clock face in front of him. "Could you please move the hands to a quarter to five?"

Her dad stared at the doctor in disbelief. "Are you bloody joking?"

"I'm not," she replied sweetly, "but as you don't like to waste time, I'm sure we can get this over with really quickly."

His mouth compressed, looking furious, her father pushed the hands one way and another. Rachel leaned forward in her seat, craning her neck as subtly as she could, to see if her father had got it right.

He had.

She released her breath as slowly as she could, a quiet exhalation of relief. That had to be a good sign.

The doctor looked neither impressed nor alarmed as she continued to go through her set of questions. Did he know the date? Could he say it? Who was the current reigning monarch? Could he stack these blocks on top of each other? Could he count back from one hundred by sevens?

Her father did all these, at first with an air of annoyance, and then with one of triumph. He was getting everything right, Rachel thought dazedly, with no problems at all. She felt another rush of relief, even stronger this time, making her weak, almost dizzy. She realised she really hadn't expected this.

"Now, one of the last things," Rebecca said with her unflaggingly bright smile. "Can you name all these objects?" She picked up a pen, brandishing it in front of him.

"A pen," her dad bit out.

Next a stapler, then a book, then a computer mouse. Her father named them all, tersely, becoming annoyed again, probably thinking she was taking the mick.

"And this?" she asked, holding up a set of keys.

"A—" Her father frowned. Stopped. Stared at them. Rachel felt as if her heart were suspended in her chest, frozen yet beating. *Keys, Dad.* She willed him to hear her, some kind of father-daughter telepathy—*as if*—but her father remained silent, staring at the keychain, his forehead crinkled, his eyes narrowed in perplexity, his expression turning mutinous, then thunderous.

"A thing to unlock a door," he finally burst out, as if he were out of breath.

Rebecca's smile didn't slip a notch as she put the keys back on the table. "Very good. Now, just a few more questions," she continued, making a note on the form she kept angled away from any prying eyes. "You said you had headaches?"

"Yes."

"How often? How severe?"

Her dad shrugged irritably. "Often enough, and bad enough that I notice."

"Have you any trouble speaking? Any slurring of speech?" She kept her gaze trained on him while he sputtered his affront.

"Slurred—! No. Of course not."

"Any trouble walking? Tripping, stumbling, that sort of thing? Feeling a little unbalanced sometimes?" She cocked her head, smiling in sympathy.

"No," her father said, but after a pause. Then, gruffly, "Not really."

"So sometimes?" she pressed. "A little unsteady on your feet, perhaps?"

"A little," he conceded, parting with the information reluctantly. "Now and again."

"And the headaches? Are they severe enough for you to take medication?"

"Some ibuprofen, maybe. Nothing more than that."

Rebecca put down her notepad and folded her hands in front of her. "Mr Mowbray, I'm going to recommend that you have an MRI. You've done very well with the questions I've put to you, but with some of your responses, especially in regard to your headaches and the loss of balance, I think it's worth having a scan just to make sure."

"Make sure of what?" her dad asked belligerently.

"Make sure everything is as it should be," Rebecca replied, her tone briskly placating. "I'll put you into our system now, and you'll get a letter through the mail about your appointment, which will be in Middlesbrough."

"Middlesbrough!" her father spluttered. It was an hour away.

"I'm afraid that's where the closest neurology services are," she replied with a smile. "They have a very good team there. You should receive a letter with your appointment date within the next ten days." It was said in a kindly tone, yet was also clearly a dismissal.

As they walked out of the room, her father straightened the cuffs of his coat, a slight spring in his step. "Well, that wasn't so bad," he said, loud enough for the doctor hear. "There's clearly nothing wrong with me."

Chapter Four

THE SUN HAD gone behind the clouds just as Rachel set out from the farmhouse later that afternoon. After dropping her dad back home, she realised she didn't want to hang around waiting for Harriet to fly at her for whatever reason she'd chosen to, and so she decided to go for a walk while her dad had beat a quick retreat to the comforts of the milking parlour.

Grabbing an old, waxed jacket and a pair of well-worn welly boots from the clutter in the hall, Rachel set off across the pasture behind the house, heading up the hill towards a stand of trees she and Harriet used to play in. Not big enough to be a proper wood, but still fun, at least, to pretend to get lost in. They'd climbed trees and built dens and chased each other, weaving between the trunks, their laughter echoing through the valley.

Those days seemed a long time ago now. How many times had she come home in the last twelve years? Rachel wondered. She could count them if she tried; it was hardly a large number, and yet she was reluctant to tally the visits, afraid of what it might show about her.

During her university years, she'd come home a *bit* more, she recalled. Always at Christmas and usually at Easter, especially right after her mum had left; she hadn't left Harriet *quite* as high and dry as she liked to remember. The truth was, Rachel had tried to hold everyone together when she'd come home during uni, making meals for the freezer and doing a big clean of the house, jollying them along as best she could, but her father had been completely uncommunicative, and Harriet had seemed so hostile.

If you want to go, go.

Rachel still cringed inwardly at that emotional scene, the first time she'd come home after their mum had left. Harriet begging her to stay and then telling her to go, while she'd stared helplessly on. *Hat, I have my exams! And you'll be gone in just a few months, too. You just have to hold on a little while longer…* Her sister had stared at her stony-faced and then walked away. Rachel had come back for Easter, yes, but not that summer, except for a couple of weeks; she'd taken an internship in London instead, which she'd felt guilty about, but it had been a good opportunity and she wasn't even sure what the point of going home had been, when neither her sister nor her father seemed happy to have her there.

As the years had gone on, it had become easier and easier to stay away, months sliding by without a single visit. Work was always an excuse; she'd had a demanding job as an entry-level financial analyst, required to work all the hours God gave to get those necessary promotions. A handful of holiday days a year meant a trip to North Yorkshire was time-consuming and usually impossible, or at least difficult enough that Rachel only did it when she had to—a few birthdays, the time Harriet had had pneumonia, early on when she'd texted Rachel that she couldn't cope, and Rachel had rushed back only to find her sister angry that she'd come at all. Well, what had she been supposed to do?

It had been three years since she'd last come home, though, the longest she'd been gone. It had just been so much easier, not to go. Not to face the hostility, and yes, the guilt. Harriet had *chosen* to stay, she reminded herself again, even if her sister always seemed to act as if she'd been heartlessly abandoned. The truth was she hadn't been. Not exactly, anyway.

Rachel had reached the brow of the hill, huffing and puffing as she squinted out at the meadows and moors rolling to the horizon in a patchwork of yellow and green. It really was all so ridiculously beautiful, she thought on a sigh. The air was crystalline clear, the sky—for once—a lovely, bright blue. A cow lowed in the distance, the sound mournful yet also holding a certain peace. The knots between Rachel's shoulder blades that hadn't had a chance to loosen in Ibiza shifted, just a tiny bit, now. Away from the house, from her father's silence and her sister's hostility, she felt as if she could breathe.

She started along the top of the hill, following an old path through the shadowy woods, the trail familiar even though she hadn't walked it in decades. When had she last been up here? she wondered as she breathed in the clean, earthy scents of cedar and pine. She, Harriet, and Ben had played up here all the time, an unlikely trio in some ways. Ben insisted he only played with them because there was no one else around; his own sister Izzy was five years older than him and way too cool to mess about in the woods.

Still, unlikely as they'd been as a friendship group, they'd all got along—she and Ben always competing, Harriet doing her best to keep up. Her mother, Rachel recalled, had had a dinner bell—a very loud warden's air raid bell from the Second World War—that she rang to get them to come home. The sound of it would echo across the valley, and she and Harriet and Ben would clamber down from trees or wade through the stream on the other side of the hill, and run home, the long grass scratching their bare legs; Ben veered off at the bottom of the hill, towards the farm whose buildings Rachel could see now, peeking through the stand of trees that separated the two properties. Those had been happy days, blurred by the mists of memory. Sometimes, because of everything that came after, she forgot they'd existed at all.

Rachel came to the end of the wood and hesitated, on the brow of the hill, as she considered which way to go—straight down and cut through the Mackeys' farm, or follow along the top to the bridlepath that led to Wood Lane and circled around before joining up with the lane that led to their two properties.

She decided on the second path. She really didn't feel like seeing Ben, and she wasn't sure he'd appreciate her striding through his farmyard, anyway. She hadn't been on the Mackeys' property since—well, she didn't even know since when. A long time. A very long time.

The bridlepath was muddy, and she picked her way along it slowly, the mud sucking at her boots, before she came to Wood Lane, a narrow track hemmed in by high hedgerows that ran all along the side of the Mackeys' farmland, before turning east towards the Mowbrays'.

She'd been walking down the road for about ten minutes when she heard the telltale grumble of a tractor behind her, and she stepped up onto the side of the lane, pressing against the prickly hedges, to let it pass. As it drew closer, her heart sank as she saw the face of the farmer sitting high above her.

Ben Mackey. And he wasn't smiling.

Reluctantly she raised her hand in a wave, because it seemed rude not to, and she expected—hoped, anyway—that he'd simply wave back and keep going. Instead, he cut the engine of the tractor so that with a groan of exhaust it rolled to a stop a mere few feet from her. She craned her neck up to see him and managed something that approximated a smile. Sort of.

"Hey, Ben."

"Hey." He regarded her silently for what felt like minutes but was probably only a few seconds. Still, it felt long. Too long. Rachel had an urge to fidget, but she kept her ground. The smile went, though. "So, you're back," he said.

Obviously. "Till Friday." She spoke brightly but also pointedly, and she wondered why she'd said it that way—almost like a warning. Perhaps it had been.

Ben's expression darkened. "We need to talk."

What? "Um, sorry?" Rachel asked. Now she was doing that pseudo-polite thing, a bit passive-aggressive. Oh, dear.

"We need to talk," Ben repeated, now sounding annoyed that he'd had to say it twice. "Are you free? I'll meet you back at the farmhouse."

"Yours…?" Rachel was still spinning from this unheard-of directive. She had not been inside the Mackey farmhouse since she was seventeen. And what on earth did Ben need to speak to her about, when they basically hadn't spoken in over ten years?

"Yes, mine." He started up the tractor again, and the rumble of its engine meant further conversation was virtually impossible. In any case, he started driving off before Rachel could even formulate a reply. What did they have to talk about? And why did she feel as if she was about to be told off?

Gritting her teeth, dread swirling in her stomach, she marched down the road in the wake of the tractor, far enough back that she didn't breathe in the dried mud it kicked up. At the gate to the Mackeys' farm, Ben drove the tractor towards the barn while Rachel, after a moment's indecision, walked towards the farmhouse. Unlike the Mowbray house's Georgian squareness, the Mackeys' farmhouse was long and low, whitewashed and rambling. Rachel recalled its slightly shabby cosiness from her childhood; the rooms of her own home had often been draughty and cold, but the Mackey farmhouse had always seemed happy and snug, filled with animals—they'd had three cats and four dogs at one point—and cheerful and busy in a way she didn't remember her own home being. Its inglenook fireplace had always had a cheery blaze, Ben's mum was usually pulling something delicious out of the Aga, and everything seemed warm and welcoming.

She waited outside the back door to the kitchen, listening to the bark and whine of the animals within, their tails beating a desperate staccato on the stone-flagged floor. After a few minutes, Ben came from the barn, his stride long-legged and firm. He wore a flannel shirt and a pair of very worn jeans; he'd taken off the outer clothes he'd worn while he'd been out in the fields.

As he came closer, his mouth twisted, although Rachel couldn't tell if it was a smile or a sneer. Sort of both.

"You could have gone inside," he said as he walked past her to open the door. The dogs rushed, surrounding her in a cheerful, frantic frenzy—two springer spaniels and a black Lab.

"Well, I didn't want to presume," Rachel replied a bit stiffly, and she bent to stroke the dogs' heads and fondle their ears. "Jack and Jill," she said, nodding to the two spaniels. "Still ticking away?"

"No, Jack died two years ago," Ben told her. "And Jill the year before that. They're from their litter, though. These are Sonny and Cher."

"Nice," Rachel replied with a small smile. "I'm sorry about Jack and Jill, though." She'd loved those dogs; Fred was from one of Jill's litters.

He shrugged his acceptance of her condolences and gestured her to come inside; he was standing in the doorway, which meant she had to squeeze past him. She did so, averting her head, trying not to breathe, not even sure why she found it so difficult. She'd forgotten how broad he was—not particularly tall, an inch or two under six feet, but muscular and strong. She swallowed dryly, cursing herself for noticing. For thinking about it. For *remembering*.

The kitchen was just as she recalled it—low-ceilinged and filled with comfortable clutter, from the tangle of boots by the door to the mess of papers heaped on the sofa against one wall.

"Cuppa," Ben said, not a question, and went to fill the kettle before plonking it on the big red Aga. A tin of tiffin was cooling on top of the Aga, and he cut two large squares, without asking, before putting them on plates and handing one to Rachel.

"Thank you," Rachel murmured, perplexed and unsettled by this seeming friendliness—although it wasn't really friendly; he didn't talk to her all the while, which was admittedly not that unusual, and there was a certain grimness to his brisk movements. This, she supposed, was simply normal Yorkshire hospitality, offered to anyone and everyone, even her.

"So how was Ibiza?" he asked, and she grimaced. Already it felt like a long time ago.

"Short," she replied. "But I'm here now."

"As I can see."

Rachel bit her tongue on any reply as the kettle boiled and Ben began to make a pot of tea. He brought it to the table, gesturing to Rachel to sit. The dogs had settled themselves on the floor, the black Lab by the Aga and the spaniels under the table, eager for crumbs.

Rachel sat opposite Ben and gave him what she hoped was a smiling, direct look. "So, what's this all about?"

"You need to stay."

Rachel blinked, surprised that she was surprised at Ben being as blunt as that. Of course he was. He always had been.

"Stay…?" she repeated cautiously, as if it were a word she didn't know, a concept she hadn't come across before, and really, she supposed she hadn't. She'd been planning on visiting more often regardless, not that she felt like telling Ben that now, but…

"Yes, stay." Ben poured out two cups of tea so strong it practically looked like coffee. He poured two large spoonfuls of sugar in his and then pushed the bowl towards her before adding a splash of milk. "Stay at the farm. For a while."

"I'm here till Friday—"

"You know that's not what I mean, Rachel."

"What do you mean, then?" Rachel asked. Here came the edge in her voice, but really, why was Ben telling her what to do? "Why, exactly," she asked, "are you involving yourself so much?"

"Because I'm concerned about Harriet. She's been holding the bag for the last twelve years—"

"What *bag*, exactly?" Rachel interjected, her voice rising. "Just because she stayed here doesn't mean she was forced to. And I have come back, you know. Sometimes."

Ben gave her a look like she was being dumb, and she *wasn't*. She knew she wasn't.

"She was just supposed to leave your dad all on his own?" he said disbelievingly, and Rachel gritted her teeth.

"Yes, because he's an adult. Children grow up and leave home, you know? That is what is called *normal*."

Ben's expression darkened and belatedly Rachel realised it sounded as if she'd been talking about him. She hadn't been—had she? "Anyway," she said, "this is really none of your business."

"It's my business, because it affects me," Ben returned levelly.

Rachel stared at him. "What do you mean?"

"Your dad can't manage the farm on his own, hasn't for a while."

She swallowed. "He's sold off a bunch of the dairy herd—"

"Even so. I've been helping out. So has Harriet. A lot. It's time you did your bit."

Why, Rachel wondered, did everyone act as if she *owed* them something? She looked down, not able to stomach the cool judgement she saw in Ben's face, and broke off a piece of tiffin, crumbling it between her fingers because she had absolutely no appetite. If she told Ben now that she'd been planning on coming back more often she knew he wouldn't believe her, and he wouldn't be impressed, anyway. It wouldn't be enough. It was never enough.

"What happened at the memory clinic, anyway?" Ben asked after a moment. "You went this afternoon, right?"

"Yes." She took a deep breath, steadying herself, because as annoyed as she was, she also felt suddenly near tears, and the last thing she wanted to show Ben was that kind of weakness. "He's been recommended for an MRI, but the specialist didn't seem to think he had Alzheimer's."

"She said so?"

Rachel shrugged, risking a look up. "No, but that was the sense I got, although…" She hesitated. "He passed everything except he forgot the word for keys. So who knows, really." A sigh escaped her, long and defeated. She'd left the appointment feeling almost as optimistic as her dad had been, but maybe that was just wishful thinking.

"When's the MRI?" Ben asked.

"It hasn't been scheduled yet." She took a breath, bracing

herself to tell him that he could butt out now, but she realised she didn't have the strength at the moment. She still felt appallingly close to tears, although she was pretty sure she was hiding it well enough for Ben not to notice. "So what are you suggesting, Ben?" she asked instead. "How long do you expect me to stay and 'do my bit', because I do have a job, you know? A flat. A life." Not really so much the life, but he certainly didn't need to know that.

Ben gave her a long, level look as he raised his mug to his lips, took a sip, and then put it down again. "As long as it takes," he said in a tone that brooked no argument.

Chapter Five

"AS LONG AS it takes?" Rachel's voice both rose and trembled. "What is that supposed to mean?"

"Your dad might not have Alzheimer's, but something's clearly going on," Ben replied in the same steady voice. "The things he can't remember, his balance being off…he's fallen a few times, not that he wants anyone to know, but I've seen."

Rachel closed her eyes briefly, not liking to think about those hard facts. "And you don't think Harriet can handle it?" she asked.

"Harriet has handled everything so far, but she's trying to live her own life too, you know, not that she's had much chance."

There was an accusatory note in his voice that made her feel like shrieking. "That's not my fault," she said as calmly as she could.

"He's your dad, too," Ben said quietly.

Not that he acted like it all that much. She cast her gaze to the ceiling and did her best not to blink. "What about my job?"

"In this day and age, can't you work remotely? For a couple of months, at least, till things are settled? I don't think it's that big an ask, Rachel, even though we all know how much you hate it here." Spoken matter-of-factly, but *ouch*. Why did that hurt so much? She *did* hate it here, and she supposed she'd been fairly obvious about it, but then so had Harriet and even Ben, about hating having her here.

Rachel forced herself to look at him again, even though it was hard, but to her surprise she didn't see the judgement she'd expected in his face but rather sympathy, and she realised that was actually worse. The lump in her throat she'd been doing her best to dissolve came back in full force. "You think things will be settled in a few months?" she managed, forcing herself to speak around it.

Ben shrugged one powerful shoulder. "One way or another."

And what was *that* supposed to mean? Did Ben think her dad had something serious? More serious, even, than dementia? Rachel knew she wasn't strong enough to ask, not right then, anyway. She didn't even want to think about it, but she had to do something…something more than just visiting every couple of months, or even every couple of weeks.

And yet…everything in her resisted agreeing with him. Just as she'd told Harriet, she couldn't work remotely. Not easily, anyway. And she had a flat, and a life in London…well a life that comprised work and more work and not much else—the odd evening out, or Saturday brunch with friends—but *still*. She didn't want to give her entire life up. More importantly, she didn't want to come back and deal with her sister and her dad, her hostility and his indifference, never mind the illness he might have, all the other potential, ensuing complications, tensions, and memories.

The memories, most of all.

"So what do you want me to do?" she asked Ben. "Just stick around for a few weeks? Harriet will love that, I'm sure. She's already acting as if she can't wait for me to leave."

"She always acts that way," Ben replied, "because you always do."

Rachel rolled her eyes, aware there might be more than a grain of truth in that statement that she was unwilling to accept. "What is this, amateur psychology hour?"

The corner of Ben's mouth kicked up although his expression remained serious, even sombre. "I suppose so."

Rachel broke off another piece of tiffin and this time she put it in her mouth, the crumbly sweetness of the chocolate and marshmallow and raisins bursting on her tongue. Ben's mum Diana had always been a fabulous baker, she recalled. "How is your mum?" she asked, needing to change the subject, at least for a few minutes.

"She's fine. Slowing down a bit, but we all are. She's helping out at the toddler morning in Mathering right now." Sounded about right, Rachel thought. Diana probably wished Ben would marry and give her a bunch of babies. Why hadn't he? He was thirty-two, the same age as her, and there had to be a fair few women around here who had their eye on him. Maybe, she thought, with an unpleasant, cramping sort of sensation, Harriet did. Maybe that's what this was about—Ben was being protective of Harriet because he cared about her.

"And the farm?" she asked, needing a distraction from that particular train of thought. "It's going okay?"

"We're making it. Just." His mouth kicked up again, this

time into a proper smile. "You're never going to make a mint farming—that's for certain."

"No," Rachel agreed with a small smile.

"So, you'll stay?" Ben said, like it was already arranged, and she wondered how he managed to do that—circle round with a sort of unyielding inevitability. Because she already knew she was going to stay, or at least try. She'd have to talk to her boss, figure out the remote working situation, maybe sublet her flat. It wouldn't be easy, but it might be doable, although in truth she wasn't even sure why she was doing it. Maybe simply because she wanted everyone to stop blaming her.

"I'll think about it," she told Ben, and he gave her a slow, sure smile that made her think he knew exactly what she'd been thinking. It was an uncomfortable, unsettling thought, that he could read her so well. That after all these years, he knew her so well. Still.

Except he didn't, not really. He knew the Rachel who had fallen for him at seventeen, who had lain in the hayloft with him, legs tangled together, dreaming up at the sky. She'd thought they would travel the world, conquer it together. Ben had had different plans.

A lot had happened since they'd realised they weren't compatible. Or, more specifically, Rachel had realised Ben wasn't invested enough in their relationship even to think about the future. Even to offer one *word* about it. His silence, after all these years, still had the power to wound her.

But this wasn't about Ben, she told herself. It was about Harriet and her dad. She'd stay until her dad got his diagnosis, whatever it was, maybe not as bad as Ben seemed to think. Yorkshiremen were always ridiculously pessimistic. And even if it was…

Well, she'd cross that bridge when she came to it. She'd figure out a way.

"All right, then." She stood up from the table with a screech of her chair. "I suppose I'll…keep you posted."

The slow smile was still there, curving his mouth, making her remember. No. She was *not* going to go there.

"If that's what you want," she added, a tiny bit belligerently, because *why* was Ben Mackey involving himself in her family's affairs, after all? More reason to think there was something between him and Harriet…

Another place she didn't want to go right now.

"All right," Ben said, easily enough. He stood up as Rachel shrugged back into her coat. She'd already turned to the door when he spoke again. "Rachel," he said quietly. She stilled. "You're doing the right thing."

Rachel opened her mouth to snap back that she didn't need Ben telling her as much, but she kept herself from it, knowing how petty it would sound. Besides, there was no point picking a fight; she was, she decided, going to avoid Ben Mackey as much as she could while she was home. Being with him was too…unsettling. After twelve years, she wished it wasn't so, but it was.

With a nod of farewell, not quite trusting herself to speak, Rachel left the farmhouse, heading across the yard and down the lane, back to the Mowbrays' farm in the distance.

AS SHE LET herself into the house, the depressing darkness of the place fell on her like a refrigerator. Why hadn't Harriet—or her dad, for that matter—done something about this house, she wondered as she kicked off her boots and shed her coat. Harriet might have bought a new bowl and a print for the kitchen, but the rest of the house was stuck in a time warp, circa 1980—or 1880, for that matter. Much of the furniture had belonged to her great-great-grandparents, heavy, dark mahogany pieces that took up a quarter of a room without being very useful.

The wallpaper was the same too, from that era, or near enough—faded flocked, some of it coming away in strips, along the stairs. And the pictures—the muddy oil paintings, the black-and-white photograph, the needlepoint sampler, none of it would be so bad, Rachel supposed, if there had been other things to lighten the atmosphere. A few modern paintings, or family photos of the four of them—even her hideous, gap-toothed school photo from her notoriously awkward stage—anything to show there was life here. There was love.

But maybe there wasn't. At least, not very much.

She walked slowly back to the kitchen, already feeling dispirited, defeated by the thought staying here for weeks, maybe even months. How was she going to bear it?

"You're back." Harriet was moving around the kitchen like a dervish, banging baking trays on top of the counter and sticking other ones in the oven. Rachel stared at her in bemusement.

"I am. But…what are you doing?"

"Baking." The *obviously* was unspoken but as clearly stated as if it had been, in a snarl.

"Cookies," Rachel surmised, because that's what was on the trays. "A lot of cookies. What for?"

"For a retirement party at the Wainwright."

The Wainwright was a local pub, named after the hill walker of old, Alfred Wainwright, who had made a path from coast to coast, St Bees to Robin Hood's Bay. Its trail went to the north of Mathering, missing the town centre and therefore the potential tourism opportunities, unfortunately.

"Oh, who's retiring?" Rachel asked, trying to be friendly, and Harriet gave her a quick, quelling look.

"No one you know."

O-kay. "You must know them, though," Rachel said after a moment.

"Actually, I don't." Harriet was slipping cookies off the tray onto a cooling rack with swift, practised ease. "Beyond their name, anyway." She hesitated and then said in a tone Rachel suspected was meant to sound offhand but clearly wasn't, "This is a professional thing."

She stared at her sister blankly. "Professional?"

"The baking." Harriet's cheeks were flushed now, and not, Rachel thought, from the heat of the oven.

"You're baking professionally?" she asked, and heard the surprise in her voice and inwardly winced. She hadn't meant to sound so disbelieving, but her sister had never done anything *professional*, as far as she knew.

And how would you really know? It's not as if you've been around.

"Yes, actually, I am," Harriet snapped. Clearly, she'd heard the disbelief, too. "It's just small stuff for now, for parties and things. I'm looking into supplying the Old Bakery, as well. With fresh bread."

The loaf she'd eaten a slice of? Rachel gave another inward wince. "Wow," she said, hearing how uncertain she sounded, even if she was sincere. "Well done."

Harriet rolled her eyes. This did not seem the best moment to say she might be staying for a while, but Rachel doubted there would be a better one. Every interaction with her sister was acrimonious.

"Did you talk with Dad about his appointment?" she asked, and Harriet blew out a breath.

"I didn't have time."

"Well, it seemed to go okay. The specialist has referred him for an MRI, but I didn't get the sense she thought he had Alzheimer's or something like that. At least…I hope not."

Harriet shot her a suspicious look. "What, then?"

"I don't know."

Her sister blew out a breath. "Okay. Well, you've done your duty, I guess."

"Actually…" This *really* didn't seem like the right time, with Harriet whirling about the kitchen, but Rachel didn't feel she could put it off. "I was thinking about staying," she said. "For a little while."

Harriet turned to face her, mouth agape, spatula in hand. "*What?*"

"For a few…weeks, maybe. You know, like you suggested." She gave the glimmer of a smile, which her sister did not return. "Until Dad gets the MRI, and then a diagnosis, if there is one."

"He might not get an MRI for months." This was said almost triumphantly, as if Harriet was looking for a reason for Rachel not to stay, which she probably was. How things had changed from when she'd first left. "You know what the waiting lists are like on the NHS."

"True. The letter should come through in the next ten days, so I can wait at least until then." Although she would have to go back to London to make some arrangements, get some more clothes and her laptop.

Harriet shook her head slowly. "Why?"

"Why what?"

"Why do you want to stay *now*?" The emphasis on *now* made Rachel think she was thinking of another time, when she hadn't stayed, and they both knew when that was.

"I want to help," she said, the words coming out stiltedly, like she didn't really mean them, and maybe she didn't. Not entirely, anyway. Why *was* she offering to stay? Because she wanted to help, or because she was tired of feeling guilty? Or was there yet another reason she really didn't want to explore?

Harriet let out a huff of disbelieving laughter. "Riiight." She turned back to the cookies.

"I do, Harriet," Rachel said quietly. She thought she meant that. She hoped she did, anyway.

"Look, I can't talk about this now," Harriet said, her back to Rachel, her voice suddenly sounding clogged, almost as if she were holding back tears. "I've got this order to fill, and these cookies have to be at the Wainwright in twenty minutes." She sniffed, tellingly, and Rachel felt a welter of emotions—sympathy, confusion, a little exasperation.

"All right, why don't I help, then?" she suggested. "What do you need?"

"Um…" Harriet looked around the kitchen a bit blankly. "Some platters. And plastic wrap. I bought the platters a few weeks ago. They're made of foil…" She looked around again, as if expecting said platters to magically appear.

Rachel tamped down on her instinctive irritation, because her sister had always been like this. Disorganised, scattered, a tiny bit hopeless. "Do you remember where you put them?" she asked.

"On the dresser." Harriet nodded towards the Welsh dresser, its surface now piled with old post—leaflets, flyers, bills. "Dad probably moved them."

She started hunting around, moving piles of papers uselessly, peering into cupboards where they couldn't possibly be.

"Do you really think Dad moved them?" Rachel asked sceptically. Their father did not bestir himself much when it came to household matters.

Harriet gave her another one of her looks. "Yes, I do, because he's been moving stuff around a lot lately, not that you'd know. Butter in the cutlery drawer, milk in with the plates, that sort of thing."

"Oh." Rachel hadn't realised.

"Like I said, not that you'd know."

"All right, fine, I wouldn't have, but I am here now, Harriet, and I am planning to stay. Do you think you can lose a bit of the attitude?" The words came of their own accord, fast and sharp.

Harriet stood up from where she'd been crouching to

look in a cupboard and blew a strand of frizzy hair out of her eyes. Her expression was more weary than hostile, for once. "I thought you wanted to help?" she asked.

"All right, I'll look. Where do you think he put them?"

"I have no idea."

Rachel started hunting around the kitchen while Harriet went back to the cookies. "Look, never mind," she said. "I'll just use some china platters. They're antique—they're retro and cool, right?" She managed a small smile, and Rachel realised how panicked she was. Baking all these cookies for this retirement do had to be a pretty big deal.

"Okay, I'll get them," she said, and went into the dining room, opposite the sitting room, and just as dreary a chamber, with the painted wallpaper, heavy furniture, dusty curtains. There was a mahogany glass-fronted cabinet full of their grandmother's wedding china, in a rather hideous maroon and dark green pattern, swirled with gold gilt, but like Harriet had said, maybe it was retro. She found two large platters and brought them back to the kitchen.

"Thanks," Harriet said, a bit grudgingly, but still, better than nothing.

Rachel helped her to put the cookies on the platters, fanning them out attractively. They looked delicious—just the right amount of gooey in the centre and bursting with chocolate chips.

"Since you've been busy with this," Rachel said suddenly, "how about I get something for supper?"

Harriet looked at her suspiciously, as if expecting a trick. "You mean tea?"

Rachel almost laughed. She'd forgotten for a moment

that she was in Yorkshire, where supper was tea and lunch was dinner. "Yes, that's what I mean. Is the Misbah still open?"

"Yeah." Harriet was covering the platters of cookies in swathes of plastic wrap. "Dad won't eat a curry anymore, though. Stomach stuff."

"Okay, what about fish and chips?"

Harriet hesitated, then nodded. "Yeah, all right."

"Okay." Why, Rachel wondered, did everything always have to feel so *difficult*? "Shall I help you take these out to the car?"

Harriet nodded, and Rachel took one platter while she hefted the other. They loaded them into the boot of the old Land Rover their dad had driven for about thirty years, and as Harriet slammed the door shut, she muttered, "Thank you."

"No problem."

Rachel stood in the yard, shivering slightly in the autumnal breeze that was picking up, as Harriet climbed into the driver's seat and started the car.

She watched her drive away, releasing her breath in a long, slow hiss, wondering if they'd made progress or just declared a truce—which was, she supposed, progress of a sort. At least it wasn't going backwards, which was something.

Rachel turned back to the house, squatting darkly under the late afternoon sky, its windows blank and unfriendly looking. Was she really going to stay here for the next few weeks, or maybe even months?

She squared her shoulders as she started walking towards

the house, making a mental list as she went of all the things she needed to do to make that happen. Because yes, it appeared she was going to stay…for better or for worse.

Chapter Six

THE NEXT MORNING Rachel came down at seven, determined to make an early start. She left her suitcase in the hall and went into the kitchen, her high-heeled boots clicking on the stone-flagged floor.

Harriet, already standing at the stove, gave her a knowing glance. "Leaving already?"

Were they back to that? Last night had felt almost—well, no, not quite friendly, but not hostile, either. Rachel had driven into Mathering—that was a blast from the past, another place that hadn't changed one iota—and picked up some fish and chips, wrapped in newspaper and smelling divine. She couldn't remember the last time she'd had proper fish and chips; she generally ate fake-healthy takeaways, salads with quinoa and lentils that tasted like their plastic wrap, chilled and flavourless.

They'd even chatted while they'd eaten; Rachel had asked Harriet a bit more about her baking gig, and while she'd been somewhat reluctant and slightly cagey about the details, Rachel had still managed to learn that her sister had been offering baked goods for parties and events for about six months. Their dad hadn't said much, and at one point he'd forgotten the word for what they were eating—fish—looking annoyed when Harriet had gently prompted him.

Rachel had been shaken by the lapse; no matter what Harriet or Ben had said, save for his brief senior moment at the memory clinic, she hadn't actually seen any real evidence of her father's memory fails until that moment, and suddenly it had all felt very real. She was glad she was choosing to stay, at least for a little while, until everything was figured out…if it could be.

But now Harriet thought she was leaving. Already. *Again.*

"I am going back to London, yes," she told her sister in a measured voice. "Just to sort some things out so I can come back long term. I should be back on Friday."

Harriet let out a sound like a snort, clearly disbelieving.

"I *will*, Harriet," Rachel insisted staunchly.

"Okay." Her sister couldn't have sounded more unconvinced if she'd tried. In fact, she probably was trying, the way she always tried, to make Rachel feel miserably guilty and at fault for everything.

Well, never mind. She had three days' respite, at least. Rachel went to pick up the kettle and fill it up, moving around Harriet, who was stirring some oatmeal on the stove. Fred wandered into the kitchen, sniffing hopefully by the stove before he plopped himself under the table.

"I saw Ben's two new spaniels," Rachel remarked as she spooned some coffee into the old, battered cafetière. "Sonny and Cher."

Harriet jerked her head around. "When did you see them?"

"I stopped by the farm yesterday, after Dad's appointment." She spoke casually, as if it had been a friendly catch-up rather than a stinging summons. She realised, as she watched Harriet, that she'd said it like that to gauge her sister's response. Why couldn't anything ever be straightforward between them?

"Did you," Harriet replied, her voice completely neutral, giving nothing away, although maybe it did, by its very neutrality. Rachel certainly didn't know what to think.

"What's the black Lab's name?" she asked. "I forgot to ask Ben."

"Brownie."

"A bit basic," Rachel remarked, half-joking, and Harriet scowled.

"Diana named him."

"Oh." Now she felt bad, as well as a bit dispirited, and she wasn't sure why. Maybe it was time to go. "I think I'll take this in the car," she said, hefting the mug of coffee that she'd poured. "Get on the road. Don't worry, I'll bring the mug back."

"Okay." Harriet sounded almost bored, focused on the oatmeal she was stirring. Rachel wasn't sure what she felt—strangely sad, a deeper emotion than her usual frustration or annoyance or even hurt, which at this moment she would have preferred. It would have been easier, less alarming, than the unsettling sense of sorrow and even grief that she felt.

"All right, then," she said after a pause. "See you Friday?" She hadn't meant to make it a question, but somehow it had come out as one.

"I'll be here," Harriet replied, in a tone that suggested Rachel was the one who wouldn't be.

"Okay," Rachel said, and then with no other reason to stick around, she took her mug, grabbed her coat that she'd hung over the chair, and walked out of the kitchen. Harriet didn't say goodbye.

All right, fine, Rachel thought, trying and failing to not feel just a little bit hurt. She was *trying,* not that Harriet noticed—or cared. She had a feeling that nothing she ever did would be enough for her sister, which begged the question, why was she doing anything in the first place?

"I'm not a quitter," Rachel said out loud as she got into her car. Although, in some ways, for the last twelve years, she had been, at least when it came to her family. She'd certainly stopped trying with the people she was supposed to love the most, beyond the bare minimum.

Perhaps it ran in her genes, she mused as she bumped down the rutted track to the lane. Her mother had certainly been a quitter, walking out when Harriet was seventeen, Rachel just one year older, and not looking back once, or so it had felt at the time.

Although she tried not to think about her mother, because it made her equal parts sad and angry, and left her feeling both fractious and empty inside. No, best not to think about her.

It was another lovely day, and the drive southward through the moors was pleasant, the rolling hills, farmhouses tucked away in valleys, glimmering under the autumn sunshine. As she hit the motorway, Rachel's thoughts turned from home to her work, her life. She was going to have to ask her boss, Danielle, if she could work remotely for an indefinite period of time, something she suspected her boss wouldn't like.

Danielle had been good to her over the years, offering equal parts tough love and sympathy since Rachel had started in an entry-level position just after university. Investment management could still seem like a man's world, and women often had to struggle to get so much as to the middle of the pack, never mind on top. Danielle had advised her to get her MBA while still working; she'd directed her to certain funds and investments that had paid off; she'd excoriated her for her mistakes while making sure higher-ups didn't hear of them.

Rachel didn't want to let her down, and she also didn't want to lose her job. Take your eye off the ball for so much as a minute and it was rolling away, forever beyond you. It was why she hadn't taken much holiday in the last three years; the trip to Ibiza had been somewhat enforced, as her company, under the guise of wellbeing, had made a new policy of employees having to take all their days of annual leave.

But a week of earned annual leave was very different from potentially months of remote working, even in this new culture where it seemed everyone wanted to go hybrid. At Wakeman and Wallace, you only worked from home if you were lazy, unambitious, or both.

With a sigh Rachel decided to grasp the nettle, and she dialled her boss's mobile on speakerphone.

"Rachel?" Danielle answered briskly after the second ring. "How's Ibiza?"

"Lovely, but I'm not actually in Ibiza anymore," Rachel replied, trying to sound upbeat and suspecting she was failing. "I came home early, due to something of a family crisis." She heard Danielle's sharply indrawn breath and she continued quickly, "Everything's fine, but my dad has had to undergo some tests. He's had some issues with memory, balance, that sort of thing."

"I'm sorry." Danielle sounded sincere, which Rachel appreciated. It was easy for a line manager to think only in terms of how personal problems affected the business, and while Rachel knew Danielle would absolutely be thinking about that, she also knew her boss cared—although, she suspected, not *that* much. She was still all about the bottom line.

"It's okay," she said, keeping her tone breezy. "But I was wondering if I could talk to you about some short-term possibilities? I need to handle some stuff back home and I was wondering about working remotely, just for a little while."

"How long?" Danielle sounded wary.

Rachel wondered whether it was better to over or underestimate. "I don't know," she admitted honestly. "A couple of weeks, to start, I suppose, and maybe only that. Maybe a bit longer."

"You know working remotely isn't the same as coming in, being seen, no matter what people like to say."

"I know." The buzz of the office, the industry gossip by the coffee machine, the occasional drink after work, talking shop…setting up an office in the gloomy dining room of her father's farmhouse was definitely not the same at all.

"Are you back in London now?" Danielle asked.

"I'll be there in a couple of hours."

"Why don't we meet for a coffee this afternoon, then? Have a chat about it all."

Rachel was taken aback, because her boss was not really a chatty sort of person. "All right," she agreed after a moment, and Danielle named a coffee place around the corner from the office, in Blackfriars, before they ended the call.

What exactly, Rachel wondered, did Danielle want to *chat* about? She hoped it was just going over the particulars of a remote working situation, and not asking Rachel to rethink her priorities, or her commitment to working at Wakeman and Wallace.

A few hours later, Rachel was back in her tiny flat in Putney, dropping her bag in the hall and looking around the space she'd decorated so proudly, and yet spent so little time in. It was tiny—a narrow living room with a sliver of balcony, a galley kitchen, a bedroom that only just fit a double bed and bureau, and a bathroom that was smaller than a public toilet cubicle. But it was hers, minus a hefty mortgage, and she'd been so thrilled to buy it, this little oasis of modernity, on the sixteenth floor of a high-rise apartment building, all glass and chrome and unnecessary skylights.

Now her flat smelled stale, and there was nothing in the fridge but a couple of slices of cheddar that had turned hardened and yellow. Rachel only had time to change into something slightly smarter, brush her teeth and add a slick of lip gloss before she headed back out to take the Tube to Blackfriars—and her boss.

Danielle was already waiting in the sleek little coffee shop by the office, a black Americano at her elbow.

"What can I get you?" she asked Rachel briskly, standing

up, purse at the ready.

"A latte would be lovely, thanks." Rachel sat down, feeling decidedly uneasy. This was not like her boss at all. Rachel had not had a single meeting with her outside her corner office with its view of the Thames from two separate windows.

Danielle returned a few minutes later, setting the latte in front of Rachel with the same brisk manner before she took her own seat.

"So," she said, the look in her eyes turning beady, and Rachel's stomach cramped. She had a feeling this was not going to be good. "Tell me what's going on," Danielle continued. "Your father has had some health issues?"

"Yes, it seems so, although I haven't been up there much to know. But a neighbour called because they were concerned, and I took my dad to an appointment at a memory clinic yesterday." This was all feeling rather personal. As kind as Danielle was, their relationship was definitely in and of the workplace; Rachel hadn't ever told her boss anything truly personal about herself. She hadn't wanted to.

"And how did that go?" Danielle asked, taking a sip of her coffee.

Rachel shrugged. "He actually did okay on the memory bits, mostly, but the doctor is still recommending an MRI. I know I could come back and then just go up on the day, and I will do that if needed, but I…I kind of have the feeling that I need to be around, at least for a little while." She glanced down at her latte; the barista had drawn a heart in the foam, and for some stupid reason it made Rachel almost want to cry. Good heavens, when had she become so emotional? She wasn't like this. She was a *machine*. At least, she'd tried to be.

Danielle had not spoken, and Rachel forced herself to look up. Her boss seemed thoughtful, her lips pursed, her head cocked. "You know if you work remotely, you might miss some opportunities," she said, more of a statement of fact than a warning. "That's just the way it is."

"I know." Elise, one of the few other female employees at Wakeman and Wallace, had gone hybrid after her maternity leave, and most people acted as if she no longer existed; Rachel suspected that for them she genuinely didn't. Out of sight, out of mind. Completely. If Rachel wanted to become a fund manager one day, or even a VP, this was not the way to do it. "It would only be for a few weeks," she said, and then forced herself to add honestly, "Probably."

"Right." Danielle did not sound convinced by the veracity of that statement. She took another sip of her Americano, and then put it down suddenly. "Do you know how old I am?" she asked, her tone turning abrupt.

Rachel blinked at her. How *old*? She realised she had no idea. Danielle looked fortyish, but in a groomed and glamorous sort of way—gel nails in a discreetly neutral colour, flawless make-up, her hair a perfect, gleaming chestnut bob. She had a trim, athletic figure and she wore classy separates that always looked very expensive and effortless. "Ah," she said, and Danielle gave her a mirthless smile.

"I'm forty-nine. Too old to have children, maybe even too old to get married. You can't teach an old dog new tricks, as they say."

What did this have to do with anything, Rachel wondered, and what did her boss want her to say to that? She had no clue, and so she simply stared, and Danielle smiled again, this time looking genuinely amused.

"I know, I know, you're wondering why I'm telling you this. I gave my life to this job, Rachel, just like you've been doing—body and soul, energy and emotion, everything. I didn't think I'd ever regret it, especially not when I got to where I have—fund manager, corner office, the works. I've always had a bit of a soft spot for you, because you reminded me so much of myself at the same age. Hungry. Determined. And so I trained you up, basically to be like me." A sigh escaped her and her gaze flitted to the pavement outside the window; a stream of people hurried by, heads tucked low, eyes on their phones, on their way home from work. "But now that I'm about to hit fifty," she continued, "my birthday is next month—I'm not sure that was such a good idea. I don't know if you should try to be like me. If anyone should."

Was her boss having a midlife crisis? Rachel struggled to think of something to say. "I've always appreciated what you've done for me, Danielle."

"I know you have." Daniel shook her head slowly. "When I was a little older than you are, maybe thirty-five, I was dating a guy. Nice guy, laid-back, not like me. He was an economics professor, and he got a job in Sheffield. Asked me to go with him. I practically laughed in his face."

Rachel tried not to squirm; this really was getting personal, and if Danielle was expecting the same level of sharing from her, well...she wasn't going to get it.

"I know, I know, it's a pretty typical story. Romance versus ambition." She rolled her eyes, smiling a little.

"Whatever, right?" Rachel wasn't sure her boss wanted her to answer, and so she didn't. Danielle sighed before continuing, "That's not even the point, though. The point is I didn't let myself even *think* about it. It was an absolute no-brainer to me, until later, much later, and then I started to wonder. Sitting up in my corner office, looking out at that incredible view of the Thames and the Shard, I wondered if I might have been happy in Sheffield. And I came to the realisation that I probably wouldn't have been. Not as I was then, anyway. So this isn't that road-not-taken sort of nonsense, at least not exactly. Because what it really made me wonder…what sort of person would I have been, would I have *become*, if I'd moved to Sheffield and chosen to be happy there? Because happiness, I've come to realise, can be a choice."

Wow, Rachel thought, this was getting quite deep. She tried to think of something to say.

Danielle leaned forward, intent now. "And more than that," she continued, an uncharacteristic throb of emotion in her voice, "I wondered if I would have been happy if I'd said yes to a lot of other things. My niece's baptism. My aunt's funeral. The holiday with university friends in Crete. I said no to a lot of things, Rachel, so I could say yes to the job."

"Right," Rachel said after a moment, when it seemed as if Danielle was waiting for a response. She supposed she knew where her boss was going with this. Say yes to something other than the job. Well, she was doing that, wasn't she? Even if it cost her. Lesson learned. Sort of.

"So what I'm saying is," Danielle finished, "that I think you should go and stay with your dad. Make those memories. Be the one who shows up, who stays. Because ten or twenty years from now, when you're sitting in your corner office—or even if you're not—you're going to wish you had done it. And you're going to wonder what kind of person you might have been, if you'd made some different choices. You won't regret the choices themselves, at least not entirely. But you'll wonder, and that can be a very uncomfortable feeling."

She lapsed into silence, her face drawn into thoughtful lines; for the first time, Rachel saw the weariness and age beneath the glossy, made-up veneer. She questioned whether Danielle didn't just wonder, but actively regretted some choices, no matter what she'd just said. Was she seeing some sort of do-over in Rachel, her protégée?

"Thank you," she said quietly. She felt sad for her boss; she hadn't realised Danielle, who always seemed so accomplished and purposeful, felt that way, but maybe everyone did, at one point or another. Maybe questioning your choices was simply part of making some in the first place. You'd always wonder.

"So yes, you can work remotely," Danielle said, straightening, back to her brisk self. "Check in every day, and I'll try to send some interesting projects your way. I assume you've got good internet up there in Yorkshire?"

"Pretty good," Rachel said, not quite honestly. It was patchy, at best, but it would have to do.

"We'll say three months to start?"

"Three months!" It hadn't, Rachel realised, actually been a question. Three months suddenly seemed like a very long time, longer than she'd ever actually been envisioning. "I don't think—"

"Three months," Danielle said firmly. "Excellent." She rose from the table, smoothing down her skirt. "Good luck, Rachel, and I hope everything goes well with your dad." She smiled in farewell as Rachel gulped and nodded, struggling to keep up. She had not expected it to be that easy, not at all. It unnerved her, that it had been. Had some part of her been hoping for Danielle to refuse, her get-out-of-jail-free card, or really, get-out-of-going-back-home?

Well, Danielle hadn't given it to her. Instead, she'd told Rachel to go back home, and with her blessing, for three whole months.

Good luck? Yes, she was definitely going to need it.

Chapter Seven

THE NEXT MORNING, Rachel headed north with a car full of stuff—several suitcases' worth of clothes, her laptop, two houseplants she'd managed not to kill—yet—and even some cookbooks she'd never cracked open, but thought maybe, *maybe* she might up in Yorkshire, for some reason.

Thanks to Danielle's perspective, Rachel was feeling determinedly optimistic, although admittedly it was taking some effort. This was an opportunity, she'd decided, rather than a duty, although admittedly it was that, too. But she was trying to see the possibilities of living at home for a little while—space to think, to breathe, to *be*. Maybe. Working remotely meant she would keep more to the usual nine-to-five hours, *and* have time to relax and enjoy herself in a way she hadn't in…well, in years, really.

That was, if she could relax in her sister and dad's presence, which was not a guarantee by any means. But maybe this could be a new opportunity there, too. Maybe she and Harriet could finally get to the root of the hostility between them, work it out, even if that prospect sounded more painful than appealing at this point.

A breath escaped her in a weary gust and Rachel narrowed her eyes as she gazed out at the road stretching north.

No, there was no guarantee about any of that, but Danielle had made her think about that, as well. *And you're going to wonder what kind of person you might have been, if you'd done things differently.* That had, unexpectedly, hit home. Hit hard.

What kind of person would she be now, if she'd come back home more, or even if she'd stayed all along? She couldn't imagine, had never even considered the possibility…just as Danielle hadn't. *It was an absolute no-brainer.*

Leaving Mathering had absolutely been a no-brainer for Rachel, even after her mum had left Harriet alone with their ornery dad. Even when Harriet had begged Rachel to stay.

"You could go to Teesside University," she'd said desperately, her hands knotted together, tears in her eyes. "*Please,* Rachel. It's only half an hour away…"

Rachel had stared at her in sympathy but also horror. She'd only been at uni for a couple of months at that point, had come running home when Harriet had phoned her, tearfully, to tell her that their mum had walked out, just before Christmas.

Leave her course, her new friends, the fun she was having, the *life* she was finally living, and for what? To coax Harriet along for her very last few months of school, make sure she got her A levels before she got to go away, the way Rachel had?

She could have done it, she knew, if she'd had to; she could have taken a term off, come back in the autumn when Harriet was leaving for uni herself. It wasn't, perhaps, as big an ask as Rachel had felt, but she'd had a sense, back then, that if she came back to Mathering she'd never, ever leave, and based on Harriet's experience, she wondered if she'd been right. And so she'd smiled at her sister, and hugged her, and tried to speak with as much gentleness as she could.

"Hats," she'd said, using her childhood nickname, trying to set her tone somewhere between sympathy and briskness. "You've got offers at Lancaster and York. You've only got a few more months to put your head down, get your A levels, and then you're out of here. I'll be back at Easter, and I can probably manage a few weekends to break things up a bit..." She'd trailed off as her sister's expression had hardened and she'd turned away. When she'd next spoken, her voice had been bitter.

"You want to go? Fine. Go. Like I care. Don't bother coming back. Ever, actually."

Rachel had stared at her sister's taut back, torn between frustration and pity. It was only a few months, after all, and Harriet was almost eighteen, not a child. Rachel was only fifteen months older than her, a little more than a year, something everyone seemed to forget, because she'd always acted like the big sister—and Harriet had always acted like the younger one. Much younger, sometimes, or so it had seemed to Rachel, as it did in this moment.

"Come on, Hats," she'd said. Begged. "I'll come back every other weekend—"

"Actually, you know what?" Harriet had flashed back. "Don't." And she'd walked away without a word, and Rachel had let her, because the truth was, she was angry at her sister's intransigence, her refusal to consider Rachel's perspective. And so, in that moment, she'd straightened, let Harriet walk away without a word, and then she'd gone herself.

She'd been so angry, and really *hurt*, that she hadn't come back until Easter, and then only for a few days, maybe a week. Another week at the end of the summer, when Harriet had been monosyllabic and Rachel had wondered if she should stop bothering. Her sister had decided not to go to university, and Rachel had told herself that wasn't her fault even if it had seemed over the years that Harriet had always, *always* blamed her for it.

Rachel flexed her hands on the steering wheel and tried to relax her shoulders and her jaw, both of which had tensed up, so she was gritting her teeth and her shoulders were nearly by her ears. Rehashing these old memories wasn't something she did very often, if at all, but it was hard not to as she drove north, towards home.

IT WAS LATE afternoon by the time Rachel drove up the lane that led to the farmhouse. The sun was already starting its descent towards the hill behind the house, the horizon a stream of serrated ribbons of colour—lavender, orange, yellow, palest blue. In the distance a sheep bleated, the sound mournful. As Rachel got out of the car and stretched, the smell of home hit her—coal smoke, animal, fresh air. She breathed it in deep, let it saturate her system. She was going to make this work.

"I wasn't sure you'd be back."

Rachel squinted through the gathering dusk to see Harriet standing on the front stoop, arms folded, unsmiling.

"I texted my ETA this morning," she said as mildly as she could, and Harriet shrugged and turned back inside.

Rachel breathed in again. Out. *She was going to make this work.* Clearly that was going to have to be something of a mantra, at least at the start. She turned back to the car, and Fred came out to sniff around her feet as she started unloading her stuff, with no help from Harriet—not, she reminded herself, that she was going to think that way.

Harriet remained in the kitchen, banging pots around as Rachel took all her stuff upstairs. She'd already moved the boxes that had been stacked in her bedroom into the fourth bedroom, which had always been used as a spare; the very fact that Harriet had used her bedroom rather than the spare for storage felt a little passive-aggressive, but she was determined to let it go. The last thing she wanted to be doing right now was keeping a list of petty slights the way her sister seemed to, but goodness, it was hard not to, sometimes.

Her bedroom, Rachel acknowledged as she unpacked her things, was unreservedly depressing—the same faded, flocked wallpaper as the rest of the house, the curtains dingy, the coverlet worn. Well, there was no reason why she couldn't brighten it up a bit, was there? Her heart leapt at the thought—why not give not just her room, but the whole house a bit of a facelift? Nothing too drastic, of course, but it wouldn't cost much to paint a few rooms, get rid of the dreadful wallpaper…maybe she'd suggest it to Harriet over supper. Perhaps it could be a project that brought them together. For a brief moment, Rachel imagined them stripping wallpaper, painting walls, all, inexplicably, to an internal soundtrack of eighties pop music. Well, a girl could dream.

With a determined spring in her step, she finished putting away her clothes, placed the houseplants on the windowsill, and made up the bed with her own linens from her flat in London. It did look a little better, she decided, insistently optimistic. This was going to work, she told herself yet again. She was going to make it work. No matter what.

Tantalising aromas of beef and vegetables were drifting upstairs by the time Rachel headed down to beard the lion in its den—or rather, her sister in the kitchen.

"What have you made?" she asked cheerfully as she came into the room. Her sister was standing at the stove, stirring a pot. "It smells delicious."

"Just beef stew and dumplings." Harriet gave her an uncertain, suspicious look. "You're not vegan or anything, are you?"

"Nope, absolutely not." Even if she did subsist mainly on salads back in London, she wouldn't here. "I didn't think you could be a vegan in Yorkshire," she teased. Surely it was a land of hearty stews and warming soups, not to mention thick slabs of sticky toffee pudding drowning in caramel sauce, Yorkshire puddings smothered in gravy… Her mother used to make those kinds of things, Rachel recalled, until, seemingly suddenly, she didn't. But why did she keep thinking about her mother?

"Can I help?" she asked Harriet, who was replacing the lid of a casserole dish on top of the Rayburn.

"You could lay the table, if you wanted." Harriet still sounded suspicious, as if she didn't trust Rachel to do such a simple thing. What had she done, Rachel wondered as she fetched the plates, to deserve such doubt? Or maybe it was what she hadn't done. Harriet probably had a whole list of the ways she'd disappointed her over the years.

But she wasn't going to think that way, she reminded herself for the umpteenth time as she set the plates on the table. "How's Dad been?" she asked. "Since I've been gone?" It had only been forty-eight hours, but for some reason it felt like a long time.

Harriet shrugged as she moved around the kitchen, wiping counters, checking pots. "The same, really."

"I don't know that I have a clear picture of what that is," Rachel remarked in what she hoped was a friendly, inviting tone. "He's not exactly forthcoming about his symptoms."

"He hides them, so I don't always know how bad it is," Harriet replied. "But like I told you before, it's the memory lapses. Forgetting words, putting things in odd places. And balance—he's fallen a few times, although he acts like it's just normal clumsiness. It isn't. I've seen him tip over when he's been standing still. There's something wrong." Her voice throbbed with emotion, and she strove to moderate it. "Something's been wrong for a while. But I told you that." Her tone was, thankfully, more matter-of-fact than accusing.

"You said months, before?" Rachel asked. She was still trying to get a handle on what was going on with her dad; every time she heard the list of his symptoms listed like that, whether it was from Ben or Harriet, she felt shaken, like someone had taken her by the shoulders and given her a good rattle. She might not have been all that close to her father, it was true, but she still loved him. He'd always *been* there—physically, if not so much emotionally; a solid, steady presence, in his own way, someone she knew she could lean on if she had to. "How many months?" she asked.

Harriet twitched her shoulders in a shrug. "I've been noticing for about six months, I suppose, but I think it went on before that. How long, I really couldn't say. You pretend not to notice, don't you?" she added, a bit bleakly. "Even to yourself."

Yes, Rachel understood all about that. She was the queen of denying things in her own mind. "And how often is he forgetting things?" she asked. "Words, for example?"

"Well, as you know, he's not much of a talker." Harriet gave the casserole another stir and then replaced the lid on the pot before turning around. "So, it's hard to say. A couple times a day, maybe?"

That much? "It must have been hard," she said quietly, "dealing with all that."

Harriet looked surprised by this remark, but then she shrugged again, the movement seeming dismissive. "I wasn't really dealing with it, to be honest," she admitted. "Not until Ben said I needed to make an appointment."

Ben did? Rachel tried to school her expression into something that wasn't—what? *Jealousy?* Heaven forbid. "You and Ben seemed to have become close," she remarked, more of a statement than a question, doing her best to keep her voice casual, although alarmingly, she realised it took effort.

"Yeah, well, when everyone else leaves, you hang out with whoever's left." Rachel tensed, readying herself for a defensive reply, but then Harriet sighed. "That's not a dig, Rachel, just a statement of fact. Izzy left too, you know. Ben and I were both alone." Izzy was Ben's older sister, and she'd been in Australia for years.

Rachel suddenly had a mental image of Ben and Harriet sitting around the kitchen table, sharing a bottle of wine, and lamenting about how everybody always left, how they were the only faithful ones, sticking it out, sticking *together*, the two musketeers of Mathering. The dagger-sharp pang of jealousy she felt, stabbing her right through, surprised her with its intensity and left her nearly breathless.

Ben Mackey? Really? After all this time? They'd been childhood sweethearts, yes, an intense, passionate, ridiculous relationship of just a few months. Well, sort of. At least, that's what Rachel had told herself, with the benefit of time, age, maturity... *It was first love. It never would have lasted.*

Of course, she'd never actually found out.

But thinking about him now, when she had, quite deliberately, not thought about him for over a decade?

It was just because she was back home, Rachel told herself. It would pass, the same way the flu did.

"Fair enough," she replied, laying another plate. "I just wondered."

"Did you?" Harriet replied, eyes narrowed, and she sounded uncharacteristically shrewd. Rachel kept her head bent so her sister could not see her expression, even though she wasn't entirely sure what that was.

Fortunately, Harriet didn't press the point, and Rachel went to call their dad for tea. It felt both odd and familiar, to walk outside in the crisp night air, feeling her way in the dark to the barn, the door opening with a creak, the sound of shifting animals rustling in the straw a strangely comforting noise, grounding her in a reality she'd let herself forget.

"Dad?" she called into the dim space, and her father straightened from where he'd been, sitting on a stool, reading the paper. Avoiding being inside with his family, as he so often did, but at this point, frankly, she couldn't entirely blame him.

As he came towards her, his left leg suddenly crumpled beneath him, and his expression turned childlike in its fearfulness as he flung his arms out to steady himself. Rachel sprang forward, grabbing him by the forearms to keep him upright.

"Dad!" Her voice came out in a panicked cry, and her father clutched at her for a few fraught seconds before he finally, thankfully righted himself.

"Sorry," he said gruffly, pulling away from her with effort. "Leg must have fallen asleep."

"Yes," Rachel agreed shakily, although she didn't think that's what it had been at all. "Must have."

Her father walked towards the house, stiff-legged and slow. "So, you're stopping for a bit, then?" he said with a sideways glance as they came to the kitchen.

"Yes, at least until your MRI."

"There's no need—"

"I want to," she cut him off, her voice firm but gentle, or so she hoped. "I haven't been around as much as I could have been, these last twelve years. Maybe it's time I was." She'd meant to speak lightly but as the words came, she realised just how much she felt them, a river of regret running through her centre that she'd always pretended hadn't existed, hadn't overflowed into every other aspect of her life.

"Harrumph," her dad replied, and Rachel had no idea if he was pleased or unimpressed, or something else entirely. He didn't say anything more and they went inside.

Harriet was dishing out the stew and dumplings as they came in, her father stooping at the sink to wash his hands. There was a piquant normalcy to the scene that Rachel couldn't remember feeling in about forever. When had things started to go sour with her mum, she wondered? When she was ten, eleven, maybe? And how had they been before that?

She remembered being happy as a small child, at least she *thought* she did, but it felt like looking at a photograph of someone else, half-forgotten, sepia-tinted with age. How had it *really* been? Did Harriet remember more than she did? Why did it feel as if there were swathes of her life that had faded or blurred or been blocked out completely?

"Are you going to sit down?" Harriet asked, sounding bemused and maybe even a bit annoyed, and Rachel realised she had been simply staring into space.

"Yes, sorry," she said, and she hurried to sit down in the same seat she'd always had at their kitchen table—second on the right.

They ate in silence, as they always ate in silence—had there been laughter and chatter when she'd been a child? Again, Rachel struggled to remember. All right, her dad had never been a bundle of laughs, that was for certain, but she had an image of his mouth twitching in a smile, the corner kicking up the same way Ben's did, both Yorkshiremen through and through.

Or was that just wishful thinking? She'd read about false memories, the way you could think something had happened simply because you'd wanted it to so much. And yet, she acknowledged, for years she'd assumed it *hadn't*. She'd assumed that her family had always been unhappy, that she'd always been desperate to get away, from the year dot.

What if that wasn't exactly true?

Her mind was still spinning with questions as they finished the meal, and Rachel began to stack plates by the sink, where Harriet was rinsing them. Their dad had gone off to the sitting room to read the newspaper, which is what he'd done every night after tea, ever since Rachel could remember. He was not a modern man, by any means; Rachel doubted he had ever cleared a plate or changed a dirty nappy in his entire experience of fatherhood.

When they'd finished the dishes, Rachel knew, Harriet would bring him a cup of tea; if she was lucky, he might mumble thanks. It was ridiculously old-fashioned and frankly sexist, but that's the way it always had been, and perhaps the way it always would be.

"Harriet," Rachel said slowly, as she brought another plate to the counter, "do you remember much about our childhood?"

"What?" Harriet looked taken aback by the question. "What do you mean?"

"I don't know. Sometimes I feel like I've forgotten things." Years of blank space that she'd filled in later, like completing old pictures in a colouring book, thinking you remembered the exact shades. What if she hadn't? Why was she even wondering that, now?

Harriet had a curious look on her face now, rather than her usual suspicious frown. "What kind of things?"

"Just how we all were," Rachel said. She didn't know how better to explain. "Were we…were we happy, do you think?"

"Were we *happy*?" Harriet looked at her in surprise. "What kind of question is that? Of course we were. At least, I think we were."

"How do you remember it?" she asked curiously.

"What do you mean?" There was an impatient, irritable note to Harriet's voice as she stacked a plate in the dishwasher with a clatter. "When we were little? I remember us being happy. We played in the woods, we went to school, we got along. *I* thought we were happy."

"And Mum and Dad?" Rachel asked after a pause.

Harriet scrubbed another plate before slotting it in the dishwasher. "Well Dad's always been your classic quiet farmer, hasn't he, not much for words or emotions, but they still loved each other. Dad used to pull Mum on his lap—don't you remember that?"

A sudden memory slotted into place—her mother giggling, her cheek pressed to her dad's shoulder as he gave that quirky little smile. She would have been little, maybe seven or eight…

"Yes," she said slowly. "I do. But…"

"But what?"

"Mum left," Rachel pointed out quietly, and Harriet rolled her eyes before averting her face, hiding her expression, her body taut as she grabbed another plate.

"I'm aware."

"I just mean…they couldn't have been very happy, if she did that?"

"She just got tired of the farming life." Harriet sounded firm, and very sure, determinedly so, although Rachel didn't think it was quite that cut and dried. "It wasn't about Dad."

"Wasn't it?" she asked sceptically. They both had to know their father was, if not a difficult man, then at least a fairly ornery one.

"Why would it be? What did he do?" Now Harriet sounded belligerent, dangerously so.

Rachel realised they were on shaky ground. They clearly had different memories, or maybe just different lenses through which they'd viewed those memories. And Harriet had been here, all this time; maybe she'd become protective of their father in a way Rachel hadn't been.

She glanced at the table, the scorch mark in the middle. Did Harriet remember that? Did she remember seeing their mum on the stairs, her head resting on her knees as her shoulders shook with sobs? She must have, because she'd so often been the one to offer comfort, giving their mum hugs, knocking timidly on the bedroom door when she wouldn't come out and they could both hear her crying, while Rachel had stayed away, furious and hurting.

Had Harriet forgotten all that? Had she chosen not to remember it? Maybe it was easier to believe her mum had been happy, until she, very suddenly, hadn't been. Until she'd left. Rachel wasn't sure she should ask about any of it. Harriet's expression was both fierce and forbidding, and she was scrubbing a plate so hard Rachel was afraid she might break it. For someone insisting they'd all been happy, she certainly didn't look it.

Maybe her own memories weren't as far off as she'd thought. Maybe it was Harriet who was misremembering, or maybe they both were, in their different ways.

"I don't know that Dad did anything, exactly," she said slowly. "I just sometimes felt that maybe Mum wasn't happy with the way things were."

Harriet blew out an irritated breath. "Then maybe she shouldn't have signed up for the farming life. It's not an easy one. She should have realised that."

Rachel blinked. "Don't you think that's a bit harsh?"

"No."

Rachel had always known Harriet harboured a resentment and even an anger towards their mother for leaving the way she did—walking out without an explanation or even a goodbye. At least, that's what Harriet had told her when she'd called, just a week before Christmas; Rachel had been in the midst of her first exams at university, trying to get her head around Harriet's anger and sorrow, her own uncertainty and surprise. She'd already moved on, she knew, even then. She hadn't wanted to go back and bail everyone out, but she had, dealing with Harriet's fury and grief, her father's stoic silence, her own yawning sense of strangeness. She'd understood her mother's reasoning, but she also hadn't, in a fundamental way. What mum just *left* like that?

In retrospect, in Rachel's view, her mother's sudden departure showed just how desperately unhappy she must have been. In Harriet's, however, it seemed to show how callous and cruel she truly was—which was odd, because when they'd been growing up, Rachel had been the one who had been irritated by her mother's low moods, and Harriet had been understanding and empathetic. Somehow, as adults, they'd switched roles, without her even realising. Maybe without Harriet realising, either.

"Do you ever talk to her?" Rachel asked now, and Harriet's eyes widened in surprised disapproval; Rachel realised they'd never talked about their mum like this. She'd been a no-go area not just for them, but also for their dad since the day she'd walked out. Talk about dysfunctional, but she supposed that was what happened when you had a family where conversation was a rare resource, a precious commodity, doled out in syllables.

"I haven't talked to her since she walked out," Harriet stated flatly, turning away.

Rachel had suspected Harriet didn't talk to their mother very much, but the admission still shocked her. It had been twelve years, after all. "Not even once?" she asked.

"No," Harriet said after a brief pause. "Not since around then, anyway."

Around then? Her sister's tone did not invite questions, but Rachel wondered if there had been a difficult conversation that had precluded future ones. "Has she reached out to you since then?" Rachel asked. Harriet shrugged her reply, which Rachel couldn't interpret.

"Do *you* see her?" Harriet asked, like a challenge.

"I have, a few times," Rachel admitted. Painfully awkward lunches every few years, where her mother looked near tears and Rachel longed to get away. Just like with going home, it had become easier not to do it at all. "Not for...a while, but I used to try to make an effort. Sometimes." It had been more than a while, she knew. It had been a couple of years, at least. There had been Christmas cards, the occasional text, nothing more. It was sad, really. Lamentable.

"Well, I have no desire to see her or speak to her," Harriet stated fiercely, her anger flaring out, high and hot. "And frankly, I'm surprised you feel the need to *make the effort*, considering you never did with either Dad—or me!"

And on that sudden, accusatory note, her voice vibrating with hurt, Harriet whirled around and strode out of the room, leaving Rachel gaping at her retreating back.

Chapter Eight

RACHEL WOKE SLOWLY, blinking in the morning sunlight, the curtains at her window rippling in the breeze; she'd left it slightly ajar last night, for the fresh air. Now, as the last, ghostly remnants of a dream began to evaporate from her mind in nebulous fragments of memory, she breathed in the cool morning air and listened to a cow low in the distance, the sound mournful yet also oddly comforting.

She'd been dreaming, she realised, of her mother. Already it was fading into fog; as so often happened with dreams, the more she tried to think about it, the less she remembered. But her mother had been there—smiling, Rachel recalled, and maybe even laughing—in a way she couldn't actually remember she had, now that she was awake.

Why had she thought of her mother like that? Was it because of her conversation with Harriet last night, which had ended so abruptly? The optimism Rachel had been determined to feel yesterday had seeped away overnight, as Harriet had barricaded herself in her bedroom and her father had kept to his newspaper, neither of them inclined to pay her any mind at all. The house had felt like a very lonely place, and Rachel had ended up watching Netflix alone before going to bed early.

Although, she acknowledged, she didn't know what else she'd been expecting—had she hoped that she and Harriet would suddenly bond over chick flicks and popcorn? Paint their nails and make cocktails? Or maybe tear down the wallpaper like she'd hoped...but she hadn't even been able to mention it.

Just because she was feeling optimistic, or trying to, didn't mean her sister was—or even wanted to. And as for her dad...well, he didn't seem to be all that thrilled she was back to stay, at least for a little while. It made Rachel wonder why she bothered, but then she reminded herself that she was trying to think differently now. And maybe eventually her dad and sister would think differently, too.

With a sigh that seemed to come from the depths of her being, Rachel sat up and swung her legs over the side of the bed. Today was a new day, and a Saturday, to boot. She didn't have to work, and away from London she didn't feel the pressure of logging a few more hours, answering a couple more emails, or doing some background research for a new investment possibility. She was away from the rat race, and like Danielle had advised, she intended to enjoy it...if she could.

She started by having a shower, telling herself not to mind that the house's water pressure left something—or really, a lot—to be desired. Washed and dressed, she headed downstairs, only to find the house empty. Her father was no doubt out in the barn, and as for Harriet...

Well, she wasn't here, either.

Rachel wandered around the kitchen, inspecting the watercolour of the Derwent Harriet must have bought, the bright red mixing bowl—these little signs that her sister had a life she knew nothing about it. *I actually have a life,* she'd thrown at her the other day, *even if you think I don't.*

When had Rachel ever said as much? But then, she acknowledged uncomfortably, maybe she hadn't had to. She knew she'd thought it, more or less, and in all honesty, probably *more*, and even though they hardly ever talked, Harriet had picked up on that. It made Rachel wonder what else her sister had picked up on.

It was something of an unsettling thought.

Turning away from the painting propped against the Welsh dresser, Rachel filled the kettle for coffee. She eschewed the very tempting loaf cooling on a wire baking rack—she wouldn't make that mistake again—for a bowl of granola and yogurt. She and Harriet should probably divvy up the cooking and shopping, she mused as she sat at the table to eat her breakfast. Otherwise, they'd probably argue about everything. They'd no doubt argue anyway, but Rachel knew she still needed to pull her weight.

Neither her father nor her sister had made an appearance by the time Rachel finished breakfast, making sure to wash and dry the dishes she'd used, and leave everything as she'd found it. It felt a little like being a guest in someone else's house, but maybe that's what she was now. It had been a long time since she'd been home long enough to think of it that way—as home.

The day was looking optimistically bright and with nothing much else to do, Rachel decided to go for a walk with Fred. He lumbered up from his place by the stairs with a wheezy groan that made her both smile and ache; he was getting old, and she'd miss him when he was gone. Funny, he'd been her dog from the start, but she'd left him when he'd just been a year old. She'd left a lot of things. Her mind skated towards Ben, and then back again. She wasn't ready to think about him yet, to open that Pandora's box of memories, each one sweetly painful. She'd managed not to think about him for twelve years; she could hold on a little while longer.

She clipped the lead to Fred's collar and headed outside, the day fresh and cool, the sun warm but the air still holding the dampness from the rain overnight. She decided to walk towards Mathering rather than up the hill behind the farm; she wanted to avoid another run-in with Ben, and she wasn't sure Fred could manage the slope.

It was three miles to the small market town, along a country lane, but about a quarter mile down, a footpath ran along the cow and sheep pastures, perpendicular to the lane before turning left and following the Derwent right into the top of town. Rachel didn't think she'd make it all the way into town, but she remembered it as a nice walk, and it kept her off the road.

Fred trotted faithfully behind her until they got to the footpath, and then she unclipped his lead and let him sniff around, walking briskly down the well-worn path, going into power-walking mode without even realising she was doing it, arms pumping, her stride long and sure.

"Rachel!" a woman called out. Her voice was familiar and full of warmth, and Rachel stopped abruptly, before she bumped into the welly-and-wax-jacket-clad woman in front of her. "You look as if you're trying to get somewhere in a hurry," Diana Mackey said, smiling.

Rachel flushed as she shook her head, conscious of the shrewd glint in Ben's mother's eyes. "No, just walking."

"Well, don't leave poor Fred behind," Diana said with a laugh, as she nodded to the space behind Rachel. "He's lagging, poor chappie."

Rachel turned to see Fred trotting slowly along, about a hundred feet behind her. "I didn't realise I was walking so fast," she said with an attempt at a laugh. Or that Fred had slowed down so much.

"It's good to have you back, Rachel." Diana's voice was warm, without any hint of accusation or judgement, but Rachel felt like fidgeting all the same. There was so much kindness in the older woman's eyes, along with that decidedly knowing glint.

"Thank you."

"Ben said you might stay for a while?"

"Until I've got things sorted with my dad."

"I'm sorry to hear he's been a bit poorly," Diana told her, sounding genuinely regretful. "I suppose it happens to us all eventually."

"Yes. I…I was sorry to hear about Douglas." Diana looked a little surprised, and this time Rachel couldn't keep from fidgeting. Diana's husband had died at least four years ago, but Rachel hadn't spoken to her since then, or even gone to the funeral. She hadn't, she realised, even written a condolence card. She thought of Danielle telling her she'd missed her aunt's funeral, and knew she'd been no better. She might have even been worse.

"Thank you," Diana said after a moment. "He is greatly

missed."

"I'm sorry I didn't go to the funeral," Rachel blurted, and then blushed. Talk about too little too late. It felt like the story of her life right now.

"London is far away," Diana replied, "and I know how busy your job keeps you."

"Yes, but..." Rachel shook her head and gazed down at her mud-splattered boots, not sure what she was really trying to say.

"Listen," Diana said, and she looked up again. "Why don't you and Harriet and your dad come for tea tonight? It won't be anything fancy, but it would be good to have a catch-up. It's been too long. Even though Harriet and your dad are right next door, I don't see them as often as I'd like to."

"Oh, that's..." Rachel stared at her helplessly. She didn't want to go to supper at the Mackeys' house and see Ben again, and yet part of her really, really did. She remembered how much time she'd spent there in her teens; the table of solid oak in their kitchen was as familiar as her own, and with no scorch mark in the middle.

"Ben will be pleased," Diana stated firmly, and Rachel bit her lip. What did Diana think about the way she and Ben had ended things? It had been so *abrupt*, a single non-conversation that had kept them from pretty much ever talking again. Why had it happened that way? Who had been the more stubborn of the two of them?

"I'm not sure that he will," she told Diana, feeling the need to be honest. "He seems to think I should have come home a lot sooner."

"I suppose Ben thinks everyone should come back to Mathering sooner than they do," Diana replied with a laugh. "He's always been a homebird."

"Yes." Something she should have realised, perhaps, when she'd been making her own plans, making her own pie-in-the-sky assumptions.

"He really will be glad to see you," Diana said, her tone turning meaningful. Rachel was pretty sure Ben would not be glad in *that* way, especially since he seemed to care far more about Harriet than her these days. Which was fine, because it had been twelve years, after all. They'd practically been children when they'd dated, and their brief romance had only lasted a couple of months. Ben had probably got over it a decade ago, at least. And Rachel thought she had too, she'd been *sure* of it, which was why the ferment of her emotions now felt so unsettling.

"So, tonight at six," Diana said, and it was not a question. "Tell your father I'll make his favourite apple crumble for pudding."

Torn between misery and a treacherous excitement, Rachel nodded. "Thanks, Diana. That will be lovely." Ish.

"Wonderful. See you then." Diana continued on her way, past Rachel to the lane and home, while she kept going towards the river. She walked more slowly, to give Fred the chance to keep up, but also because memories were seeping into her mind like water into cloth. You could pretend it wasn't happening for only so long, and then suddenly you were soaking wet.

Ben, at the sixth form disco, the February of their final year, one elbow propped on the bar, sipping his pint of beer, his brown eyes glinting gold over the rim of his glass. Rachel had been clutching a fruity cider—kiwi strawberry or some such, a real girly-girl drink—trying to look worldly-wise even though she was anything but and this was Ben. *Ben*, who knew her better than just about anyone, who had been her constant companion through childhood, until they'd started secondary school and he'd suddenly become mysterious and remote.

Rachel still remembered the first day of year seven, when they'd waited for the bus at the end of their shared lane, both of them looking nervous and uncomfortable in their stiff new uniforms—black blazers and grey flannel trousers, a skirt for Rachel that had made her legs look like pipe cleaners. The collar of her blouse had cut into her chin and the stiff straps of her backpack had chafed her shoulders. She'd felt self-conscious in the short, narrow skirt and oversized blazer; her mother had bought one two sizes too big so it would last, and she was pretty sure she looked ridiculous in it.

When they'd climbed onto the bus, some part of her had assumed they would sit together, even though they hadn't really spoken at the stop; the week before they'd biked into Mathering before coming back to Ben's and eating pick 'n' mix in his lounge, while watching telly. They were still *friends*.

But then Ben had slid in next to a boy he played rugby with, from the town club, and Rachel, who had been about to follow him into the seat before realising there was no room, had flushed and stumbled past, while the boy he was sitting with had snickered.

"Hey, Ben, is that your *girlfriend*?"

"What?" Ben had sounded both incredulous and utterly disdainful. "No *way*."

Her cheeks bright red with mortification, Rachel had walked to the back of the bus and slid into an empty seat. She'd clutched her backpack to her chest and tried not to cry.

Ben hadn't talked to her at school once for the next six years. When they'd seen each other back at the farm, he'd been friendly enough, in a reserved sort of way; occasionally, with Harriet in tow, they got back some of the old camaraderie although it felt a little forced, without the careless ease of childhood.

But otherwise, it had become a mutually agreed and never talked about fact that they simply weren't friends at school, at *all*, a fact that stung bitterly although she did her absolute utmost never to show it did. Ben hung out with the rugby lads; Rachel drifted between the geeky group and a few loners who attached themselves to her simply so you could have someone to sit with at lunch, friendships born of expediency and not much else. She hadn't been able to make friends the way Ben had, and that had made her miss him all the more.

Over the years, school had become something to excel at academically but endure socially; never one to have the confidence to saunter up to a gang of girls, her few friends in primary school had melted away to other groups, and Rachel had struggled sometimes not to feel completely, agonisingly alone. By the time she took her GCSEs at sixteen, her eyes had been on the prize of leaving Mathering for good. Find somewhere else, somewhere where people understood and even liked her. Home had become a place to dread, thanks to her mother's unhappiness, which hung like a shroud over their house, and university had begun to beckon, a siren song of new opportunities and personal reinvention.

So when Ben had given her that long, lazy look at the sixth form disco—she'd only gone at all because a friend had invited her; she'd thankfully made a couple of genuine ones during A levels, at long last—she hadn't known what to think. Why wasn't Ben ignoring her the way he always did at school, his gaze skating over her as if she were actually invisible? It had never, over the course of five years, ceased to hurt.

"Nice dress," he'd said, without any snickering or snark the way some of the other lads might have, and Rachel had pressed one hand down the form-fitting red dress of some stretchy material that her friend Beth had let her borrow. It was the most revealing thing she'd even worn, and she'd felt self-conscious even though Beth assured her she was a knockout in it. "It's perfect for your dark hair and eyes, and you've got a figure like a supermodel," she'd said enviously. "I wish I looked that good in it!"

"Nice shirt," Rachel had blurted to Ben, and he'd looked surprised because he was wearing a plain button-down in light blue, but then he'd smiled and said, "Thanks," and somehow, they started talking and when he asked her if she wanted to dance, Rachel had felt as if she were floating.

Ben Mackey was finally paying attention to her at *school.* She felt seen in a way she never had before, everything in her buzzing and alive. They'd danced twice together, and Ben had kept his hand on the dip of her waist when they headed back to the bar for a drink. Rachel's head had been spinning from the cider but really mostly from Ben, from the way his hand slipped from her waist to her hip before he dropped it to pick up his pint.

The evening had ended without them dancing again or even talking, and Rachel had tried not to feel utterly flat by the lack of attention or promises. It had just been a dance, she reminded herself, no big deal, and she'd be gone from Mathering in a few months, anyway. She'd already had an offer from Exeter; she'd been counting the days till she could go…until Ben had danced with her.

And she might have abandoned her plans completely, Rachel acknowledged as she stopped, breathing hard, by the River Derwent, where the footpath turned left towards town. The river rushed by her in a cheerfully burbling stream, but in her mind's eye she was seeing Ben's broad back, just a few months into their brief relationship, as he'd flung hay into a stall, his knuckles white around the pitchfork, refusing to turn around, even to say anything, while her heart had splintered into a thousand pieces.

After a yawning minute of silence, Rachel had finally turned around and walked slowly out of the barn. She hadn't spoken to Ben again for six months, when she'd come back after her mum had left, and then only the briefest and tersest of hellos. The next time they'd spoken had been—when? Several years later, at least, maybe after her university graduation, when she'd come home to pack up for her move to London. And then a handful of brief, awkward conversations since then, but really, the number of times she'd spoken to him at all was negligible, indeed.

Really, Rachel thought, the man had ignored her for most of her life. So why did the prospect of seeing him again fill her with that old, fateful mix of longing and hope? Some things, it seemed, never changed.

With a sigh, she called to Fred and headed back down the footpath the way she'd come, towards home.

Chapter Nine

"COME IN, COME *in*!"

Diana Mackey was all effusive warmth as she welcomed the Mowbrays into the cosy kitchen of her home. It had been something of an effort to get her sister and father to agree to come; when Rachel had said she'd accepted the invitation, Harriet had harrumphed that she might have had plans.

Exasperated, Rachel had turned to her. "All right, yes, but *do* you?" she'd asked.

"No," Harriet had admitted a bit grumpily, "but I might have."

Their dad had even been worse. "Why would I want to go there?" he'd demanded, as irascible as ever.

"Because the Mackeys are our neighbours and friends," Rachel reminded him as patiently as she could. "And Diana said she's making your favourite, apple crumble."

"Hmpph," her father had said, sounding like Harriet, but they'd both agreed to come, and Rachel had wondered why it was so hard. Wasn't Harriet friends with Ben, if not more than that? Hadn't he been helping out on the farm? Why were they so reluctant to see him? Or were they just reluctant to fall in with any of her plans, out of principle, or maybe just out of habit?

She was reluctant, Rachel knew, even as her heart raced with something treacherously like excitement as she hugged Diana and then shed her coat, trying not to look around for Ben.

"Oh, Harriet, you shouldn't have," Diana exclaimed as Harriet handed her a freshly baked loaf, wrapped in a tea towel. "But I'm very glad you did. How is the baking going?"

"Slowly," Harriet admitted, "but it's coming along."

Diana glanced at Rachel, smiling. "Has your sister told you all about her baking endeavours? Very clever of her. Everyone is talking about her cookies."

"I've heard a little," Rachel replied, hating how awkward she seemed, not knowing what was going on with her own family. "But I hope Harriet tells me more." She tried to smile at her sister, but she looked away.

"Ah, here's Ben," Diana said as she set the loaf on the table, and Ben ambled into the kitchen, clearly fresh from a shower. His hair was spiky and damp and he smelled of aftershave—the same one he'd always used, an old-fashioned scent of bay rum. Twelve years later and it still made Rachel's heart skip a beat. She looked away from the sight of him, afraid she was already blushing. Good gracious, what was *wrong* with her? She really shouldn't have trawled through all those memories this afternoon, torturing herself with their painful poignancy.

It had been like taking out a photo album from the deep recess of her mind, letting herself linger over each snap, so now she was filled with nostalgia and a sense that those days were a lot closer than they actually were. She needed to get over herself, Rachel thought crossly, before acknowledging the person she really needed to get over was Ben.

Except she *had*, eons ago. She really, really had.

"Supper will be ready in a few minutes," Diana said as she opened the door of the Aga and peered in. "Cottage pie—just needs to bubble a bit more, I think. Ben, why don't you get everyone drinks and we can go into the sitting room for a bit? There's a fire—I thought it was getting a bit nippy out."

Ben glanced from her dad to Harriet to Rachel, his gaze seeming to linger on hers a beat longer than necessary. She'd spent far too long choosing her outfit for this evening, and finally settled on a pair of smart black cigarette trousers, and a red turtleneck sweater in soft cashmere. London clothes, and too dressy for a kitchen supper in a Yorkshire farmhouse, but they'd felt a little bit like armour, and she knew she needed that. She needed to create a distance between herself and Ben in her own mind, because memory had blurred that space far too much.

"Rachel?" Ben asked. "What can I get you?"

"A glass of water, please," she replied, and suppressed the urge to clear her throat.

"Oh, come on, now," Diana interjected, smiling. "We're celebrating, aren't we?"

"Are we?" Harriet interjected, sounding surprised, and Diana wagged a playful finger at them all.

"Yes, we are! Your sister's home. Families together. Of course we're celebrating."

Harriet's mouth pursed rather sourly but she didn't object. Rachel tried not to cringe, because she was pretty sure her family was *not* celebrating her being home.

"All right, then," Ben said easily. "What can I get you, Rachel? A can of Kopparberg?" She blinked because that was what she'd been drinking at the disco all those years ago. Why on earth was he mentioning it now? Was she imagining that teasing, knowing glint in his eyes?

"Open a bottle of wine, you silly boy," Diana said, and Ben's mouth quirked up at one corner as his laughing gaze met Rachel's for a beat longer before he turned away to fetch a dusty bottle from the rack by the boot bench.

Rachel had an urge to press her hands to her cheeks, which she feared were flaming. She had not expected that flirty little encounter…if that was even what it had been. She felt as if she'd dropped down a rabbit hole into a land of memories and wished-for scenarios from her teenaged years…the nights she'd spent lying on her bed, dreaming about Ben Mackey! Thank goodness he would never know. Even when they'd been dating, ever so briefly, she'd never told him how long and hard she'd crushed on him. And she certainly wasn't about to now.

Ben opened a bottle of red with a smiling flourish and poured both her and Harriet glasses, while their father opted for his usual lager. As they headed into the sitting room, Rachel risked a glance at Harriet, who had relaxed a little, and thankfully wasn't looking so sour. Had she completely got the wrong end of the stick, thinking something might be going on between her and Ben? They seemed comfortable enough, chatting about the farm, but she didn't get the sense of any lingering looks or secretive, knowing glances. Not after the way Ben had looked at her…except *had* he looked at her that way? Or had she been imagining it all, some unfortunate wishful thinking?

Rachel felt as if she were seventeen again, and it was not a particularly nice feeling. She sipped her wine and let Harriet and Ben keep up the chat, too uncertain and confused to contribute much at all. She was glad when Diana took the cottage pie out of the Aga and called them all to the table, and she went to sit at the far end, away from Ben's usual seat, except after she'd sat down, he moved around to sit next to her, close enough that his thigh nudged hers as he settled into his seat.

What on earth was going on?

Diana doled out the pie and then started to engage Harriet in conversation about her bakery business while their dad methodically ploughed his way through a hefty portion of cottage pie. Ben turned to Rachel as she toyed with a forkful of pie, wondering why on earth she felt so nervous. So alive.

"So, how does it feel to be back home?" he asked, low enough that no one else could hear, so their conversation felt private.

"Strange," Rachel admitted. She found she couldn't quite look at him. "It makes me realise how long it's been."

"Twelve years, since you've been back for any length of time." For once it didn't sound accusatory.

Rachel risked a glance towards him, surprised to realise how close he was, his head bent towards hers to hear her better. She could see the golden glints of stubble on his jaw, and when she breathed in the scent of his aftershave, she felt dizzy. *Oh, help,* she thought. *Help, help, help, I can't react this way.*

"Have you been keeping count?" she asked and was glad her voice came out light.

"What if I have?" Ben replied, and Rachel felt jolted, as if she'd missed the last step in a staircase—or put her finger in an electric socket.

What was *that* supposed to mean? And how was she meant to respond to it? Having no idea what to say, Rachel shoved a forkful of cottage pie into her mouth. She saw Ben's tiny smile from the corner of her eye, and she wondered if he was messing with her for his own amusement. What else, really, could be going on? She knew he didn't like her like that anymore. Maybe he never had, since he hadn't tried very hard—or even at all—to make her stay.

Fortunately, Diana brought them both into the conversation then, telling Rachel about a ceilidh in Mathering next week.

"It's for charity," she said, "and I do hope you'll go. Ben's going, aren't you, love?"

Ben relaxed back in his chair. "Wouldn't miss it for the world," he stated dryly.

"And Harriet, you'll go, dear, won't you?" Diana pressed.

"Um, maybe," Harriet hedged. "Depends if I have an event on then…"

Rachel doubted she did, but she understood her sister's reluctance. Mathering's country dances were usually popular with the over-sixties, who danced with impressive vigour, and very few people younger than that. Rachel knew they kept trying to get the area's few twenty- and thirty-somethings involved, or at least had in the past, but as far as she could tell, they'd yet to be successful.

"For charity, remember," Diana pressed, and then turned to their dad. "Peter, you'll go, won't you?"

"What?" he barked, looking positively alarmed. "A ceilidh? I don't think so. Never been much of one for dances." And was even less of one now, Rachel suspected, with his balance issues.

Diana laid a hand on his arm. "You don't have to dance," she promised. "And it will do you good, to see the young people about."

"Will there be young people?" Harriet asked sceptically, and Diana gave her a mock glare.

"At least the three I see here, I hope! We are trying to get them involved, you know. Do say you'll come, Peter. It is for charity, after all."

Rachel suppressed a sudden bubble of laughter at the look of pure panic that crossed her father's face, and Diana's rather shrewd glance in return. She was reminded that they'd been neighbours for forty years—their families for generations before that; Douglas Mackey's family had farmed here for almost as long as the Mowbrays had. Had Diana and her mother been friends? Rachel realised she couldn't actually remember, although she thought they must have been.

"Well, I don't know," her dad replied as he tugged at his collar. "Maybe."

In Diana's book it was as good as a yes, and with a satisfied smile on her face she went to get the promised apple crumble.

Rachel glanced at Ben again, but he'd leaned over the table to address Harriet, his expression animated. They were talking about some local craft fair, and Rachel didn't know the first thing about it. She tried not to feel left out as she rose from the table to help Diana clear.

"Oh, you don't have to do that, love," Diana protested as Rachel brought several dishes to the sink. "You'll get that smart outfit dirty."

Rachel flushed, trying not to feel even more left out. "It's not that smart," she half-mumbled, and Diana gave a protesting cluck.

"Looks very smart to me," she replied.

From behind her, Rachel heard Ben murmur, "Too smart for Mathering, maybe."

Harriet gave a snort of laughter in return, and Rachel saw them share a complicit glance that had her cheeks burning once again.

Ouch. She did her best to school her expression into something neutral as she finished clearing the table while Ben and Harriet continued to chat about the craft fair, having seemingly dismissed her after that stupid Mathering remark. Had he *needed* to say that, she wondered bitterly, especially when he'd been teasing, even flirting with her earlier? But of course that was all it had been—teasing. She was an absolute muppet, to consider taking it seriously for so much as a second.

The realisation shouldn't have hurt nearly as much as it did. Rachel *knew* that, but she still couldn't keep sudden tears from stinging her eyes, a ridiculous lump from forming in her throat. It was hard enough to have Ben act as if he hated her; it was much harder when he acted as if he didn't. She stood on the edge of the kitchen, watching as Diana fetched the ice cream from the freezer while Ben got the bowls and Harriet, at Diana's instruction, started to serve, the three of them chatting all the while, and suddenly Rachel felt as if she couldn't be in that room, feeling like such an outsider, for a minute longer.

She excused herself, barely aware of what she was saying, before hurrying out of the kitchen to the bathroom she knew was down the hall. It still had the same wonky latch that wouldn't quite fit, she saw as she let out a muffled laugh that turned into something almost like a sob. Good *grief.* She was really losing the plot, she thought with a lurch of panic as she reached for some loo roll to blow her nose. There were just too many memories and feelings rising up and reminding her of who she was, who she'd chosen to be—her mum, her sister, her dad, Ben; the girl she'd left behind, the woman she'd become. It all felt like too much.

So much for her optimism.

A light tap on the door had Rachel tensing. *Please, don't let it be Ben...*

"Rachel? Sweetheart?"

It was Diana, sounding so kind and concerned that Rachel wished she could quietly disappear and never, ever return. If Diana had come out after her, realising she was upset, then everyone else—well, Harriet and Ben, at least—must have seen that, as well. They were probably talking about her right now, and she didn't know which would be worse—their condemnation or their pity.

"Rachel," Diana said again, and a stern note had crept into her voice, reminding Rachel of when she'd been younger, when she and Harriet and Ben had got up to all sort of antics, demolishing an entire batch of cookies Diana had left out on the range...

Slowly, with deep reluctance, she opened the door. "Sorry," she said, knowing she couldn't hide her reddened eyes or the ragged tone of her voice. "I was just having a moment."

"Oh, you poor lamb." Without another word or a second's hesitation, Diana pulled her into a warm, comfortable hug—the hug of a mother. She smelled of cinnamon and soap and her body was soft and welcoming in all the right places. Rachel found herself putting her arms around her as she hugged her in return, wondering when she'd last been hugged like this. When she'd felt so accepted, just as she was.

"It's hard coming home," Diana murmured as she stroked her hair. "Of course it is."

And even though Rachel knew Diana could not possibly know all the particulars, she still felt she understood the gist. "Especially," she managed with a sniff, "when it doesn't feel like home."

Diana pulled back to give her a look that was equal parts severe and gentle. "Rachel Mowbray, this will always be home to you."

"Not when other people like to act as if it isn't," Rachel returned with her first display of spirit in some time. "And when I'm constantly reminded of how long it's been since I was back, properly. I did come back, you know, a few times. I counted and it was at least, well, five." She blinked and looked away, realising how pathetic she sounded, before she turned back to Diana with flagging defiance.

Diana pursed her lips, and Rachel could practically hear her mind ticking over. "Is that how it is?" she murmured, half to herself. "Well, some people are still smarting, I suppose."

Rachel had no idea what that was supposed to mean, and she decided she wasn't going to ask. "Thank you," she said, "for being so kind." And then she steeled herself to walk back into the kitchen, and face her family—and Ben—again.

Chapter Ten

RAIN RAN DOWN the windows like tears as Rachel brought her laptop and work bag into the dining room at half past eight on Monday morning. She'd decided to set up her office in here, to be as out of the way as possible, since the kitchen was clearly Harriet's domain, and the sitting room didn't have a table.

It was a chilly, austere room, with its dark mahogany table and two large cabinets full of dusty china, but at least the view of the moors, now obscured by the misting rain, was lovely. After a difficult twenty-four hours, Rachel was recovering her optimism through sheer force of will.

The meal at the Mackeys' had, in the end, been both interminable and bearable; she'd come back into the kitchen with a smile on her face and managed to talk to Diana all through dessert about the older woman's various volunteering efforts, even agreeing to help out at the mums and toddlers morning—shudder—one day soon. She'd also avoided so much as catching sight of Ben in her peripheral vision, and she'd pretty much ignored Harriet, as well. It felt like the only way she could survive the rest of the evening, after they'd seen her rush off to the loo near tears, like some teenaged drama queen.

When they'd walked back down the lane to their own farm, she'd chatted to her dad about the dairy cows, barely listening to his answers because it took so much strength of will not to talk to her sister. Not to think about Ben. What a basket case she was becoming. That was what home did to her, she supposed.

On Sunday morning, lying in bed, she'd reviewed the whole evening with a cooler head, managing to give it a dispassionate analysis. So Ben had flirted with her, just a little. She supposed he wanted a little payback, after she'd swanned off to university so long ago, not that that was how it had actually happened. But he might see it like that, after all this time. And so, Harriet and Ben were friends. Rachel hadn't got the sense there was something more there, at least not yet, but what of it? It made sense for them to be friends, since they'd both stayed in Mathering. She wasn't jealous, she acknowledged. What she felt was more complicated than that; it was a sense of missing out, of having taken a turn in the road without realising she was doing so, while everyone else went another way, linking arms and laughing. She thought about Danielle, who had wondered what sort of person she might have become, and knew she'd been thinking that, as well.

What if she'd stayed in Mathering? What if she'd married Ben? Of course, such prospects were both alarming and absurd; at seventeen she'd wanted to experience life, to have adventures, not stay home and never do anything at all, or worse, turn into her mother, unhappy and essentially alone, even when she was married. Rachel had always known she needed to leave this place, with a bone-deep certainty, but this wondering about what-if was starting to drive her crazy, and so she decided to stop. Draw a line under it all and move on.

She spent Sunday unpacking and then going for a long, invigorating walk with Fred, who promptly passed out in his bed, basically comatose, after being dragged up hill and down for three hours. Harriet had been busy in the kitchen, their dad in the barn; Rachel had the suspicion that they would all spin in their own separate orbits for as long as she was home, unless she challenged that status quo.

Well, maybe she would, but not quite yet. She needed to build up her reserves of strength, of self, because coming back to Mathering had made her feel like that shy, insecure seventeen-year-old girl all over again, and she needed to figure out who she was now, not just who she'd been then, before she took any steps with the people in her life—her dad, Harriet, and maybe even Ben, although at the moment Rachel thought she'd do best by avoiding him completely.

It had worked for twelve years, after all. Hadn't it?

And so, by Monday morning, she felt brisk and efficient, setting up her laptop, wearing her work clothes and proud of her *smart outfit.* Yes, she was, indeed. Why shouldn't she be? This was who she was, who she'd chosen to become. She wasn't going to be ashamed or apologise for it, even if it was, like Ben had said, too smart for Mathering.

Maybe Mathering wasn't smart enough for her.

Already Rachel could hear Ben's voice, dry and mocking. *That was exactly the problem, wasn't it?*

No, no, no. She wasn't going to buy into his narrative, his so-called *truth* even, because that was not the way it had happened. Taking a deep breath, Rachel sat down at the dining room table and opened her laptop, felt a rush of reassurance at the sight of its screen flickering to life. Work. She needed to work.

She'd been a financial analyst for Wakeman and Wallace since she'd graduated, inching slowly but surely up the corporate ladder. She loved what she did; she loved the needle-in-the-haystack hunting for a good investment opportunity amidst all the masses and masses of dross; she loved studying columns of figures, pages and pages of financial data and figuring out what it all meant. She loved when she found a good opportunity that nobody else had, but almost as much she loved waving a red flag at something that looked too good to be true, and usually was. She loved being good at something, at feeling productive and useful, at knowing what she did worked and was right.

It gave her focus, it gave her confidence, it gave her identity and purpose. If that was too much for a mere job to give a body, well, too bad. She needed it. She *craved* it. And as Rachel fired up her laptop and started checking her emails, she felt something settle inside herself, an anchor coming to rest on solid ground, bringing her back to shore. *This* was what she did, who she was. For a couple of days, being back home, she'd felt shaken, and Danielle's ready agreement to have her commute from the deepest reaches of North Yorkshire had made her start to doubt who she was, what she wanted, but no.

Right here, in front of her computer, crunching the numbers, was where she belonged. In that moment, Rachel thought she'd see her dad through to his MRI and be back home within a month. What on earth had she been thinking, coming up here for some undisclosed amount of time? That was crazy talk. Crazy thoughts.

She worked solidly for three hours, barely moving in her seat, as she answered emails, set up a conference call, analysed some fresh data for an investment opportunity a client was curious about. Her brain was buzzing and her shoulder blades ached—those knots were back—but she felt good, important and useful in a way she hadn't been since she'd rocked up to Mathering a week ago. Thank goodness for the change.

A little after eleven Rachel stretched, closed her laptop, and then decided to venture to the kitchen for a much-needed cup of coffee. The house was quiet, making her wonder if Harriet had gone out, perhaps to deliver more baking, only for her to come to a surprised stop in the doorway of the kitchen. Her sister was sitting at the kitchen table, her head in her hands, a tissue screwed up in one fist.

"Hats—" The nickname came unthinkingly, but at the sound of her voice, Harriet jumped up as if she'd been electrocuted. The look she shot Rachel was one of both misery and fury, and she whirled away from her to hide her very clearly blotchy face.

"Harriet," Rachel asked gently, "what's wrong?"

"Nothing." Harriet's voice was muffled as she moved around the kitchen, tidying up needlessly and avoiding Rachel's eye.

"Something," Rachel argued, keeping her voice gentle. It had shocked her, to see Harriet in tears, or very nearly. She was so used to her sister's anger, she hadn't let herself think about what might be underneath that far easier emotion.

"Why do you care?" Harriet replied, and instead of the old hostility, her voice just sounded weary, which Rachel realised was far worse.

She took a step into the kitchen. "I do care," she said quietly. "Even if I haven't seemed as if I do. That's why I am here."

"I thought you were here to boss Dad around," Harriet replied with some of her former spirit. "It's nothing to do with me."

"That's not true." Rachel tried to keep the hurt from her voice. "I came home because of Dad, it's true, but I stayed…" She stopped, because suddenly she wasn't sure she wanted to continue. How could she explain the complicated tangle of feelings that had brought her back home, especially when she doubted them herself?

"You stayed…?" Harriet prompted, with more than a touch of sarcasm, and Rachel suddenly decided to be honest, *totally* honest. Why not? What, really, did she have to lose, when it came to her relationship with her sister? A depressing thought, perhaps, but unfortunately a true one. The closeness they'd once had as children was sadly long gone.

"I stayed because it felt like the right thing to do," Rachel stated before adding matter-of-factly, "And because I thought that if I did, maybe you'd stop blaming me for everything."

"What!" Harriet's jaw dropped as her eyes blazed righteous indignation. "Wow, thanks. Thanks *a lot.*"

Rachel suppressed a short sigh. All right, maybe she shouldn't have been *that* honest. She wasn't even sure she meant it, anyway. Not entirely, at least. "Do you think we could stop fighting," she asked, "for just a few minutes?"

Harriet let out a hard laugh. "You ask that after telling me I blame you for everything? How could I, when you're not even here ninety-nine per cent of the time?"

"I'd say it's more like ninety-five," Rachel replied rather flippantly, and was rewarded with the very tiniest quirk of a smile. Beneath her prickles, her sister had a soft heart. She had, Rachel realised, always known that, really. It was just they'd both built layers of armour to protect themselves, and it was hard to peel them back.

"More like ninety-six," Harriet returned, just as flippantly. "Or really, ninety-six and a half."

Rachel gave a sudden burst of laughter, like a bubble escaping her. She shook her head slowly as Harriet smiled, her expression almost, strangely shy. "Harriet," Rachel asked, "why were you crying?"

Harriet looked away. "I wasn't."

"Yes, you were." Rachel kept her voice gentle; she realised then just how much she wanted to know. How much she wanted to *help*. "Your eyes are red, and your face was blotchy. It's not now," she added quickly, before Harriet could fly at her, although for once her sister did not look as if she were working herself into something of a rage. "But you were crying, Harriet. You have to admit it. Won't you tell me why?"

Harriet hesitated, nibbling her lip, and then she let out a long, weary sigh. "I don't even know," she said, and while it felt like at least part of the truth, it also sounded like an excuse.

"You must know at least a little," Rachel said, and her sister shrugged, the movement seeming restless.

"The Old Bakery doesn't want my bread. I suppose that's what kicked it off."

"They don't? But it's so delicious." Rachel tried for a smile. "I should know."

Harriet let out a tired laugh as she acknowledged Rachel's quip. "Yeah, well, they decided it was easier to make their own. Then they don't have to worry about whether my bread is compliant with all the hygiene regs and stuff like that. Or so they told me. It's not that big a deal, I suppose, but I was really hoping for a proper, ongoing contract. Not just these parties and events and things like that, where I think people are really just doing me a favour."

"A favour? What do you mean?"

"Sometimes I think everyone in Mathering feels sorry for me," Harriet stated bluntly. She looked up to give Rachel a direct, bleak look. There was no accusation in it, no condemnation or judgement. She was just stating fact, one that thudded through Rachel because she'd never thought that way before…and yet why shouldn't she have? *She'd* pitied her sister, more or less, for staying in Mathering.

"Why would they feel sorry for you?" she asked now.

"Because I've never got my act together, have I?" Harriet tried for another laugh but this time she didn't manage it. "Kicking around here since school, never had a proper job or a decent boyfriend. Everyone looks at me and thinks 'loser'. And this isn't a pity party," she said, with something of her old fire. "*I* don't think I'm a loser. I'm just saying that's how it is."

Slowly, her mind reeling from this information, Rachel eased herself down into a chair at the kitchen table. Harriet folded her arms, looking mutinous. She probably regretted saying so much, but Rachel wanted to get to the bottom of it, if she could.

"You're hardly the first person to stay in Mathering," she pointed out after a moment. "Far from it. Most people do. I've always felt the odd one out for leaving."

Harriet shrugged. "But I was going to leave, too, wasn't I? Just like you did."

"Why *did* you stay here, Harriet?" she asked. It was a question, she realised, she'd never actually asked before, maybe because she hadn't wanted to know the answer. "You had uni offers. You could have gone, like you were going to."

"Actually, I couldn't have." Harriet glanced away. "I didn't take my A levels."

"What?" Rachel stared at her in blank incomprehension. "What do you mean you didn't take your A levels?"

Harriet glanced back at her, smiling a little although her arms were still folded, her jaw set. "Exactly that. I didn't take them."

"But..." Rachel shook her head slowly. "How did I not know this?"

"You were busy at university, and then that internship in London. You didn't come back home all spring, when I would have had my exams."

"I know, but..." Surely she would have *asked*. She must have texted Harriet on results day. Been involved, at least that much. "Did I text you?" she asked abruptly. "When you got your results?"

"Yes, you asked how I did, and I didn't reply, and you didn't follow it up. When you came home a week later, I just told you I'd decided not to go, because, well, I suppose I had."

"Yes…" Vaguely Rachel recalled a conversation, Harriet shutting it down after she'd asked. She supposed she should have pressed, dug deeper into it all, but she hadn't. She'd left for her second year of uni a few days later with a sigh of relief.

"I'm sorry," she said quietly. "I should have known about that."

Harriet shrugged. "I didn't tell you when you asked."

"Yes, but…" She'd known something was off. She could have asked. "Why didn't you take them?" Rachel asked.

"I don't know, really." Harriet glanced down, tucking her chin low. "I meant to. At least I think I did. But it was a tough time, after Mum left. Maybe it shouldn't have been—I don't know. If I'd been you, I'm sure I would have got on with it all much better. But I didn't." She drew a breath, squared her shoulders. "And I'd failed my mocks in February—couldn't concentrate at all then. My teachers were telling me I'd really have to get my head down and work hard, and I wasn't, I *couldn't*. I started having anxiety attacks, and when it came to the day of the first exam…I just couldn't face it. At all. I realised I'd rather not take them at all than fail them, and so I didn't show up. And after I didn't show up for the first, it was easier not to show up for the second and then the third." She blew out a breath. "I'm not sure I really wanted to go to university, anyway. I always found the prospect pretty terrifying, to be honest."

"Why did I not know any of this?" Rachel asked, knowing the question was directed as much at herself as at Harriet. How could she have not known something so big, so fundamental? Had she already been that disengaged, just months after their mum had walked out? She'd come back for Easter, she remembered, but she'd bustled around the house, making meals and doing laundry and, she suspected, feeling put upon.

"I tried to tell you, a little bit." When she'd begged her to stay, Rachel thought, or later? Had there even been a later? She couldn't remember now, if Harriet had texted her, if she'd called. It was all a blur—university, coming home, moving on. "But I didn't go into it," Harriet conceded, "because I knew what you'd say. 'Just get on with it, Hats. Uni is brilliant. Just a few more months at home and then you'll be free.'" It was, Rachel knew, *exactly* what she would have said. "I know you might have meant well," her sister finished, "but frankly that wasn't going to help me at all."

Rachel felt winded, like she'd been sucker-punched. She'd always known, on some fundamental level, that her sister had struggled back then, more than either of them, it seemed, had ever wanted to acknowledge.

Rachel glanced down at the table, trying to sort through her jumbled feelings. She'd told Harriet that she'd come home because maybe then she'd stop blaming her for everything, but right now Rachel felt as if maybe her sister hadn't blamed her enough.

"I'm sorry," she said at last, because those felt like the only words she had to offer. "I'd tell you I wish I'd known all that, and I do, *now*, but I'm not sure I wanted to, back then, if I'm completely honest." She made herself look up at Harriet, who was gazing back at her, her expression weary and resigned, but at least not overtly hostile.

"No, I don't think you did," she agreed. "And that is actually something I don't blame you for. Anymore, that is. I definitely did, though, back in the day. I was pretty angry with you."

But she wasn't still? Rachel wondered. Because Harriet had certainly seemed angry with her recently. She wasn't going to press the point, though. They were both silent, lost in their thoughts, and for once the mood didn't feel fraught with tension. Rachel knew this was only the beginning, the first conversation of what she hoped would be many more. She still didn't know why Harriet had been crying, or why she hadn't left in the twelve years since she hadn't taken her A levels, but those questions and answers could wait, for now. They'd taken steps together here today, steps she was very glad of. She thought of Danielle saying how she'd wondered what sort of person she might have become if she'd done things differently, and Rachel thought that right now, at last, she was starting to answer that question about herself.

Chapter Eleven

A WEEK AFTER her conversation with Harriet, the letter for her dad's MRI appointment came through the letterbox, fluttering onto the floor. Rachel picked it up and opened it before taking it into the kitchen where Harriet was baking a batch of cookies for another party, this one an eighteenth birthday.

"Dad's appointment," she said briefly, putting the letter on the table. "His MRI is a week from Thursday."

"That's quite soon, really," Harriet remarked. She dusted her hands on her apron before picking up the letter and studying it.

They were both silent, absorbing the fact of the appointment, its necessity. Over the last week they'd managed to find an even keel, a careful balance. Rachel didn't press too much, and Harriet didn't fly at her. They'd worked out a schedule for shopping and cooking, with Rachel pulling her weight as much as Harriet was. It was working, Rachel thought, for the most part. No, they hadn't yet bonded over manicures and mocktails or shared a tub of ice cream during a Netflix marathon, but maybe those things would come in time. Although maybe they wouldn't; Rachel hadn't exactly been a mocktail-and-manicure type girl before now, so why she would be with her sister, she wasn't sure. But still, baby steps. Their relationship had made some progress, and hopefully it would continue to do so.

And yet...Harriet put the letter back on the table and they both stared at it. The reality of what it meant felt like a weight pressing down on Rachel. She could pretend she'd come back to right old wrongs, to get close to her sister, be a family again—but the hard fact of the matter was she'd come back because there was something wrong with her dad, and the evidence was right here on the table, not to mention in the events of the last week she'd tried both to handle and ignore—her father's debilitating headache one afternoon, when he'd had to lie down in a dark room; the time at supper when he'd forgotten the word for salt. The way he walked now, so stiff-legged, holding on to things sometimes, as if afraid he might topple over.

Something was really wrong, Rachel knew, and they needed to find out what it was. As for when they did, what would happen then, well...that was a problem for another day.

"Should we both go?" Harriet asked. "Or do you think he won't want to make a big deal of it?"

"An MRI is kind of a big deal, though." Rachel shook her head. "I don't know. I think he's forgotten about it, actually. He left the memory clinic convinced there wasn't anything really wrong with him, just because he knew how to tell the time and who the reigning monarch was."

"But there obviously is," Harriet replied quietly, and Rachel nodded.

"Yes, there is."

Again, they fell silent, absorbing what this meant—even if Rachel didn't think they could know what it would mean, not fully, until they had a diagnosis, and neither of them seemed willing or brave enough to truly consider what that might be, although vague possibilities swirled in her brain. Would Harriet stay in the house, if…

No, she didn't even want to think about it. Her dad might not have been the cuddliest father on the planet, but he was still her *dad.* As frustrated as she'd been by his remoteness over the years, she didn't want to lose him completely. Or lose this house, the only place she'd ever really called home, even if she'd hardly ever come back…which reminded her of that letter from the bank she'd seen, when she'd first arrived.

"Harriet," she asked suddenly, "when I was moving the boxes from my room, I saw something from the bank about a mortgage. Do you know anything about it?"

"Dad got a mortgage on the house," Harriet replied with a shrug.

"A mortgage?" Rachel couldn't hide her surprise. "Why?"

"Because he couldn't make ends meet. You know we have half the number of dairy cows we did before, right?"

"Yes, but—"

"It's really tough to make a living from farming these days," Harriet continued. "It's part of the reason why I wanted to get this bakery thing going. To help out with expenses. And because I like baking," she added with a small, wry smile. "I'm not that altruistic."

"So there's a mortgage on the house," Rachel stated, her mind focused on that one unpalatable fact. "How much?"

Harriet spread her hands out wide. "Honestly? I have no idea. Ben helped him with the paperwork."

"*Ben?*" For some reason this felt like a betrayal. Ben was getting all up in her father's financial business? Was this part of the reason why he'd said she had to come home? Why hadn't he told her about it? It annoyed Rachel that her neighbour knew more about her family's financial affairs than she did.

"He's been really helpful, Rachel," Harriet said quietly. "When Dad's been down with one of his headaches, Ben's done the milking with me, even though he's got all his own work."

Rachel took a steadying breath. "I wish you'd told me that Dad was thinking of getting a mortgage on the house," she said, trying to keep her voice mild even though part of her felt like raging the way Harriet once might have. "Or that *he'd* told me. That's a really big deal. Having this house free and clear—"

"What," Harriet interjected, an edge to her voice, "are you worried about your inheritance?"

"No," Rachel returned evenly, "but I'm worried about Dad struggling to make his mortgage repayments, especially if the farm is already in the hole financially. If he'd needed an influx of cash, he could have come to me."

Harriet raised her eyebrows. "You've got that much lying around?"

"Some," Rachel allowed. She felt as if they were veering towards one of their old arguments, and she wanted to avoid it. Things had been going well this week, mostly. "Probably not enough. Look, it's obviously too late to worry about it now," she said in what she hoped was a conciliatory tone. "Maybe I'll talk to Ben about it, find out more."

"Go right ahead." Harriet turned away, still sounding in something of a snit.

Rachel stared at her sister's back, a new thought creeping over her with unease. "You and Ben have become close, it seems," she remarked, keeping her voice as casual as she could. Her sister, however, wasn't fooled.

"We've always been friends, if that's what you're asking," she replied with a short laugh.

"I wasn't asking anything—"

"Ben and I have never been a *thing*, Rachel," Harriet cut her off. "And we never would be. He's always been yours." She spoke matter-of-factly, without rancour, without regret.

Shock blazed right through Rachel, and she felt her cheeks heat, her body tingle. "He's not mine," she said somewhat unsteadily.

"Well, he's not anybody else's—that's for certain," Harriet replied.

Rachel knew, absolutely, that she shouldn't fish for information, and yet she couldn't quite help it. "He's dated women, though, over the last twelve years," she said, more of a statement than a question. More than she'd dated, surely, although that wasn't saying much. A handful of first dates, men she'd matched with online and never saw again, one or two who had made it past that, but only by a little.

Harriet shrugged. "There's been a few casual girlfriends, it's true, but no one's lasted more than a few months, if that." She glanced back at Rachel, her eyes glinting. "Are you still holding a candle for him, then?"

"What?" Now her cheeks really were scorching. Rachel resisted the urge to press her hands to them. "No. Absolutely not. And I wouldn't think he was for me. I'd—I'd hope he wasn't."

"Well, you were the one who left, after all," Harriet replied, without any sting to the words, although Rachel felt it all the same. "You broke it off."

"That's not—" She stopped, took a breath. She wasn't going to go into the breakdown of her relationship with Ben right now, with Harriet. Some things were better remaining private. "It's all water under the bridge," she said instead, her tone dismissive, final. "*Way* under the bridge. But I will talk to him about the mortgage."

RACHEL DIDN'T GET a chance to talk to Ben until the next day, when she finished work a little early and headed down the lane to the Mackey farm just as dusk was settling. Her dad was settled inside with his newspaper, having finished the afternoon milking, and Harriet was on supper duty, so Rachel had slipped out with Fred, trying to act as if she were just taking him for a walk rather than heading straight over to the Mackeys'.

"That dog has never had so much exercise," Harriet had remarked rather shrewdly as Rachel had clipped on the lead, making her think her sister suspected where she was going.

She was just talking about business matters, she reminded herself, even as Harriet's matter-of-fact statement kept echoing through her head. *Ben's always been yours.*

He certainly hadn't felt like hers when she'd waited, in agony, for him to tell her not to go, or at least *talk* about it, figure out a future they could both have, and he'd stayed determinedly, obdurately silent. All it would have taken was a single word, at that stage, and she would have stayed. All her dreams would have been wrecked in an instant. Why hadn't he said it? *Don't, Rach. Stay with me.* She would have melted like butter—she knew she would have. She would have stayed in Mathering, and then what?

She wasn't really regretting the choice she'd made all those years ago, was she? No, Rachel decided as the Mackeys' farmhouse came into view, she wasn't. But that endless moment of silence when Ben had shown just how little he thought of her still had the power to sting, to wound. A lot.

The dogs set up a chorus of barking as Rachel came to the kitchen door with Fred, a light automatically flicking on outside as she raised her hand to knock. Ben opened it before her fist had touched the wood, and Rachel blinked at him, discomfited by his simple presence. He'd stripped off his outer layers, the boots and the overalls and the fleece-lined jacket, and was dressed in jeans and a Henley-style long johns shirt that hugged his biceps and muscled chest. His hair was rumpled and sticking up in front, and stubble glinted on his jaw and chin. He didn't look surprised to see her, although Rachel hadn't told him she was coming.

"Hey." He stepped aside so she could come in through the door. "I just got in. Mum's out tonight at the WI—you weren't looking for her, were you?"

"No." Was she imagining that lazily flirtatious note in his voice, the way she'd convinced herself she'd imagined it last time? Why would he be flirting with her after all these years, anyway? Just because he could?

"So it was me you came to see?" Ben asked, and now he definitely sounded flirtatious. Either that or she was losing her mind. Rachel bent down to unclip Fred's lead, and also to hide her blush. She'd been in a state of near-constant embarrassment and anxiety since running into Ben on his tractor. She'd really thought this unhelpful awareness of him, of his body, his smell, even, would have abated by now. A lot.

"I wanted to talk to you about some stuff with my dad," she said as she straightened, once she trusted her voice to sound level and her body not to respond to his, even if that shirt was obscenely tight. She could see the outline of his *pecs*, for heaven's sake. It was very distracting.

"Okay." Ben's voice was easy and slow, but she thought a slightly guarded note had crept into it. He went over to the Aga and opened the door to peer inside. "Mum's left me a lamb casserole," he said over his shoulder. "You fancy some?"

A jolt went through her at the thought of sharing a meal together. Almost like a date. No. *No.* "That's okay," Rachel replied, "Harriet's making supper."

"Are you sure?" Ben asked, a note of challenge lilting his voice as he closed the door to the Aga and turned around to face her. Fred was sniffing around the table while the other dogs had settled into their usual places. "I've got that bottle of red already open, as well, from our dinner the other night." He raised his eyebrow, a slow smile curling the edges of his mouth.

Rachel blinked as the image of them sharing a meal together developed details, tantalising ones. Wine, candlelight, murmuring voices… *No, Rachel!* "I didn't know you drank wine," she said, a bit stupidly, but her brain was buzzing, and it had become hard to think.

Ben shrugged expansively. "Sometimes I do." Again with that lovely little quirk of a smile. "I assume you don't just drink Kopparberg, anymore, do you? You did have a glass of wine the other night."

For a second she pictured herself at that disco, bottle in hand, heart thumping. She felt like she was that girl again, and the realisation was alarming. "No," she admitted after a moment. "Definitely no more Kopparberg Cider for me."

Ben reached in the cupboard for two plates. "How about it, then?" He raised his eyebrows, the plates now in his hands, and Rachel felt a sudden, fizzy sort of recklessness take hold of her, buoy her spirits—and her bravery. The kitchen was so cosy and warm, the lamb casserole smelled wonderful, and a glass of wine actually sounded like heaven. And yes, *Ben*. He was the most tempting part of that scenario, for sure.

"All right," she replied with what was meant to be a careless shrug but felt more like a nervous twitch. "I'll just text Harriet to let her know not to wait."

"Seems like you two are getting along," Ben remarked as he set the table and Rachel slid her phone out of her pocket and thumbed a quick text: *Eat without me. I'll be back later.*

"More than we used to," Rachel replied, sliding her phone back in her pocket. "Although I don't know how much that's saying, really." She paused, and then admitted quietly, "I didn't actually know she'd never taken her A levels until recently. I can't believe I hadn't twigged that earlier."

Ben shrugged as he reached for two wine glasses and poured them both generous measures. "Well, she never told you, did she?"

He spoke like someone who had known the truth for a while, and Rachel felt a little splinter of—what? Not jealousy, no, but not a good emotion, either. Something sharp and prickly that had lodged in her insides as she pictured Ben and Harriet in this very kitchen, eating a lamb casserole and sharing a bottle of wine along with their old secrets. *Ben was always yours.* But was he? Was he, really?

"No, she didn't," Rachel said after a moment, "but I never pressed her about her results or anything. She told me she'd changed her mind about university, and I left it at that. I should have realised there was more to it."

Ben handed her a glass of wine, and as she took it her fingers brushed his, and a twang of awareness, of *longing*, ricocheted right through her, far too strong for that barest of touches. *Oh, help.* That physical awareness really hadn't abated at all. If anything, it was getting stronger by the second. "I'm glad we've talked about it now," she continued, praying her voice sounded steady, "but it feels like I missed the boat more than I realised before. More than I let myself realise, I suppose." She took a sip of wine, enjoying the velvety smoothness of it as it coated her throat, the way it instantly relaxed her, at least a little. "Anyway," she said, wanting to move the topic on.

"Sounds as if you two have had some chats." Ben's gaze, his eyes glinting gold in the dim light of the kitchen, met hers for a moment that lingered on, neither of them looking away although Rachel felt that she should. "That has to be good."

"Yes, I think so." She finally broke his gaze and took another sip of her wine. This time, however, she choked, spluttering helplessly, her hand pressed to her mouth as her eyes streamed and, mortifyingly, she splattered Ben with drops as she continued to cough and wheeze.

He took her glass from her before she spilled it and then patted her back, firmly at first, no more than the usual medical necessity as she recovered her breath, and then with a slow, circular rubbing, his fingers tracing the knobs of her spine, in a way that made Rachel feel as if she were melting inside, turning boneless and watery.

"I'm all right," she managed after a moment, her voice hoarse, and she stepped away on shaky legs, her whole body ablaze with sensation. Ben, seemingly unaffected, dropped his hand and then retrieved her wine glass, handing it back to her with a small smile.

"You sure?" he asked, his voice touched with both amusement and concern.

No. "Yes." She took another sip, this time carefully, swallowed it slowly with a small sigh of relief. She'd been here five minutes and she felt like a wreck. She really, really needed to get a grip. Immediately, if not sooner, because this was meant to be a business chat, about her dad and the mortgage and the farm, not…

Not what it was. Except what was it? She had no idea if half of this, no, *all* of it, was in her head. The desperate, fevered imaginings of a lonely heart. *Ugh.* That made her feel so pathetic.

"Anyway," she said again, this time a bit desperately. "About my dad."

Chapter Twelve

"WHAT ABOUT HIM?" Ben asked, his voice sounding mild—deceptively so, Rachel thought. She thought she detected a slight edge underneath the smooth tone, the easy manner, as he moved into the sitting room where a log fire was already burning comfortably, the room warm and welcoming and so very familiar.

She couldn't count the number of times she'd snuggled up on the sofa with Harriet and Ben to watch movies, a big bowl of buttery popcorn between them, Diana coming in to make sure they weren't too scared by *Ghostbusters* or *The Goonies*, classics from their own parents' childhoods. They'd taken off all the cushions and pillows more than once to make a huge den that had collapsed on top of them while they'd been helpless with giggles; Diana had never seemed to mind the mess. They'd had sleepovers, the three of them lined up like sausages in sleeping bags in front of the fire, passing out around midnight after declaring they wouldn't sleep all night.

The memories bombarded her, one after the other, sweet and poignant and yet somehow painful, too. She'd forgotten about it all, or at least buried it too deep to let herself recall it in any detail. Worse than that, Rachel realised, she'd as good as thrown it all away. The friendship, the wonderful certainty of feeling known by another human being. Known and accepted.

"Rachel?" Ben prompted as he settled himself in the armchair by the fire. "What about your dad?"

But suddenly she didn't want to talk about her dad, not like that, anyway. She didn't want this to be about *business*. They'd been friends, once. Good friends. The years of ignoring each other in secondary school, the abortive romance that came after didn't change that; it added complexity to their history but it didn't alter it completely.

"Never mind that for now," she said as she sat in the sofa opposite him, letting the fire warm her right through. "Tell me what's going on with you."

Ben raised his eyebrows, but beyond that his expression didn't change. Rachel knew he had to be surprised, even if he didn't show it. When had she last asked him about his life? When had she last talked to him at all, properly? The years stretched behind her, endless and empty.

It wasn't as if she had no friends in London, she reminded herself; she had some old uni friends and work acquaintances she did things with—went to wine bars or Pilates classes, the occasional spa day or birthday party, but there was a certain expediency about it, a transactional nature to each and every of those relationships. It certainly wasn't like this, sitting in front of a fire with a glass of wine, being okay with the silence.

Well, *sort of* okay with it. Why hadn't Ben said anything?

"What's going on with me," he repeated neutrally, his tone naturally giving nothing away. "Not much, besides the obvious. The farm keeps me busy, but you know that already."

"Yes, I suppose." Although she felt like she didn't know much about anything anymore, and certainly not about Ben. She took a sip of wine. Did he have hobbies? A girlfriend? "What about other stuff?" she asked. "You must have something going on in your life, other than the farm."

He quirked one eyebrow at her in challenge. "Do you? Other than work, I mean?"

She lowered her glass, startled by the question. *Did* she? "Well, no," she admitted after a pause. But then she was a financial analyst, she told herself, not a farmer. But maybe that didn't make much of a difference. "Not really."

Ben stretched out his legs in front of him. "The farm has taken up pretty much all my time, especially since Dad died. He did a lot more than I realised, until he was gone." He spoke matter-of-factly, but there was a remnant of sorrow in his voice, an old grief.

Rachel gazed at the bright, flickering flames of the fire as she recalled Douglas Mackey, a typical Yorkshire farmer, stalwart and stoic, but with a sudden, booming laugh, and an easy affection with his children and wife. Rachel could picture him absent-mindedly slinging an arm around Diana in the kitchen as he sipped from a mug of tea, ruffling Ben or Izzy's hair as he passed by.

"I'm sorry I didn't go to his funeral," she said, and when she turned to look at Ben, she saw he looked entirely non-plussed in a way that made her stomach dip unpleasantly.

"I didn't expect you to," he replied after a second's un-easy pause.

Rachel had a sudden desire to squirm in her seat, to look away. Ben had spoken without rancour, without any of the accusations that so often hovered in the air between her and Harriet. Just a simple statement of fact. *I didn't expect you to.*

And the truth was, he shouldn't have, because she hadn't even considered coming. Harriet had texted her that Douglas had died after a short battle with cancer—only a couple of months—and Rachel had felt a fleeting sense of sorrow and then pushed it away, focused on the future. *Her* future.

She took another sip of wine, trying to organise her thoughts, to figure out her feelings. Was she hurt by Ben's seeming indifference, or disappointed in herself, that that was the choice she'd made all those years ago? A no-brainer, just like Danielle had said.

"I wish I'd come," she said suddenly, a confession, and Ben leaned forward.

"Do you?"

He held her gaze, and the moment spun on, intense, a little uncomfortable, seeming to encompass more than his father's funeral. A lot more. Rachel swallowed dryly. "I feel like I missed a lot of things," she said after a moment, and for some reason it felt like something of a cop-out, although she wasn't sure why.

Ben eased back in the chair, his expression ironing out to blandness. "Well, you did." Another statement of fact, and for the first time that evening Rachel felt herself prickle with annoyance.

"I did have a job, you know," she said as mildly as she could. "A very demanding job."

"Trust me, I know."

"What is that supposed to mean?"

Ben was silent for a few seconds while Rachel waited, wondering if they were actually arguing. No, she decided, not yet, but it was close.

"I'm not sure this is a valuable discussion to have at this point," he finally said, his tone resigned, and Rachel prickled all the more.

"Maybe I should be the judge of that."

He expelled a long, low breath as he raked a hand through his hair, causing it to stand up all the more. "What do you want me to say, Rachel? You made it very clear, over the years, again and again, in fact, that you had no intention of coming back home. That you were completely over Mathering and everybody here, and that you had a very important and busy life in London. So yes, I know all about your *demanding job*."

Rachel stared at him, her lips slightly parted, colour flooding into her face as she absorbed the terrible sting of his words. The worst part was, he hadn't even been saying it to hurt her. Again, just another weary statement of fact. He met her gaze with a steady one of his own, his shoulders moving in a little 'so what' sort of shrug.

Rachel scrambled to think of something to say, how to respond. She felt flayed, and worse, utterly exposed. She hadn't realised that was how Ben saw her—shallow, self-important, *annoying*. How Harriet saw her too, probably, and maybe everyone else in Mathering she'd left behind. She didn't think she'd ever *said* as much, had she? She hadn't droned on like an absolute prat about how busy and important she was back in London, had she?

Except, maybe she had, out of the defensiveness and insecurity that came roaring back every time she came home. She cast back over the admittedly few interactions she'd had with Ben over the years, and had a sudden, squirming recollection of when she had told him about the demands of her job. Six or seven years ago, when she'd come home for Christmas and seen him at the midnight service at the parish church on Christmas Eve. He'd looked so crisp and clean in a forest-green flannel shirt, pressed jeans; cleaned-up farmer was a really good look for him. And she'd felt vulnerable and lonely, remembering how he'd rejected her all those years ago, and so yes, she'd acted as if she was far more important than she was.

But not just that, Rachel knew. She couldn't excuse her braggadocio on insecurity alone. She'd wanted him to be sure she'd forgotten him. She'd wanted to make certain he knew just how much she'd moved on. She had a sudden, scorching image of her sliding out her phone mid-conversation and thumbing a quick text, just to look important. To *feel* important.

For heaven's sake, she must have been *insufferable.*

Rachel realised the moment had stretched on, the only sound the crackling of the fire. She tried to think of something to say, and came up utterly empty.

"Well," she finally said, her voice faint, her tongue feeling thick and dry in her mouth. "It's not actually as demanding as all that."

Ben let out a soft huff of laughter. "Has it changed, then? Have you?" he asked, and there was an intimacy to the questions that made Rachel blush, even as part of her resented him asking it. Was she the one who had to change? *Improve*, while everyone in Mathering got to stay the same and like it?

"I don't know if I've changed or not," she told him. "Maybe you have."

"Maybe I have," he agreed easily enough, and just like that her twinge of annoyance evaporated.

She stared at him openly, honestly. "I suppose I was a bit insufferable," she said, trying to sound wry, but the words came out a bit bleak.

Ben smiled and shrugged. "We're all insufferable, in our own ways, aren't we?"

"That's generous of you."

"I can afford to be generous. A lot of time has passed. It's water under the bridge, right?"

Which was exactly what she'd said to Harriet, and yet somehow Rachel realised she didn't like Ben saying it. Was he talking about them, as a couple, or just life in general? Well, there was only one response she could give, and so she gave it. "Yes," Rachel said, managing a smile even though she feared her voice rang hollow. "Water under the bridge."

Ben rose from his chair. "I think that casserole's probably ready to eat," he said, and he reached out a hand to help her up from the sofa. Rachel took it, trying not to react visibly to the slide of his warm, dry palm against hers, the way his fingers tightened over her hand as he hauled her to her feet. The scent of his spicy aftershave that made her senses swim, *still.* When he was so close, she could remember exactly how she fit in his arms, how her cheek had rested right above his heart, against his broad chest.

Stop. Stop this right now.

Swallowing with what she feared was an audible sound, Rachel turned and followed him blindly back into the kitchen.

She reached for the pottery jug on the windowsill by the sink that Diana Mackey had always used for water, and filled it while Ben took the casserole out of the Aga, bubbling away in its Le Creuset stockpot that had to be at least thirty years old, a deep, burnt-orange colour, and one Rachel remembered well from the many meals of her childhood that had been spent in the Mackey kitchen.

"So," Ben said once they'd sat down and he was dishing out a generous helping of lamb and carrots and potatoes swimming in rich, rosemary-scented gravy, "you came over here to talk about your dad."

It felt like a reminder as well as a repositioning of their conversation, of themselves. No more semi-deep stuff about the past. Well, good, Rachel told herself, even though she felt, weirdly, considering how painful and awkward that conversation had actually been, disappointed.

"Yes, I did." She cleared her throat the way she did before she started a business meeting. "Harriet mentioned that my dad took out a mortgage on the house, and that you helped him with it."

Ben blinked, unrepentant, matter-of-fact. "Yes, I did," he parroted back at her.

"Why did he take out the mortgage?"

Ben raised his eyebrows in a faintly well-duh sort of way. "Because he needed an influx of cash."

"What for?"

"He sold off half his herd a couple of years ago and once that money was gone, he wasn't making ends meet, so he needed to figure out something else."

Rachel looked down at her plate, toying with her fork as she speared a piece of succulent lamb, seasoned with rosemary. "Surely there are other ways of raising capital," she said. "Taking out a mortgage on a property you own free and clear is generally not advisable."

"Well," Ben said, and now his tone possessed that slight edge again, "it was his choice."

"But the repayments—"

"He was planning to pay it off when he sold off the rest of the herd," Ben cut her off. "It was about the same amount, so it would all work out in the end."

"What?" Rachel stared at him in surprise. "Sell off the entire herd? He never said anything about that to me." Ben shrugged, and she knew what he was thinking. *Why would he?* "But if he sells off the herd..." she began slowly, unable to finish. *There wouldn't be any more farm.* The Mowbrays had farmed this part of Yorkshire for over two hundred years. Was it really going to end with her dad?

"Who's going to farm the land?" Ben asked, his tone turning almost gentle. "Or milk the cows? You're in London, and Harriet can't manage the farm on her own. I don't think she wants to, even if she might not say as much. Your dad was being pragmatic, that's all. He wanted to keep farming as long as he could, hence the mortgage. But by the time he wasn't able to farm anymore, he was intending to have everything in order. No mortgage, so you and Harriet get the house free and clear, along with the land."

"I don't care about the house," Rachel protested, thinking of Harriet's barb about the inheritance. "It's not about the money."

"Well, it was about the money for your dad," Ben replied evenly. "He wanted to make sure to pay all his bills, but he also wanted to keep farming as long as he could. He loves it, you know." His voice was quiet. "He'll miss it."

Rachel stared down at her plate. A lump was forming in her throat, and she needed it to dissolve. She definitely did not want to cry in front of Ben. "His appointment for an MRI came today," she said in a low voice, still gazing at her plate.

"That's good."

She tried to nod but couldn't quite manage it. She forced herself to ask, "Do you think there's something really wrong with him?" Ben was silent for a moment, and Rachel risked a look up, even though her eyes were swimming with sudden tears. "I mean I know there's something, but something properly serious. Do you?"

"Do you?" he asked, and the gentleness in his voice undid her. A tear slipped down her cheek and she dashed it away quickly.

"Sorry—"

"Don't be sorry, Rach." She couldn't remember the last time he'd called her that, not since their school days. Her vision was too blurry to see him, but she heard his chair scrape across the stone-flagged floor, and then, to her shock, his arms were around her and he was pulling her up into a tight hug, and her damp cheek was pressed to his chest just as she'd remembered, so she could feel the steady thud of his heart, and it felt like the most reassuring sound in the world.

Rachel drew a shuddering breath, knowing she should pull away but not quite able to make herself. It felt far too nice to be held in Ben's arms, to feel the warm and comforting touch of another human being. When had she last been held like this, save for Diana's brief hug at that dinner? She had friends in London, yes, but there was a sterility at the centre of her life, an emptiness that she felt now more than ever, when she was in an embrace with someone she cared about.

You don't still care about Ben, her sensible self reminded her rather frantically, but her heart was saying something very different.

"The thing is," she said after a moment, her cheek still against his chest, her voice wavering and wobbling all over the place, "I told myself he wasn't a very good father in some ways. He was so distant, a lot of the time. He never really tucked us into bed or played with us. He always seemed as if he'd rather be in the barn than in the house with his family. But he was still *there.* I still depended on him, without even realising that I was."

"He was your dad," Ben said simply, as if that explained everything, and maybe it did. He was resting one hand on the small of her back, and his palm felt warm and sure through the material of both her shirt and jumper. As they stood there together, unspeaking, he began to move his hand in slow circles, his thumb brushing the base of her spine, and a sudden, fierce longing blazed up inside Rachel until she felt as if it would consume her; it would burn her right up, into sparks and cinders.

She pulled away from him, just a little, to look up into his face. Her heart was thundering, and her body was flooded, *flooded* with an immediate and desperate need. She couldn't remember the last time she'd felt so strongly, so fiercely. She wanted to kiss him. She *had* to kiss him.

Ben glanced down at her, and she felt as if she could fall into the glinting depths of his golden-brown eyes. Everything in her tensed, strained, *yearned* as her lips parted and she came up on her tiptoes, her head falling back a little. Ben began to dip his head towards hers, that glinting gaze focused on her lips. Her eyes fluttered closed. *Yes, this was happening. Yes…*

And then she felt his hands move from her body to her shoulders and he set her away from him, like he was pushing in a chair.

Rachel's eyes flew open. She stared at him for a second, registering the look of firm decision in his face, with only the barest flicker of regret. Realisation scorched through her, along with a deep humiliation that felt more like grief.

For a second she couldn't speak, couldn't think. She could feel a mortification, but—worse—a deep, pervading sadness.

"Rachel," Ben said, and his tone was too close to pity for her to be able to stand it.

"No," she said, although she didn't even know what she was saying no to.

"Rachel—"

"No, look, I need to go." Even though she knew, in her head if not her heart, that running away like a scalded cat was just about the worst thing to do right now, and definitely the most revealing, Rachel couldn't keep herself from it. She had to get out of there, *now*. "Harriet's expecting me," she babbled as she reached for her coat and thrust her arms through its sleeves, making sure not to glimpse Ben so much as in her peripheral. She grabbed Fred's lead and clipped it to his collar. "And I've actually got a lot of work to do, you know, with my very important job." She'd meant to sound lightly self-deprecating, but it came out pointed and sharp, her voice vibrating with hurt. Heavens, but she was making everything a million times worse, and yet she just couldn't seem to stop. She'd pressed the self-destruct button without even meaning to, and she was now on that ominous course with no way to step on the brakes.

"Rachel," Ben said for a third time, and now he sounded exasperated.

"Sorry, have to dash!" Her voice came out high and bright now, so she sounded like a positive lunatic. "*Bye-ee!*" And then she was hurtling out the door, dragging Fred along with her, across the farmyard, grateful that the darkness cloaked her, and wishing it could swallow her whole.

Chapter Thirteen

"IT'LL BE FUN," Harriet said, without any enthusiasm at all.

Rachel stood in front of Mathering's village hall, a squat building of Victorian red brick on the banks of the Derwent, feeling mutinous. The cheerful, slightly manic strains of a ceilidh band could be heard from within, along with the occasion burst of raucous laughter and the stamp of feet.

"I'm not going."

"Rachel." Harriet sounded sympathetic, but also a little exasperated. Rachel had been dragging her feet all evening, first with getting dressed—Harriet had made an effort with a denim skirt and some lippy, while she'd flatly refused to wear one of her so-called *smart outfits*, settling for jeans and a jumper. Then she'd balked when it was time to go, insisting they couldn't leave their father behind. Despite the agreement he reluctantly gave to Diana to attend, he was now claiming a headache—Rachel wasn't entirely convinced—and was firmly installed in his armchair in the sitting room, in front of their ancient TV, watching *Mastermind* and reading the paper.

"We have to go," Harriet reminded her, far from the first time. "We promised Diana, and she's expecting us."

"I don't like leaving Dad—"

"He's fine, and we'll be back in a couple of hours at the most. Plus, he can call us if he needs us."

Rachel knew their father was too proud to do that. She also knew he would probably be fine, but she still didn't like leaving him alone. And, she acknowledged, she didn't like being here, on a wet Wednesday evening, about to face a whole load of people she'd rather not see. Especially one in particular.

"I don't care," she told Harriet, folding her arms and sticking her lower lip out, as stubborn as a small child.

Harriet sighed. "What is the big deal? It's just a ceilidh."

"I actually hate ceilidhs. Like, really hate them." Rachel spoke matter-of-factly, without emotion, even though everything in her was wincing and cringing with awful, squirming horror and humiliation. She *couldn't* go in there. She absolutely could not.

It had been a week since her meal with Ben and that absolutely mortifying moment she could not bear to think about, and so, quite simply, she hadn't. She'd focused on work and spending time with Harriet that wasn't overtly hostile, and sometimes even friendly, and making meals and taking long walks with Fred and absolutely avoiding Ben Mackey in any way, shape, or form. But if she went into the village hall, she knew she'd see him. And then she'd see the pity flash across his face, and she just couldn't bear that. She'd run away from him once before to avoid that awful look. She could do it again. Easily.

"Rachel," Harriet said. "Sorry, but you're being a bit ridiculous."

"I'm not."

"You *are*. What's the big deal? So you have to dance Strip the Willow with a few pensioners." She raised her eyebrows, shrugging. "Big deal. There are worse things, surely." Harriet's eyes narrowed as she looked at Rachel. "Unless there's *another* reason you don't want to go…?"

Darn Harriet for her sisterly Spidey sense. Rachel could see the thoughts ticking over in Harriet's head, putting two and two together and making about twenty-seven…which, unfortunately, was right, more or less. Or really, she thought bitterly, thinking of how Ben had so firmly pushed her away from him when she'd been desperately hoping he'd kiss her, making a big fat zero.

"No reason," she said as firmly as she could, knowing she'd been backed into a corner, and probably the only way to get out of it was to come out step dancing. "I've just never been very good at dancing."

"Who is?" Harriet returned, rolling her eyes, and then she grabbed Rachel by the elbow and more or less marched her into the crowded hall.

The music, fiddle and flute, Scottish small-pipes and guitar, drum and even accordion, all set up on the small stage on one end of the hall, was powering through a merry tune as a caller gave instructions in a jovial tone, to the beat of the music, one hand slapping his thigh, and couples whirled and flew around them, breathless and laughing. Rachel immediately looked for the bar.

"There's Diana," Harriet remarked, her tone resigned. "And she's heading this way with a beady look in her eye. I think she's going to make us dance straight away."

No, no, no, no. Rachel looked around wildly, seeking escape. Diana, all well-meaning, steely bonhomie, would instruct Ben to partner Rachel for the next round or reel or whatever it was. And then they'd be twirling the Gay Gordons and trying not to look each other in the eye. At least, she would be trying. Heaven only knew what Ben would be doing.

"I'm getting a drink," she announced, and slipping from her sister's grasp, she walked swiftly in the opposite direction of Diana Mackey, straight to the bar. "Gin and tonic, please," she announced to the fiftyish, comfortable-looking woman behind the bar, one elbow propped on it as she gazed at Rachel with a faint smile on her lined face. She looked vaguely familiar, but Rachel was trying not to remember the faces or names of the people in the room, most of whom looked familiar. She could not handle the onslaught of memories, or the prospect of several dozen 'so you're back, eh?' conversations. "And make it a double," she added for good measure.

The woman reached for a glass. "That kind of night, eh?" she remarked with a chuckle. "I'm not surprised, Rachel Mowbray, after all this time."

Greeaaat. Rachel closed her eyes briefly before snapping them open. "Do I know you?" she asked bluntly, and the woman chuckled again as she poured two generous measures of gin into the glass.

"You should do. I taught you year three."

"Mrs Coombs," Rachel stated dully, and the bartender nodded.

"That's the one."

"Are you still teaching at the school?"

"Retired last year."

Rachel nodded slowly before she steeled herself to turn and face the room. How many people here did she know but had tried to forget? The faces of her past, the people who had known her as Rachel Mowbray, gawky, geeky try-hard, before she'd become glossy and successful and self-assured. Who all saw right through her now, and always had.

"Here you go, love," Mrs Coombs said. "That'll be four pounds fifty."

"Do you take card?"

The other woman just chuckled, and Rachel wondered if she'd thought she'd been joking. Didn't everyone take a card these days? It was cash that was usually the problem.

"Here you go," a voice said to her right, and to her horror she watched Ben hand the woman a fiver. He turned to Rachel with a steely smile that didn't reach his eyes. "It's on me."

"I don't—"

He reached for her arm. "We need to talk."

"We really don't." Rachel could feel Mrs Coombs's avid curiosity like a laser on her back as she shook off Ben's hand and took a large, much-needed gulp of her gin and tonic. "There's no need to make a scene," she said to Ben in a low voice, and he raised his eyebrows.

"You're the one making a scene, not me."

"Thanks for gaslighting me there," she snapped. "I don't want to talk to you, Ben." She stalked away from the bar, aware her whole body was trembling. She took another sip of gin, grateful for the way the alcohol burned down her throat and through her system. She was in dire need of some Dutch courage, especially as she could hear and even feel Ben's long strides coming after her.

She knew she was just making things worse, acting so angry and emotional and *hurt*. She was making it look like she really cared about Ben, and she didn't. She *didn't*.

"Rachel." His voice was low, rich, deep, with that faint Yorkshire burr. Rachel felt her shoulders start to work their way up to her ears. She'd reached the far wall of the hall, and there was nowhere else to go. Nowhere to hide. She was going to have to talk to Ben, and she had no idea what she could say, how she could salvage her absolutely wrecked dignity.

She let out a long, low breath of resignation before she slowly turned around to face him. He was eyeing her with exasperation, his hands braced on his hips, feet apart, like Atlas surveying his world. He looked nice, too, in a button-down shirt of dark blue chambray and a pair of jeans, his usual dressy outfit, it seemed. She wondered if he only had one pair of nice jeans, and for some reason that thought made her smile.

Ben arched an eyebrow. "Are you able to talk sensibly now?"

"Don't patronise me, please," she replied, glad she sounded calm, at least. "I've been talking sensibly all along."

They stared at each other for a long moment, a childish game of blink where neither of them wanted to admit defeat and look away. Rachel's eyes started to water.

Ben finally dropped his gaze, running his hand through his hair. "Rachel," he began, his gaze on the floor. "Look,

I—"

"There you are!" Diana's voice cut through the crowd and made Ben fall silent as his mother bore down on them like a ship in full sail. "We're doing the Cumberland Square and we need you to make up an eight."

"What? No—" Rachel began, only to have Diana slip one arm through hers, another through Ben's, the gesture seeming cosy but with a grip like a vice.

"Finish your drink, dear," she said, and Rachel had no choice but to toss back the rest of her drink, her throat burning, eyes watering, as Diana marched them towards a waiting group of dancers.

Rachel stood there rather miserably as everyone got into position, Ben standing silently next to her. They would be partners for the whole dance, and, Rachel recalled with a sinking sensation of dread, this was the number where two pairs of dancers went into the middle, and the men lifted the women up and swung them around before dancing back to their places. She was dreading the experience with every fibre of her being.

The music started up and the caller began to shout out instructions in a jovial voice. "Right, grab your partner and swing her round! Time to waltz, back to back!"

Ben put one hand on her waist, taking her rather limp hand in his other. A tiny smile quirked his mouth as he glanced at her. "You don't have to look quite so much like you're being tortured."

"But I am being tortured," Rachel returned, trying for a quip but it came out like a quarrel. She put her free hand on Ben's shoulder, and they started to whirl and gallivant about, reminding her just how much she did actually hate these country dances, with their forced, manic jollity.

Thankfully, it wasn't really possible to talk, between the music and the dancing, and Rachel didn't have the breath anyway. Plus, she was doing her best not to make eye contact with Ben, because his face was far too close. She was also trying not to inhale too much, so she didn't smell his aftershave, which was difficult because the dance required a fair amount of exertion.

She steeled herself for the rush into the middle, when the men locked their hands behind her and the other woman's backs, and they rested their arms on top of the men's while they were spun around, their feet lifting off the floor. If you had a modicum of grace, the move looked both easy and cool, like a human spinning top; if you didn't, it looked like two blokes straining to heave up two heifers.

Fortunately, Ben and the other man, whom Rachel didn't recognise, were up for the challenge, and while Rachel knew she was far from graceful, at least she was spun around without looking she was going to give a guy a heart attack. Still, she thought she'd rather do just about anything else, except maybe talk to Ben.

And she knew, she absolutely knew, that he would corner her as soon as this dance was over and demand explanations, or worse, give a painful one of his own. *I'm sorry, Rachel, but I just don't feel that way about you anymore. I thought you knew that.*

Just the thought of it made Rachel cringe inwardly, an internal squirm that made her wince visibly.

"Did I hurt you?" Ben asked in concern as he set her

back down on her feet, and Rachel could only shake her head.

Did you hurt me? Yes, but not in the way you mean, and I am definitely not going to go there.

Another endless few minutes and the dance was finally over, and as the other couples drifted away, Rachel realised just how much of a reprieve it had been. Ben definitely wasn't letting her go; he was still holding her hand, his grip much like his mother's.

"We need to talk," he stated firmly.

"Fine," Rachel replied, because she knew they'd have to, sometime. Fortunately, the dance had given her enough time to come up with an angle, and the alcohol fuelled her courage to put it in action. "Why don't we go outside? I can't hear myself think in here."

She marched ahead without waiting for him to respond, determined to gain the upper hand. The back door of the hall had been propped open for air, and Rachel slipped through it and out into the alley that ran along the side of the hall, dark and damp and not particularly pleasant. There was a smell of drains and rubbish, and the brick wall that hemmed them in trickled with slimy-looking water.

"Rachel—" Ben began, before she turned around, one hand flung up, palm outward.

"Wait. Let me speak first."

Ben frowned but then he jerked his head in a curt nod and Rachel took a deep breath before continuing, "Please don't feel you have to explain your actions the other night, when we had supper," she said, her voice stiff, her body rigid. "I was feeling rather emotional, what with my father and his health concerns, and frankly, just being back here in Mathering. It brings up a lot of memories, a lot of old feelings." She tried for a rueful smile, and thought she'd managed it. "It reminds me of who I was, even though I'm not that girl anymore."

"No?" Ben interjected, the word sounded as if it had been bitten off and spat out.

"No, definitely not," Rachel replied firmly. "So, sorry, it all got a bit much for me, and I was carried away for a moment. But that's all it was. So, you definitely don't need to worry, and we don't need to talk about it, because it is absolutely never going to happen again."

"Good to know," Ben replied after a brief pause. His voice was toneless, his expression typically inscrutable.

Rachel let out a breath that she told herself was relief. "Okay, then," she said, and Ben jerked his head in another curt nod. It seemed their conversation was over. "Right," Rachel said, for no reason, while Ben simply stood there, utterly immobile, reminding her of a brick wall. He still hadn't spoken, and Rachel decided she might as well leave it. She'd said what she'd needed to say. She gave a jerky sort of nod of farewell, and then she slipped past him back into the noisy crowd of the hall.

Another dance had started, and Rachel glimpsed Harriet dancing with someone she didn't recognise, a guy about her age, tall, with dark hair. Quite handsome, actually. Her sister's head was thrown back, her cheeks were pink with exertion, and she looked happy and carefree. Rachel didn't want to disturb her or kill the mood, but as she stood on the side of the hall, she knew she felt far too flat and even sad to stay at the ceilidh for another moment longer.

Her conversation with Ben, its clarity, should have brought relief, but it hadn't, or at least not yet. She felt even more mixed up than before, and strangely dispirited. She decided she'd walk home; it was three miles, but she could use the time to clear her head, especially after bolting down that double G&T.

She slipped out of the hall without so much as meeting anyone's eye and headed out into the night that felt chilly and damp. It was just turned October, and it felt it. Rachel buttoned up her coat and quickly texted her sister to tell her she was heading back, and then, with her hands in her pockets, she struck out down the Pickering Road, towards home.

It took forty-five minutes to reach the farm, walking briskly, her head down against the wind that had kicked up. She tried to keep her mind blank, but memories kept slipping through the cracks, taking up residence where she definitely didn't want them to be.

The first time she'd danced with Ben, at that sixth form disco years ago, she'd felt dizzy with excitement, with happiness. Afterwards, she'd wondered if he was going to go back to ignoring her, but then, a few days later, at the bus stop on the way home—Harriet had stayed after school for a club, so it was just the two of them—he'd asked her if she wanted to see their new puppies. They'd walked silently up the lane and into the Mackeys' barn, where their springer spaniel Jill was set up in her own stall, eight squirming little puppies all around her. Rachel had dropped to her knees, squealing in delight at the sight of them.

"Can I hold one?" she'd asked eagerly, and Ben had scooped up one of the puppies, cradling it close to his chest before he'd handed it to her. Rachel had oohed and aahed and kissed its tiny, velvety nose. When she'd looked up from the puppy, her breath had caught in her chest because Ben was looking at her with a blaze of intent in his eyes. She'd simply stared at him as, very slowly, he'd leaned forward and then brushed his lips against hers. The puppy had scrambled out of her hands as her mind had spun and her heart had thundered and she'd felt as if she might actually explode with happiness.

Three months they'd had together, as a couple. Three pretty perfect months at the end of sixth form, before she'd had to get her head down for exams and then when she'd resurfaced, everything had changed.

We can still be together, she'd told him, her voice wavering and then breaking as he'd continued to pitch hay, his back to her, not saying a single word. *I'll be back for holidays, the whole summer. Ben?*

He hadn't replied, hadn't said anything at all. Rachel had stood there, staring, waiting, desperately hoping, and she'd got absolutely nothing back.

Is this it then? She'd finally flung at him, meaning it as a challenge, a dare, and he'd nodded, the same curt jerk of his head that he'd given tonight. Knowing she was going to cry, to sob, and not being able to bear having him see her, she'd whirled out of the barn, ran all the way home, and basically never talked to him again…until now.

And look how that turned out.

With a sigh, Rachel opened the front door of the farmhouse, determined not to think about Ben anymore. Not to remember. All around her the house felt cold and dark, its room bleak and depressing with their old furniture, the peeling wallpaper, the dispiriting sense that nothing here ever actually changed.

"Dad?" Rachel called softly as she walked back to the kitchen. It wasn't that late, but her father liked to go to bed early. "Are you still up?"

The kitchen light was still on, and as she came in, Fred ran up to her, whining in a way she'd never heard him before. Frowning, Rachel stroked his head, before noticing that the tap was still running.

"Dad?" she called again, and this time she heard the edge of fear in her voice. She went to the sink to turn the tap off, and that's when she saw him, crumpled on the floor, unconscious.

Chapter Fourteen

RACHEL SAT ON the hard plastic chair in the A&E waiting room of James Cook Hospital in Middlesbrough, one knee jiggling manically. She chewed her lip, which already had a bloody welt in it, and checked her phone for about the twenty-seventh time. The last several hours had felt like a complete blur. When she'd seen her dad lying there on the floor, she'd dropped to her knees and frantically checked his pulse, which, after a few fraught seconds, she'd thankfully felt. He hadn't looked good, though, his skin papery white, a great big bump on his poor head, a trickle of blood dried down his cheek.

She'd called 999 and then waited by his side, willing him to wake up, her mind feeling as if it were full of static. What had happened? And how could she have left him alone for so much as a minute?

On the way to the hospital in Middlesbrough, an endless hour-long journey where she'd fortunately been allowed to accompany her father in the back of the ambulance, she'd texted Harriet to tell her what had happened, and then they'd rushed her dad into A&E while she'd sat here in the waiting room, having no idea what to expect.

She'd been sitting in this chair for over two hours, and

she still hadn't heard from Harriet. Rachel thought about texting Ben, but then realised what a stupid idea that was. Still, she *wanted* to text him; she wanted him to be here. Even stupider. But it was hard handling this alone, because just like she'd told Ben, even though her dad had been distant, he'd been *there*, and she wasn't ready to lose him. Not by a long shot.

It might have just been a bump on the head, she reminded herself, not for the first time, and nothing necessarily more serious than that. He'd been at the sink, he'd lost his footing, and he'd hit his head on the corner of the counter. It could happen to anyone.

"Miss Mowbray?"

Rachel looked up to see a youngish nurse in blue scrubs smiling at her in a way that made her think it was bad news.

She stood up quickly, wincing at how stiff her body was from sitting for so long. "Yes?"

"The doctor will see you now."

She followed the nurse through the swinging doors into A&E, and then into a curtained-off cubicle with a bed that was empty, stripped of its sheets. For a second Rachel's heart stopped and she felt like she couldn't breathe. *Had her dad…*

"He's been transferred to the neurology ward," the nurse explained quickly, her eyes crinkled in sympathy. "The doctor wants to speak with you."

"Okay," Rachel managed shakily. Her heart was racing, and her limbs felt watery. She eased herself onto a chair by the bed, the vinyl creaking and squeaking underneath her, and made herself take several slow, even breaths. A full twenty minutes passed before the doctor, a man in his late thirties with sandy hair and a tired smile, came into the cubicle.

"Miss Mowbray, Peter Mowbray's daughter? You brought him in?"

"Yes, please call me Rachel." She half-rose from her seat before the doctor waved her back down and perched on the edge of the bed, a clipboard resting against his knees.

"Your father was unconscious due to the injury he sustained to his head, which I don't think is particularly serious in itself," he told her, and Rachel couldn't keep her breath from rushing out in a gusty sigh of relief.

"Oh, thank—"

"But I'm afraid there are other issues I am concerned about," the doctor continued, silencing her completely. "When he regained consciousness, he was disorientated, which was to be expected, but it became clear that the disorientation was more significant than simply from the bump on his head. I also saw from his medical records that he'd been having some issues with balance, memory, and speech?"

"Well, yes," Rachel confirmed. She wanted to add some sort of caveat but there wasn't one. "He's scheduled to have an MRI tomorrow, actually."

"Yes, I was pleased to see that. Hopefully we can get some answers for him soon." He gave her a smile that was kindly enough but didn't reach his eyes, which looked tired and even sad. Rachel felt a frisson of dread take hold of her, swirling in her stomach.

"What do you think it is?" she made herself ask. "That's wrong with him, I mean?"

"I couldn't possibly offer a diagnosis without an MRI," the doctor said, but his tone was hesitant, and Rachel leaned forward.

"I know that, absolutely, of course. But if you *had* to guess...can you just let me know what we might be dealing with here?" She tried to smile but couldn't quite manage it. "He went to a memory clinic a couple of weeks ago, but the doctor there didn't seem to think he had Alzheimer's or anything like that. At least, it didn't seem like he did, based on how he was able to answer the questions." But the doctor *had* recommended him for an MRI, and clearly something was going on with her dad. Why had she kept pushing it to the back of her mind, doing her best not to think about it, even when it had been staring her full in the face?

Because you do that with a lot of things.

"Please?" she asked the doctor, an edge of desperation entering her voice. "Just an idea of what you're concerned about?"

"From the symptoms described, I'd be looking to see if he might have a brain tumour," the doctor told her after a pause. "But whether it is benign or malignant, slow or fast growing, I couldn't possibly say, without an MRI and potentially a biopsy."

A brain tumour. As she stared at the doctor, the professional sympathy she could see in his face, Rachel knew she wasn't really surprised by this news. *This* had been the possibility no one had been willing to talk about, when it seemed he didn't have some sort of dementia. This was the possibility that had been there all along, except she hadn't wanted to see it. Ben had, though, she thought, knowing the truth of it absolutely. He'd suspected something like this and hadn't said as much, maybe because he knew she couldn't take it.

"I'm sorry," the doctor said, when Rachel realised she'd been simply staring at him. "I could be wrong."

"What happens now?" she asked. It took effort to form the words; her tongue felt thick in her mouth, her brain fuzzy. It was nearing midnight and she was utterly exhausted.

"We'll keep him here overnight for observation anyway," the doctor said, "and he'll have the MRI as scheduled tomorrow. After that, he'll either stay in hospital, if the consultant he's assigned decides that's the best course, or he'll be released back home until the MRI results come through, which usually take a few days."

"Okay." Rachel nodded mechanically. "Can I see him?" she asked.

"Of course. I'll have one of the nurses direct you to the neurology ward." The doctor rose from the bed and Rachel from her chair; she still felt as if her brain was buzzing, every thought difficult to form, impossible to hold on to.

She followed the doctor out of A&E; he left her in the waiting room with a murmured goodbye and she realised she'd forgotten to thank him. A nurse bustled up to her and gave her the directions to the neurology ward, which Rachel couldn't follow at all.

She nodded and mumbled her thanks before walking over to the hospital's main foyer. The card and coffee shops were shuttered, one of the staff was mopping the floor, and a weary-looking security guard sat at the reception desk.

On stiff legs Rachel walked to the bank of lifts and studied the list of departments posted by their gleaming doors. *Short stay surgical, renal services, gastroenterology, breast and endocrine surgery, respiratory medicine, acute…*

The words blurred before her and she took a deep breath, let it out slowly. A woman glanced at her as she pushed the up button. "You all right, love?"

Rachel turned to see a woman in her sixties with a short bob of bright pink hair looking at her in concern.

"I'm looking for the neurology ward," she said, and the woman frowned.

"Neurology?" She glanced at the board with its list of wards and then pointed to low down on it. "Looks like it's ward twenty-four, neurology and stroke. Is that what you're looking for?"

"Yes, I think so." Rachel felt as if the words were coming from far away, outside of herself. She forced herself to meet the woman's gaze. "Thank you."

The doors pinged open and they both stepped in. "Ward twenty-four is on the first floor," the woman said, pushing the corresponding button. "I'm on the second, coronary care unit."

"*Oh—*" Rachel began, and the woman smiled and shook her head.

"It's all right, love. Husband had a heart attack, and it looks like he's going to need a triple bypass. But you have enough to be getting on with, it seems." Her voice was kind, almost tender, and Rachel felt the rush of gathered tears, the pressure in her chest and the lump in her throat.

"I do," she whispered, and then the doors pinged open.

The first floor of the hospital was clearly dedicated to

those in most need of care—Rachel passed an intensive care unit, and then another, for cardiothoracic cases, before coming to the neurology ward. She was buzzed in, and a nurse showed her to her father's bed, at the end of a ward, the cubicle curtained off.

Rachel stepped inside, taking in her father's frail-looking form with a sickening lurch of her heart. How could he look so *small*, all of a sudden, his hair so wispy, his face so pale? He was in a hospital gown, which made him look terribly vulnerable; she could see the sharp angles of his collarbone poking through the gown, the white stubble on his chin and cheeks.

As she pulled the curtain closed behind her, with a rattle of its rings, her father opened his eyes.

"Rachel!" His voice sounded raspy, and he struggled to sit up, only to fall back against the thin pillow, irritation crossing his face. "I just fell and bumped my head, that's all. Why have they got me in this ridiculous get-up?"

"It's a hospital gown, Dad." Rachel tried to smile even though she feared she was very close to crying. Her father, she knew, would not want to see her tears. "They're keeping you overnight for observation. It's your MRI appointment tomorrow, so we would have been coming to Middlesbrough anyway. Saves you a second trip."

A frown crossed her father's face. "I don't need an MRI."

"We talked about it, Dad, remember?" She kept her voice gentle but firm. "Just to check everything is okay."

"Everything *is* okay. And even if it isn't..." He turned his face away from her, to stare stubbornly at the curtain, as if he were looking out a window, at some view beyond. "Maybe I don't want to know."

Which was more or less what Harriet had suggested. "If it is something that can be picked up by an MRI," Rachel said quietly, "then the doctors might be able to treat it. Wouldn't you want that?"

Her father turned back to face her. "Treat what, Rachel?" he asked bleakly, and she knew if she blinked, a tear would fall.

"I don't know," she whispered. "They don't know, Dad."

"They think it's a brain tumour, don't they?" he asked flatly.

"Maybe," Rachel replied after a pause, her tone hesitant. "How did you know? Did they tell you?"

"No, but I'm not an idiot. I can put two and two together the same as anyone else, even if I have been forgetting things sometimes."

"It might not be that," Rachel offered. "And even if it is, a lot of brain tumours are treatable." Or so she'd heard, somewhere, sometime, although she couldn't remember any specifics because none of it had applied to her or her life.

Her father nodded slowly. "We'll just see what they say tomorrow, I suppose," he said, sounding both resigned and stoic, and then, to Rachel's horror, his face crumpled, just a little, before he forced himself to smooth it out back into his usual irascible expression. "Never mind," he said with an attempt at briskness that he didn't quite manage. "Are you driving home tonight?"

"I came in the ambulance," Rachel replied, realising only just then that she did not have a lift home.

"Will Harriet pick you up, then?"

Harriet still hadn't replied to her text. "I don't have to go home," Rachel told him hesitantly. "Since I'd be coming back tomorrow, anyway. I could stay here, with you."

The look of naked hope that blazed across her father's face was nearly her undoing. Then he shrugged. "There's not much room. I don't think you'd be too comfortable."

"There's a chair," Rachel replied, "and it reclines. I'm sure they're used to people staying over. I think I'd be okay."

Her father gave another twitchy sort of shrug. "As you like," he said, and for the first time Rachel felt as if she could see beneath that stubbornly indifferent exterior, to the surprisingly tender vulnerability beneath. Had it been there all along, and she'd just never seen it? Never felt it?

"I'll stay," she said.

The nurse on duty was happy to give her a blanket and pillow, and then showed her to get the chair into a reclining position, next to her father's bed. Rachel thought this was probably the closest she'd ever been to him; they were practically lying side by side. As she set up the chair as best as she could, her dad drifted off to sleep, his jaw slack, his face looking so *old*. She gazed at him for a moment in silent sorrow, before the wasp-like buzzing of her phone had her quickly stepping out of the cubicle.

"Harriet?"

"*Rachel!*" Her sister sounded both tearful and panicked.

The nurse at the station gave Rachel a rather stern look, and mouthing an apology, she hurried to the visitors' lounge where she could take the call in private, without disturbing anyone.

"Rachel—"

"I'm here."

"*Where?*"

"At the hospital in Middlesbrough."

"Is Dad okay? What happened? My phone died at the ceilidh so I didn't see your text until I got home, and I saw you and Dad weren't here..." Harriet trailed off, sniffing.

"Sorry," Rachel said, knowing that must have been a frightening moment for her sister. "He's okay, at the moment. I think he must have fallen and bashed his head, but they said it's not a serious injury."

"Oh, thank—"

"But," Rachel cut her off, just as the doctor had done to her, "they're keeping him in overnight for observation, and for the MRI tomorrow. And the doctor thinks he might...he might have a brain tumour."

"What..." The word rushed out of Harriet in a whispered breath.

"It makes sense, doesn't it?" Rachel replied quietly. "With his symptoms, and it not seeming entirely like dementia? I mean, nothing is for certain yet."

"I know, but..." Harriet was silent for a moment. "I don't know why," she said finally, "but I didn't think about something like this."

"No, I didn't either, not really."

They were both silent for a moment, absorbing the possibility. "Do you want me to come?" Harriet finally asked. "I could drive over right now—"

"No, don't, it's late. I told Dad I'd stay with him here and take him to the MRI tomorrow. There's no need for both of us to be there." Harriet didn't speak, but Rachel felt a suddenly frosty silence from her all the same. "I mean, come if you want to," she added, and realised that she'd just made it—whatever *it* was—even worse.

"I'm sure you can handle it," Harriet replied stiffly. "Will Dad be coming back tomorrow, do you think?"

"I hope so."

"All right."

Another silence, this one only very marginally less frosty. "I'll see you tomorrow, then," Harriet said, and hung up.

Chapter Fifteen

BY EIGHT O'CLOCK the next morning, Rachel was gritty-eyed, her body stiff and aching with fatigue. She'd managed to snatch a few hours of sleep, but it had been no more than dozing, broken by the constant interruptions of nurses coming to check her father's stats, or someone else's on the ward, squeaky doors or wheels of trolleys, the sudden beeps or buzzes of various machines. She hadn't realised how little sleep could be got in a hospital, never mind while curled up in a chair.

The nurse was kind enough to give her a toothbrush and mini tube of toothpaste, and while her father was still sleeping, Rachel went to the bathroom to wash her face and brush her teeth, trying to feel a little less like the walking dead. She went down to the foyer to get a lovely strong Americano from the coffee shop, and a cup of tea for her dad, strong and sugary just as he liked it.

As she stood by the counter, waiting for the barista to make her coffee, feeling tired and achy and longing for a shower and a change of clothes, she wondered how much of her life would be spent in hospitals. Was this the beginning of a new normal, days and even nights spent with her dad while he awaited some kind of treatment? The future yawned in front of her, uncertain, potentially awful. And yet…she was glad she was here, she realised. She was *glad* she'd come home. This, she thought, even though it was hard and painful and sad, was something she did not want to miss.

"Americano and tea for Rachel?"

Rachel blinked the world back into focus. "That's me," she said. "Thanks."

Back up on the first floor, the neurology ward was coming to life, after the quiet of the night shift, when the lights had been dimmed and interruptions kept to a minimum—although, Rachel had found, that was a matter of opinion.

Now, however, visitors were arriving, some looking shell-shocked like her and others seeming like old hands. A care assistant was pushing a trolley with breakfast trays on it, and someone else was mopping the bathroom. The curtains of most of the cubicles had been pulled back so Rachel could see the other patients—some of them seeming like her dad, older but without too much seeming wrong with them, while others were clearly experiencing more difficulty. She averted her eyes from a man who looked only to be in his forties or so, but was paralysed all down his left side, probably after a stroke, his face frozen in a sort of rictus grimace.

Her dad was awake as she came into the cubicle, looking as tired as she felt. "I got you a tea, Dad," she said, and put the cup on the table by his bed.

"That was nice of you," her father said gruffly. She knew he didn't like depending on anyone, needing things.

"Your MRI isn't till noon," Rachel told him. "So, we have some time to wait." She'd already emailed Danielle to explain the situation; she'd been planning to take this morning off anyway, but she'd hoped to be back at her desk later in the day. Now she wasn't sure that would happen.

Her father carefully reached for his cup of tea, his movements laboured and jerky. Rachel held her breath, wanting to help but knowing it would annoy him. He took a sip successfully and she let out her breath in a slow, silent release.

"If it's bad news," her father said abruptly, "I don't want you girls making a fuss."

"And what," Rachel asked, smiling a little, "would a fuss entail?"

"You know," he said in his usual, irritable way. "Getting all upset. Flapping around."

"If it's bad news, Dad, of course we're going to be upset." Already she could feel a lump forming in her throat—again—and she swallowed past it. "But I promise no flapping."

"No need for you to be upset," her dad said, not looking at her. "It wasn't as if I was a very good father to you."

Shock had Rachel gaping at him for a moment. "Dad..."

"No need to talk about it," he told her dismissively. "I did my best, but I suppose I could have done better, especially after your mother left."

They had never, ever talked about her mum's leaving. It was as if she'd ceased to exist when she'd walked out that door, and in any case, Rachel had already been gone, mostly. "Maybe this is a conversation you need to have with Harriet," she said quietly.

"She knows." Her dad sighed and rested his head back against the pillow. "It's not a comfortable feeling, looking back on your life, wondering what you could have done differently."

"No, I don't suppose it is." She'd had some of the same thoughts, albeit on a less dramatic scale. "But it might not be bad news, Dad. You're not at death's door quite yet." She'd meant to lighten the mood just a little, but her father simply shook his head.

"I have some regrets," he stated slowly, his gaze distant, and Rachel tensed, because he had never, in all her memory, talked like this. Her father wasn't the kind of man who had regrets, or at least who acknowledged them. He was the kind of man who simply soldiered on, silent and stoic.

"I think we all have regrets, Dad," she said after a moment. It was, she knew, a bit of a cop-out, because while part of her was intensely curious to know what his regrets were, another, larger part did not have the emotional bandwidth to deal with any potential revelations, not on top of a sleepless night and a potentially difficult diagnosis.

His jaw tightened as he kept his gaze averted. "Some are worse than others."

Oh, help. She took a deep breath, steeling herself to ask, and then chickened out. "That's understandable," she murmured instead, and then the nurse drew the curtain with a cheerful "good morning" as she came in to take her father's blood pressure. Rachel sat back in her chair with an intermingled sense of both relief and disappointment and sipped her coffee.

THE NEXT FEW hours passed with laborious slowness, as her father became irritable, then silent, and then thankfully drifted to sleep, and all the while Rachel struggled not to feel irritable or drift off to sleep herself. She yearned for a shower; why had sleeping in a chair made her feel so *dirty*?

She watched other visitors come and go; in the cubicle next to them an elderly woman became fractious, fretful, and her husband gently soothed her, his voice tender yet with a tone that made Rachel think this had happened many times before. Across the ward, a patient was wheeled into an empty cubicle; he was young, not even twenty, with part of his hair shaved, no doubt for some surgery or other.

So much sorrow and suffering, worry and fear, and yet also so much love. Rachel saw it in the mother of the boy who sat by his bed, smiling and holding his hand even though Rachel knew she had to be terrified. Or the husband of the woman next to her dad, who gently wiped her mouth after she'd taken a sip of water.

She felt as if she'd lived—and aged—a year, a century, by the time a nurse came to wheel her father away for his MRI.

"He'll be gone an hour at least," she told Rachel with a smile. "We'll text you when he's ready to come back to the ward, in case you want to leave the hospital."

"All right, thank you. See you soon, Dad." She waved at her father who gave a grunt in response, and then he was gone, and Rachel felt as if there were an emptiness whistling right through her. She decided to take a walk around the hospital grounds; it was a beautiful day, the sun shining through the windows at the end of the ward, and after so many hours in the artificial light and filtered air, she felt the need to stretch, to breathe.

Outside the air was surprisingly balmy, an Indian summer at the start of October. There wasn't really anywhere to go except along the pavement around the hospital buildings, and so Rachel set off, glad for the fresh air, the chance to stretch her legs.

She'd been walking for ten minutes or so when her phone buzzed, and she saw, with a jolt of shock, that it was Ben—she'd programmed in his number after he'd called her in Ibiza, so she wouldn't be taken by surprise that way again. For a second, she deliberated about whether to take his call, and then decided she wanted to.

"Ben?" she answered after she'd swiped.

"Hey." The low rumble of his voice was so familiar, so…so *dear*. It shouldn't be, Rachel knew, but it was. "Are you okay?"

The fact that he was asking if *she* was okay, and not her dad, made her eyes sting.

"Yes," she said, and her voice wobbled just a little. "I think so. My dad's having the MRI right now."

"Harriet said they thought it might be a brain tumour."

"That's what the doctor said, but of course we don't know yet."

"I'm sorry, Rachel." He sounded so regretful, so genuine, that she had to blink rapidly.

"Thank you," she whispered. "I thought maybe you'd suspected something like this."

"I wondered." He sighed. "But it's still crap."

"We don't know for sure," she protested quickly, only to fall silent when Ben did not reply. "We'll get the results in a few days."

"Will he be able to come home today?"

"I'm not sure. Maybe."

"Do you need a lift?"

Rachel hesitated, because of course she did, but she also suspected she should ask Harriet. She feared her sister was feeling cut out, even though Rachel hadn't meant her to be. She just hadn't wanted her to have to make an unnecessary journey late at night. "I don't know if Harriet was planning on coming," she said, only for Ben to reply, "She's got a big baking thing on this afternoon. Scones for some tea shop in Pickering."

"Oh, wow—" Harriet hadn't told her about that.

"I can come." He sounded firm and decisive, almost bossy, and although Rachel knew that in the past his tone might have made her hackles rise, now she only felt relieved—and glad.

"Thank you," she said simply. "I'll text you when I know if he's allowed to come home today."

As she ended the call, she realised she felt just that little bit better—and less alone.

TWO HOURS LATER, her dad was back from his MRI looking pale and tired but acting as irritable as ever, and the doctor was assuring Rachel that he could be discharged that afternoon; they would call with the MRI results within the week.

Another couple of hours after that, Ben was striding into the ward, smiling and looking as if he could conquer the world. Rachel, meanwhile, felt as if she could collapse into a heap. She suspected she smelled like stale coffee if not something worse, and her hair was definitely greasy. Suddenly she wished she hadn't agreed for Ben to pick them up, except despite her hair and smell, she was glad. She wanted him here, even if she wasn't about to let him know that.

"Hey, Mr M," Ben said with an easy smile for her dad. "You want to get out of this place?"

Her father looked at Ben with both affection and relief. "Do I ever," he said.

It took a bit of paperwork and rigamarole, but a short while later Rachel was pushing her father's wheelchair out to the front of the hospital while Ben drove his Land Rover up. As she helped her father into the passenger seat—help he accepted irritably but accepted all the same—she let out a weary breath, glad to have got this far.

As she climbed into the back of the rover, moving aside a bunch of papers as well as a pair of muddy boots, she thought she might have the longest bath ever upon her return. Ben kept the chat with her father light as they drove home, until her dad drifted off into a doze and Ben met Rachel's gaze in the mirror with a small smile.

"Guess I tired him out," he said softly.

"I don't think I've ever heard you talk so much," Rachel returned with an answering smile. The tension she'd felt from before, when they'd been at the ceilidh, seemed to have disappeared, at least for now. Maybe it would return once this immediate crisis was over, but she was grateful for the reprieve, however short that turned out to be.

They remained in a companionable silence for the rest of

the journey back to Embthwaite Farm, and her dad stirred awake as Ben pulled up the rutted lane that led to their adjacent properties.

"Home already?" he mumbled, before straightening, running one hand through his wispy hair.

Harriet wasn't home yet from her baking gig, and so Rachel helped her dad to the living room—he insisted he didn't need to go to bed—and settled him with the TV on and a cup of tea.

"Do you want one?" she asked Ben as she headed back to the kitchen. She was surprised at how easy it felt to ask him; somehow the events of the last twenty-four hours put her little snit about him not kissing her into lamentable perspective. *Big deal,* some part of her subconscious had told the rest of her panicky self. *Get over it.*

"I would, but I need to get back," Ben said, already at the door. The part of her that had felt so mature and affable suddenly shrivelled up and died. Okay, maybe she was still in a snit. Sort of.

"Okay, of course," Rachel said quickly, trying to sound like she didn't care anyway, that she wasn't mad, or heaven help her, *hurt* by his refusal of a simple cup of tea. For heaven's *sake.*

"Another time?" he asked, cocking his head, and Rachel nodded, managing a smile, feeling a bit better.

"Another time."

After Ben had left, she sank into a chair at the kitchen table, feeling boneless with exhaustion. She needed a bath, which she should start now, because it took about half an hour to fill up their old, claw-footed tub. A cup of tea in a deep, hot bubble bath, she decided. That was just the ticket.

She went upstairs to fill the bath, and when she came downstairs, she saw Harriet had come in the back door to the kitchen and was dumping empty trays onto the counter.

"Harriet! I didn't hear you come in." She smiled a greeting, but her sister seemed focused on what she was doing. "How did the baking go? Ben said you were supplying scones to a tea shop in Pickering?"

"Yep." Harriet didn't look at her and Rachel let out a weary sigh. She was not in the mood for any surly theatrics, and she really didn't have the energy to hash out what had been meant to be a simple phone conversation. She decided to grasp the nettle. "Look, I'm sorry about how I sounded on the phone yesterday. I didn't mean to make it seem like you weren't needed or wanted at the hospital. That certainly wasn't the case."

If she thought that speaking so plainly would help, she was to be disappointed. Harriet jerked her shoulders in a shrug and kept unpacking, without so much as a glance at Rachel.

"*Harriet.* Please."

"What?" Her sister looked up, a spark of challenge in her eyes. "What do you want me to say, Rachel? I *know* you didn't mean it like that. That doesn't mean it didn't achieve the same purpose."

She was too tired for word games. "What is that supposed to mean?"

Harriet let out a heavy sigh before shoving her hair back from her forehead with one hand. Baking in a hot kitchen had turned it into a frizzy halo. "I just mean, it's always been you and Dad. Even when you haven't been here."

What? For a few seconds, Rachel could only stare. "What are you talking about?" she asked finally. "It hasn't always been me and Dad, Harriet. I haven't been back properly in years."

"Did you listen to what I said?" Harriet returned wearily. "'Even when you're not here.'"

Rachel lowered herself into a chair at the table, shaking her head in instinctive denial of such a distortion of past reality. "That's just not true."

"You don't even see it. You never did." Harriet spoke without bitterness or recrimination, and somehow that made it worse. It forced Rachel to take what she was saying seriously, because it wasn't an insult or accusation hurled in a moment of temper or hurt. It was simply stated as a matter of fact. All these *facts*, bombarding her, barraging her.

"Okay," she said after a moment, although she was still reeling. "Why do you say that?"

"Because it's true."

"Explain what you mean, please."

Harriet gave another heavy sigh before turning towards the Rayburn. "For this I'm going to need a cup of tea. Do you want one?"

Rachel thought of the bath running upstairs; she had another twenty minutes or so before it was filled, but she wasn't sure how long this heart-to-heart was going to last. Harriet seemed in the mood to bare secrets, and Rachel knew well enough that short-changing this conversation in any way was not a good move. Even if she was tired and emotional, and she desperately needed to wash her hair. "Sure," she said, doing her best to inject a note of enthusiasm into her voice. "Thank you." She rose from her chair. "Let me just turn off the bath, and then we can talk." She paused and added with deliberation, "Properly."

Chapter Sixteen

BY THE TIME Rachel came back downstairs, the bath only a third of the way filled, Harriet had made a pot of tea and brought it to the table on a tray, with a couple of mugs, a jug of milk, a pot of sugar, and a few leftover scones. She'd clearly gone to some effort, and Rachel was touched. She was also filled with trepidation, because clearly this was going to be a Big Conversation, and she thought they'd already had several of those. What more did she have to discover, about the past she thought she'd known, because she'd always remembered it a certain way? Harriet seemed to have a different version of events, and one that had as much relevance to reality as Rachel's did. Their experiences had differed in a way she'd never even realised, as had their perspectives.

"This looks lovely," she said as she sat down. "Thank you, Harriet."

Harriet let out a little laugh. "It's not much. The scones were left over, anyway." She began to pour the tea as she remarked mildly, "You don't have to walk on eggshells around me, Rachel. I know I was a little frosty on the phone, but I get that you didn't mean anything by it. I really do."

"Okay." Harriet, it seemed, had mellowed out since Rachel had come back home, just as she had, albeit in a different way.

"So, where to begin?" Harriet put milk and sugar in her tea and then stirred it slowly. "Maybe it's easier if I give it to you in a nutshell. You've always been Dad's favourite child, and while I've generally made peace with that, sometimes it stings. There." She smiled as she took a sip of tea. "Maybe this conversation won't be as long as you're dreading."

How, Rachel wondered, did her sister always seem to know what she was feeling? She wished she could say the same, but she wasn't sure she could. "Dad's favourite child?" she repeated, eyebrows raised. "How do you figure?"

Harriet shrugged. "In a million different small ways. He never came to my parents' evenings when we were at school, for one."

"He didn't?" Rachel couldn't hide her surprise. Her dad had come to most of hers. Not with much enthusiasm or interest, as far as she recalled, but he'd *been* there. Mostly.

"No, he didn't. Not a single one." Harriet stared at her directly. "And, you know, I sort of got it, even as a kid. He had one parent conference in him, I think, and he chose yours."

"He could have alternated," Rachel replied quietly. She felt humbled, and unsettled, and also vaguely guilty, although she knew it wasn't her fault. Was it? "How did I not notice that?"

Harriet shrugged and reached for a blueberry scone, breaking off a large chunk. "It's not necessarily something I would have expected you to notice, as a child."

"Yes, but…" She still felt she should have. "What else?"

she asked, looking at her sister directly.

Harriet popped the chunk of scone into her mouth and chewed thoughtfully. "He always asked about your day at teatime, never mine," she said after she'd swallowed. "And if that sounds petty, like I was keeping count, well, sorry, but that's how it was. He just wasn't interested in me, Rachel." Harriet's expression briefly turned bleak. "He never has been. I don't really know why."

"I didn't feel he was all that interested in *me*," Rachel protested. "He's spent more time in the barn than the house. He missed a lot of things—sports days and stuff like that." She shook her head slowly. "I never really felt that he was all that interested in what I was doing or how I felt."

"Well, he was—is—a Yorkshireman and a farmer. He was never going to *emote*. But he was certainly more interested in you than he was in me."

"I never saw it that way. I'm not saying that's not how it was," she added quickly, "just that I never saw it." At all. And yet...memories began to filter through her subconscious, so vague and faint she couldn't be entirely sure that they were real. Sitting with her dad on the sofa as they watched *Pointless*. Where had Harriet been? Coming into the barn to fetch her dad for tea, having him smile at her and call her 'Rachel girl'. Had he had a nickname for Harriet? Him sitting by the side of her bed when she'd been ill with the flu, one large, callused hand resting on her hair. *Get better, Rachel girl.* Had he done that with Harriet?

"I know you didn't," Harriet told her. "And I understand why he was more interested in you than me, really. You're the oldest, and you're so much like him."

Rachel reared back a little. "That's not exactly a compliment, is it?"

"It's not an insult, either," Harriet returned with a small smile. "You're driven and focused, just like he is. I know it looks different as an investment manager or whatever you are than as a farmer, but you both have the same steely core."

Rachel took a sip of tea as she tried to organise her clamouring thoughts. "Why did you stay, Harriet," she finally asked, "if you felt that way? I mean, you certainly didn't owe him anything."

Harriet looked down at her lap, her hair falling in front of her face to hide her expression. "Well, like I told you, I didn't take my A levels. I didn't really have a lot of options."

"I know, but…you could have lived with Mum, maybe?"

The tension this suggestion caused a feeling like a tautening of the very air. "She didn't offer," Harriet stated flatly.

Something else Rachel hadn't known, although she supposed she could have guessed easily enough. Their mother had walked out without so much as a forwarding address. Rachel hadn't spoken to her after she'd left for more than a year, and then it had been a short, stilted, painful conversation. After a while, they'd managed to meet, and they'd found a distant sort of rapport.

"Did you *want* to leave?" she asked, realising as the words came out of her mouth that it was a question she'd never actually asked her sister.

"I don't know." Harriet raised her head, her expression ironed into something like resignation. "I suppose I didn't let myself think about it too much. It never really felt like a possibility." She broke off another chunk of scone, but this time she simply crumbled it between her fingers, onto her plate. "I don't want to blame Mum and Dad for being screwed up or something like that," she said slowly. "I'm an adult. I need to take responsibility for my choices, and I chose to stay."

"And I chose to leave," Rachel returned quietly. Danielle's words, full of regret, whispered through her mind. *The person she could have become.* "Sometimes I wish I hadn't," she said, the words surprising her—and yet not.

"Do you really?" Harriet looked and sounded understandably sceptical. Rachel knew she had never indicated as much in any way before; in fact, quite the opposite. "You always seemed like you wanted to bust out of here."

"Yes, I did." Rachel knew she couldn't deny that. "I suppose it's more in retrospect. What would I have been like, what would we have been like, if…" She couldn't make herself finish that thought.

"I should never have asked you to stay," Harriet said abruptly. "When you came back from uni that first time after Mum had left. I know I shouldn't have. I think I knew it at the time. I just felt…scared, I suppose. And lonely."

Rachel swallowed hard. All right, it seemed as if they *had* needed another Big Conversation, after all. "I'm sorry," she whispered. "I should have handled that better. Even if I hadn't stayed, I could have come back more often. Been more involved. I think I felt guilty and that made me stay away. That's no excuse, but—"

"It wasn't like I was a little kid, Rachel," Harriet returned with a wry smile, "even if I felt like one sometimes. I wasn't your responsibility. I think I just wanted to be."

"And since then?" Rachel ventured to ask, since they were having such a massive heart-to-heart. "You've seemed pretty angry with me, over the years."

"I have been," Harriet admitted baldly. "Being angry feels stronger than being hurt. And the more you stayed away, the...*angrier* I became." She sighed. "Not the most mature reaction, I know, but whenever you came back you seemed like you had such a busy, important life in London. Like you didn't want to be here."

Rachel grimaced as she nodded her acknowledgement of that unfortunate truth. "And you seemed like you didn't want me to be here," she replied gently. "Which unfortunately, I do understand."

Harriet shrugged. "A vicious cycle, I suppose."

"Yes. And I know I'm at fault in perpetuating it." She took a deep breath. "I'm sorry, Harriet, for letting you down."

"I guess I let you down, too," Harriet replied. "I'm sorry."

They stared at one another a bit uneasily. Yes, it had been a vicious cycle but one, perhaps, they now could break. Maybe it was already broken. Rachel knew there were still more conversations to have, more steps to take, but she felt as if they'd truly got somewhere, somewhere she hadn't even realised they needed to be, although she supposed she should have guessed. She'd thought things had been going okay with her sister for the last few weeks, but now she realised just how much had remained unspoken. How much she'd been willing to leave unspoken, because the unfortunate truth was, she'd always preferred avoidance to confrontation, running away to staying put.

But now, for better or worse, she *was* staying put.

"We need to talk about Dad," Harriet said heavily. "About going forward."

"Yes." Rachel steeled herself. She knew there was no point protesting that he didn't have a diagnosis yet; the last few days had shown her absolutely that her dad needed help. That something had to change.

"We'll have to cover the milking, for a start," Harriet said, and Rachel jolted a bit in surprise.

"I didn't even think about that," she admitted. "Who did the milking this morning?"

"I did, with Ben's help. But I can't do it every day. It takes a couple of hours, and then again in the afternoon, plus arranging with Ray, who does the deliveries."

"Ben told me that Dad was going to sell off the rest of the herd to pay the mortgage," Rachel said quietly. "Did you know that?"

Harriet shook her head. "But I'm not really surprised. Neither of us have ever wanted to take on the farm in that way. He knew that. But until he does sell it, or we do, the cows need to be milked."

"I can help with that," Rachel stated, and then bristled just a little when Harriet arched an eyebrow in obvious scepticism.

"Can you?"

"I have milked a cow before, Harriet." They'd had to learn, as children, and Rachel actually hadn't minded it, because it had been one time when her father had been interested and invested in being with her…except it seemed he had been all along, at least more than he'd been with Harriet. How had she not seen that? Felt it? Maybe she had, but she'd let herself forget. It was easy, she was beginning to realise, to forget things when you felt hurt. In any case, there was time to reflect on that later. Right now, they needed to think about practicalities.

"It's a little different now, you know," Harriet told her. "With the new milking machines. It means it's quicker, but you have to know how to put the suction cups on—"

"I'm sure I can figure it out, or you or Ben can show me," Rachel replied. "I can't ask you to do all the milking, and I'm willing to do it."

"Okay." Harriet nodded in acceptance, and Rachel let out a breath. They might have had a Big Conversation, but it seemed there were still some fairly tricky moments to navigate. At least it seemed to be getting easier.

"Is there anything else that needs doing?" she asked.

"Well, just the obvious," Harriet replied. "Feed the cows, clean their stalls, clean the milk bottles…"

It sounded like a lot of work, and Rachel still had a full-time job, even if it felt like the last thing she was thinking about just now. "For how long?" she wondered aloud. "Till Dad is back at it, do you think?"

"I have no idea." Harriet was silent for a moment. "I mean, depending on his diagnosis, he might not be back at it, Rachel. That's something we have to consider. And arranging to sell the herd will take weeks, at a minimum."

Rachel massaged her forehead as she felt a headache throb at her temples. Managing a dairy farm was not something she had the time or even the inclination to do, and yet she wasn't about to back down now. "Okay," she said, even though she had no idea how she was going to go about this. "Maybe I could ask my boss if I could take some time off work."

"I can scale back my commitments too," Harriet offered, and Rachel nodded, knowing Harriet had just as much of a right to a life of her own as Rachel did, if not more so.

Harriet's been holding the bag for a long time.

"Don't scale back too much," she told her sister. "It sounds like this baking gig of yours is just getting going."

Harriet looked surprised, and Rachel knew that was not something she would have said, ever, in the past. "Well, sort of," she admitted almost shyly. "The tea room in Pickering was a nice one to pick up. They might become a regular thing."

"That's great, Harriet." Rachel smiled at her, feeling genuinely pleased. She was glad her sister had something she seemed passionate about, something she could build into a career. "I'll email Danielle right now," she said firmly as she rose from the table. "Then we can make a proper plan."

AFTER SHE'D SENT the email to Danielle, Rachel decided she needed to clear her head. As much as she wanted a bath, the water was now barely tepid and her head felt too full of thoughts to have a soak; she felt the need to move.

She changed into a fresh set of jeans and a fleece and called for Fred as she put on her boots. "I'm just going to the top of the hill," she called to Harriet, who was still in the kitchen. "I'll be back in a bit."

Outside the day was still warm, the air like a balmy caress, the sunlight a benediction as Rachel headed behind the house towards the hill, Fred trotting faithfully beside her. She walked with purpose, like she had a destination to reach, a place to go, and maybe she did.

She felt as if she had to reframe her whole life, her whole *self*, in light of all she'd learned, and the most surprising thing of all was that didn't feel like a bad thing.

She took a deep breath, letting the fresh air fill her lungs. She strode quickly up the hill, arms swinging at her sides, huffing and puffing and feeling her heart beat hard and fast and strong. Fred trotted behind her, huffing and puffing a bit too, and when she reached the top, she wondered why she had been walking so quickly to get there, and yet somehow, she was glad she had.

Rachel turned around to face the view—the farmhouse below, smoke curling from its chimney, nestled in the dip of the valley, the barns behinds it, the pastureland rolling out in a carpet of green to the lane. From here she could see the slate roof of the Mackeys' house and the back of their barn, but not much else. A tractor cut through a distant field beyond, and she wondered if Ben was riding it, going about his work, day after day in this place.

Once that would have been anathema to her. Harriet was right, Rachel knew; she *had* been busting to get out of here for most of her childhood. She'd felt hemmed by her mother's unhappiness, her father's distance, the other schoolchildren who saw her as gawky and shy and strange. The smallness of Mathering, a community where people knew what you were doing before you knew yourself. Where no one would let you be anything than what they thought you were.

Oh yes, she'd been longing to escape it all. Exeter had felt like a breath of fresh air, a world where she wasn't known, where she could be anyone she wanted to be. London had been the same, but by the time she'd been working awhile she had started to wonder, without actually articulating her thoughts, that maybe it could be *nice* to be known, for people to remember you from when you were small, and see you as more than a cog in a vast machine, one more anonymous soul in the sea of strangers that was a city.

Another deep breath to fill her lungs and then out again, as she surveyed this tiny and beautiful corner of Yorkshire—the rolling moors in a patchwork of brown and green, the Derwent winding its way gracefully through the hills, the rooftops and grey stone of Mathering in the distance, all underneath a pale blue sky.

For once, Rachel thought, she wasn't hightailing it out of this place, running away from the people she was meant to love because she was too scared or too angry or too tired to deal with the messy complications relationships inevitably came with. For once, she was staying.

For how long, she didn't know, but she let that open-ended idea settle inside her as she started back down the hill. Whatever happened, whatever came next, she promised herself, she was going to see it through.

Chapter Seventeen

"ALL RIGHT, YOU."

Rachel gave the cow she was milking what she hoped was an encouraging look as its large, soft brown eyes blinked back at her. "This doesn't hurt, I know it doesn't, and I *can* do this, because Harriet showed me." It was five o'clock in the morning the day after she and her father had returned from Middlesbrough, and just as she'd promised Harriet, she was doing the milking. Or she would be, as soon as she steeled herself to attach the suction cups to the cow's swollen teats.

It had been a long time since she'd been this close to a cow.

In fact, despite what she'd told Harriet with such assurance, she couldn't remember *when* she'd last been near a cow. Yes, she'd helped her dad with the milking, *sort of*, but the truth was he'd done most of the work and she'd simply sat and watched. When Harriet had shown her how to do it yesterday, seeming uncharacteristically, briskly capable about it all, Rachel had watched and nodded and said yes, of course she could do it. Part of her had even been thinking, shamefully, that she could do anything her sister did, only better.

Old habits died hard, it seemed, because already Rachel

was pretty sure she couldn't be better than Harriet at this.

"All right, let's do this," she told the cow, and leaned forward to attach the milk cup to a teat. She'd already released the rubber stop and turned the whole contraption, which looked something like an octopus made of metal and rubber, upside down, and now she just had to connect it to the cow…the cow which mooed and danced a few steps away.

"Now, don't *do* that," Rachel implored the beast. "We're friends, right? And you want to be milked. Think how good it will feel…" All right, maybe best not to go down that route. "Come on," she said, and reached forward again. Once more the cow took a few prancing, alarmed steps away. The *moo* she gave this time sounded like a warning.

Rachel sat back on the milking stool with a groan. Already her back was aching, and she hadn't even started yet. She had sixty cows to deal with, so she really needed this cow to cooperate. Unfortunately, she didn't seem to have received the memo.

"Need help?" Rachel tensed and then turned to see Ben slipping through the barn doors and shedding his coat. He was wearing a flannel shirt and waterproof trousers, and the smile he gave her was both knowing and full of mischief.

"No-o," Rachel replied, hearing the hesitation in her voice. Her instinct was never to ask for help, but she couldn't deny she was glad to see Ben. "I'm just about to start."

"They sense your nervousness," he told her seriously, although he was smiling. "You've got to be firm but gentle with a cow."

"That almost sounds dirty," Rachel quipped, and he let

out a laugh.

"None of those types of farmer jokes, please." He started rolling up his sleeves over his powerful forearms as he reached for one of the ankle-length rubber milking aprons hanging on a hook by the door. "If we work together, it will go faster."

"Don't you have your own work to do?" Rachel asked. Ben didn't keep dairy cows, but he had a lot of sheep.

"I've already been up for an hour." He grabbed a milking stool and sat next to her, close enough so she could breathe him in, along with the scent of the barn—hay and animal, a sweetish, dusty scent that was not unpleasant, once you got used to it. "Here. Let me show you," he said, and attached all four cups in about six seconds.

"Why are you so good at that?" she exclaimed with a laugh. "You're not even a dairy farmer."

"Well, it's all of a piece, isn't it," Ben replied easily, and Rachel gave a little huff of sound, half amusement, half amicable annoyance. "And," he added more quietly as he moved to the next cow, "I've been helping your dad a bit."

"Yes, thank you for that. Harriet said you helped her with the milking yesterday, too—I have to admit, it didn't even cross my mind."

"I'm not sure why it would," Ben replied as he kept moving down the line of cows while Rachel simply sat there and watched.

"You mean because I haven't been around much," she stated, not a question.

Ben lifted one shoulder in a shrug as he kept working. "Are you going to help me here," he called, "or are you just going to stare at my backside?"

And a very nice backside it was, Rachel thought as she rose from her stool. "All right, show me how to do it," she said, and he beckoned to her with one finger.

"Come here."

She came with a small smile on her face, because there had been something almost intimate about his tone, and even though they'd parted rather tensely at the ceilidh, everything felt different now—or maybe it was just her who felt different, because she knew she did. She was no longer in self-protective mode, running away rather than engaging, blustering rather than being. She came towards him, and he shifted over on the stool so she could perch on the other half of it, and it was not a large space. Their thighs were pressed together from hip to knee, and her shoulder and breast brushed his body as she leaned forward, everything in her tingling from the contact.

Ben, however, seemed completely focused on the darn cow.

"Now watch," he murmured, and Rachel had to use all her energy to focus on the process of attaching cup to teat, rather than the warm, solid male body next to hers. "See?" he said, straightening so his shoulder pressed more firmly against hers. Her mind felt fuzzy. *Why* was he so unaffected?

Then she remembered. She couldn't believe she'd forgotten for even a moment. He'd rejected her when she'd wanted him to kiss her. Pushed her away from him firmly. He might as well have said 'no thank you' aloud. Of course he wasn't affected now.

"Yes, I see," she managed, and she stood up, trying to

make the movement natural rather than abrupt. Ben wasn't fooled though, because he twisted around to look at her, a frown settling between his brows.

"Rachel…?"

"I'll get going with the next one," she said, turning away from him. Amazingly, she found she could do it now. She certainly wasn't nervous about a *cow*, not when she felt that cringing mixture of humiliation and hurt that she'd fooled herself into believing she'd moved past.

They worked in silence until all the cups were attached, and then, after they'd washed their hands and dried off, Ben went back to his coat by the door and produced a thermos and two tin mugs. "Voila."

"Is that tea?"

"Of course."

"You think of everything," Rachel managed, but her voice came out a little false. She was still cringing inside, even though she was trying not to.

He frowned again, cocking his head to one side. "You okay?"

"Yeah. You know, tired. And a bit strung out. But I'm okay." She nodded her head a few too many times.

"Get this in you," Ben replied, and handed her a cup of warm, sweet tea. Rachel took it, cradling the mug between her hands, grateful for its warmth. "How's your dad holding up?"

"He's been in bed for most of the time since he came home from the hospital. He seemed tired, but I don't know if that's emotional or physical."

"Probably both."

"Yes."

They stood and sipped in silence for a while, while all around the cows did their business.

"And if it is something serious?" Ben asked finally. "What are you going to do?"

"I'm going to stay," Rachel replied firmly. At least she knew her own heart on that. "I've missed enough of my dad's life already. I'm not going to miss any more."

He nodded slowly, looking thoughtful. "Your fancy company back in London won't mind you working remotely for a bit longer?"

"I don't think so." Rachel shrugged. "And anyway," she added a bit recklessly, "I don't have to be tied to them forever." Ben raised his eyebrows, looking both surprised and sceptical. Rachel wasn't even sure why she'd said such a thing. She'd been with Wallace and Wakeman for nearly ten years; she'd never even thought about leaving. "I mean, I don't think it will come to that, of course," she said, deciding a quick backtrack was the best option.

"Of course." Ben nodded slowly, seeming as if he expected her to say exactly that. "Well, it's good to have you here," he finished as he downed the last of his tea.

Rachel heard herself returning spikily, "Is it?"

Ben slowly lowered the mug from his lips and stared at her. Rachel stared back, even though she could feel herself flush and she hadn't meant to say something so prickly and provocative.

"What," Ben asked slowly, "is that supposed to mean?"

"I don't know."

"Yes, you do."

She bit her lip and then decided to be honest. Why not? What did she have left to lose when it came to this man? "The other night," she admitted, casting her gaze downwards because she could be honest, but she couldn't look at him while she was. "You didn't seem to think it was good to have me around then." She kept her gaze firmly fastened on the floor as she waited for Ben to respond. And waited. And waited.

"It wasn't quite like that," he said at last. She couldn't tell anything from his tone, but still, *quite*?

"Then how was it?"

He sighed, not a sound of impatience or weariness, but one of deep thought. "You were emotional," he said finally. "Vulnerable. I didn't want to take advantage of you."

"That's some pretty emo talk for a Yorkshire farmer," Rachel returned with some asperity.

Ben let out a huff of something like laughter. "This is the twenty-first century, Rach. It's not all 'ey up, fetch me my tea, tha' daft apeth.'"

Rachel had to laugh at the thick Yorkshire accent he'd put on. "Translation?" she asked as she finally looked up with a smile.

He feigned shock, staggering back a little. "What's a bonny Yorkshire lass like tha'self not knowing such a thing?"

"'Something like hello, I'd like some tea please, darling?'" Rachel returned with a smile, and Ben nodded soberly.

"Aye, now the lass has the hang of it, ey reyt."

She laughed again and then shook her head, determined to keep being honest, even though it was hard. "I wasn't *that* vulnerable, Ben. I don't believe you."

He was silent for a long moment, and she took a sip of tea, steeling herself.

"Well," he said finally, scratching his cheek, "I suppose it wasn't just that."

"No?"

"I've got my pride," he admitted. "I can just about take being turned down once, but not twice. And I didn't fancy being your bit of rough, if that's the way you were thinking."

"What!" There was so much in that statement that Rachel needed to unpick, to argue with, because he clearly had the wrong end of several sticks. "First of all," she said, "I didn't turn you down, *you* turned me down, back then."

Ben's mouth dropped open. "What—"

"Second of all, I have never, ever suggested that you could be my bit of rough! What a thought. You're not even that rough, Ben Mackey, I'll have you know." She glared at him, although she wasn't, she realised, feeling all that angry. She was feeling strangely exhilarated. "And third of all, you didn't even say any of this on the night, so it's all a bit after the fact, isn't it?"

"You didn't give me a chance!" he exclaimed, flushing. "You hightailed out of there like a—like a bat out of hell! What was I supposed to do?" He looked so aggrieved that Rachel had a sudden urge to laugh.

"What you were *supposed* to do," she replied, hardly able to believe she was actually saying such a thing, "was kiss me senseless! That was what I wanted! That's what I was so clearly asking for, so none of this telling me I was *emotional*."

"*You* said you were emotional, at the ceilidh," Ben fired back, taking a step towards her. His face was flushed, his eyes glittering. They were fighting, except, Rachel knew, they really weren't. She didn't think she'd ever felt so alive, every nerve end singing.

"What was I supposed to say," she tossed back at him, "when you had so clearly rejected me? Was I supposed to get on my knees and beg? I have some pride too, you know, Ben Mackey!"

She poked a finger in his nicely muscled chest, and quick as a flash he captured her hand in his, drawing it against his heart. Rachel's breath caught as she stared at him with wide eyes, her heart thundering in her chest.

"What do you mean," he asked in a low voice, "that I turned you down, back then? Because that's not how I remember it, Rachel Mowbray. At all."

Her mind was *buzzing*. Her whole body was. "You never asked me to stay," she whispered.

"You were so set on going," he replied, his voice so low she had to strain to hear it, even standing right in front of him. "You *told* me you wanted to go to Exeter. You knew I was never going to leave the farm."

"There is such a thing as long-distance relationships. I said as much—"

"You really wanted that?" he returned, his hand clasping hers tightly. "You wanted to spend three years toing and froing, your heart in one place, your mind in another? I *knew* you, Rachel. You wanted your freedom. This isn't a case of simple misunderstanding, one conversation gone wrong. That's just revisionist history."

"Maybe," she allowed, unable to tear her gaze from his. She knew there was more than a little truth in his words.

"But you didn't say a single word, Ben. Not one word. Do you know how…rejected…I felt?"

"Do you know rejected *I* felt?" he returned, drawing her closer to him so their hips bumped. "You were going off to this exciting new world, and you were *fizzing* with it. I was just staying here in bloody Mathering, pitching hay."

"Why didn't you say anything?" she pressed, her voice little more than a croak. "You didn't even turn around."

"Why do you think?" he demanded raggedly, which was no answer at all, but Rachel had no time to protest because then he was kissing her, kissing her in a way he never had before, with a wild, almost frenzied passion, his hands in her hair, driving her forward until her back was pressed against the barn wall, and her mind blurred in the most wonderful way as she kissed him back with all the passion she knew she felt.

The next few seconds, or maybe even minutes, passed in a blaze of sensation—lips, hands, bodies, breathing ragged and wanting.

And then—

"Rachel," Harriet called, the barn door squeaking open, and then, in true Yorkshire brogue, "Eh, by gum!" She backed out again quickly, but the moment was broken. Ben stepped back from her, raking a hand through his untidy hair while Rachel struggled not to slide to the floor, boneless and weak.

"Oh dear," she said after a moment, and Ben frowned.

"Oh dear?" he repeated, a bit warily.

"I only meant Harriet saw us," Rachel explained as she tried to straighten her clothes, her thoughts. "Don't be paranoid."

"Once bitten, twice shy," he replied as he straightened his own clothes. Somehow his shirt had got untucked, even underneath the rubber apron—had she done that? She must have. She had a vague yet wonderful recollection of sliding her hand up the smooth muscles of his bare back.

"Don't, please," she said, shaking her head. She didn't want to have any recriminations or rehashing of their past. Not now. "Can't we just...let this be?"

Ben frowned. "What do you mean?"

"I'm not sure," she admitted. "Just...life is short. My dad's situation has made me realise that more than ever. Can't we just...enjoy this?"

"And what," Ben asked, "is this?"

"I don't know," Rachel replied honestly. "Us, in some form, I suppose. Can we just see...how it goes?"

Ben stared at her for a moment. "I'm not really sure what you're asking," he said finally.

"I'm not, either." She let out a shaky laugh, because she felt wonderful and alive but also incredibly vulnerable, admitting this much. "All I know is we got tied up in knots last time we had to think about the future, and who would be where, how it would work." Although they'd never even got as far as discussing any of that. It had been the conversation they'd never had. "Can't we do it differently now? Live day by day, enjoy each moment, and see what happens?"

"Are you asking to have a *fling*?" Ben asked, with something like disbelief.

"Well, not necessarily," Rachel said quickly. She wasn't ready to commit—or not commit, as it happened—quite that much. "Don't jump the gun! I just...I like it when you kiss me."

A tiny smile tugged at his mouth and his eyes glinted whisky amber. "I like it, too," he admitted, which thrilled her.

"Okay, then."

"Okay?" He raised his eyebrows in query.

"You could, you know, kiss me again," she suggested hesitantly. As ballsy as she'd just been, she still felt incredibly insecure about all this. "And then we should probably deal with these cows, and head into the house before Harriet has a conniption."

"All right, then," Ben replied. His smile was slow as he drew her towards him, and her head fell back before his mouth settled on hers. This kiss was as different from the last as was possible—leisurely, deliberate, *tender*. She felt as if he were kissing her soul, and at the same time as if he was both possessing and cherishing her.

After an endless moment, he broke the kiss and stepped back. His gaze was steady and warm and very sure. Rachel felt a silly, sloppy sort of smile spread across her face, and Ben gave a little chuckle. She felt, she thought, very, very happy.

"Right, then," Ben said, pronouncing it the Yorkshire way, *reyt*. "You can handle the rest? I should be off."

"Oh—" Rachel heard the pulse of disappointment in her voice.

"I'll see you later?" he returned gently. "Maybe for tea?"

Tea, the Yorkshire word for supper. "All right, yes." She nodded, the smile back on her face. "Yes."

Ben leaned forward and gave her her third kiss of the morning, this one hard and fast, like a seal. "Bye, then," he said, and then he was out the door, and Rachel was left alone with about sixty cows.

Chapter Eighteen

HARRIET WAS STIRRING a pot of porridge, her back to her, as Rachel came into the kitchen.

"The milking's done," she said as she took off her coat. "And Ray's loading up the deliveries."

"Is that all you have to say?" Harriet turned around, eyebrows raised, a knowing and rather devilish smile on her face.

"Well." Rachel found herself smiling back, unable to keep herself from it and not, she realised, even wanting to. "I suppose you saw Ben and me..."

"I certainly did." Harriet sounded smug, and Rachel let out a little laugh as she shook her head.

"I don't know what it means, exactly," she warned her sister as she started to take off her boots. "We're just...we're just going to take it day by day."

"That sounds sensible," Harriet returned, but her smile had slipped off her face and she was now frowning a little.

"What?" Rachel asked.

Harriet turned back to the pot of porridge, stirring it slowly. "Just don't break his heart, Rachel," she said quietly. "Not a second time."

Rachel stood there, one boot on, one boot held in her

hand, as she stared at her sister. "I didn't break his heart a first time," she finally objected. "If anything, Harriet, he broke mine."

"But you're the one who left."

It was what Ben had said, and Rachel knew it was true, technically, but…it hadn't quite been like that. It certainly hadn't felt like it.

"I doubt his heart was broken," she tried to scoff. "I mean, Ben was one of the cool kids back in school."

"Cool?" Harriet glanced back at her. "He had his rugby lad friends, I suppose, but I wouldn't say he was *cool*."

Well, Rachel thought, *she'd* found him cool, seriously cool, but maybe that was just because she so obviously hadn't been—shy, awkward, lonely geek that she'd been back then. But Harriet, in the year below, had had more friends than Rachel had—a whole gang of girls she went around town with, or sprawled in the sitting room, eating crisps and watching telly, while their mother had, as she so often had, retreated upstairs to her bed. Maybe, to her, Ben had never been that cool. He'd just been…Ben.

"Anyway," Harriet said as she doled the porridge into bowls, "his heart *was* broken. I know because I was here, and you weren't. He moped around for ages—although I don't think *mope* is really the right word. He was as grumpy as a bear, snapping at everyone, that is if he said anything at all."

Rachel sat down to take off her other boot. "Maybe he was," she allowed, "but so was I, Harriet. Heartbroken, that is. I didn't just swan off to Exeter without a care in the world."

Harriet arched an eyebrow in blatant scepticism. "Sorry,

Rachel, but from where we were standing, that's what it looked like. At least," she amended, "that's what it *felt* like."

She put two bowls on the table, along with a jar of honey and a pot of coffee. "I'm taking this up to Dad," she said, gesturing to a tray she'd made up, complete with porridge, tea, a plate of toast, and the newspaper rolled up on the side. "We can talk more when I get back down, if you want to."

Rachel watched her go, wondering what it was that drove Harriet to keep caring for her dad even when she'd clearly felt so unloved for so long. Was it duty, sacrificial love, or a hope that eventually he would appreciate her?

Or was that, Rachel wondered, what drove *her*? Because no matter what Harriet had said, she hadn't felt all that close to her dad growing up. Yes, he might have gone to her parent evenings and not Harriet's, but he'd barely said a word at them and had seemed as if he didn't want to be there. But, she supposed as she sat down in front of a bowl of porridge, at least he'd gone.

When Harriet returned just a few minutes later, Rachel realised she hadn't had time to organise her scattered thoughts about Ben Mackey. She hadn't even processed the three kisses they'd shared, each one spectacular in its own way. Or his agreement to take it day by day, or what that even meant, or would look like.

As for broken hearts...well, if their hearts *had* both been broken, they were mended now. Mostly. But in danger, Rachel knew, of splintering again, those hairline fractures never healed properly, after all. At least hers hadn't.

"So." Harriet bustled back into the kitchen and sat down opposite Rachel, digging into her porridge with relish. "Tell me about you and Ben."

"There really isn't much to tell."

"No? Because when I ventured into the barn, it was looking pretty hot and heavy to me! I backed out of there right quick, let me tell you."

"It was just a kiss," Rachel protested, even as she felt her cheeks warm. "I don't know, Hats," she confessed. "I feel like I can't even think about any kind of future. I know Ben is as much a part of the landscape here as this house is, or the hill behind us, or, I don't know, *anything*. And my job—my life—is in London." She stopped abruptly, because until she said it out loud, she hadn't realised just how bleak it sounded. They were two very different people, with two very different lives.

"There are solutions to that problem," Harriet replied, spooning honey onto her porridge, "if you want there to be."

And what, Rachel wondered, would those solutions be? A long-distance relationship? Her moving back to Mathering? She knew Ben would never move to London—she couldn't even imagine such a thing—and as for her moving here…well, back she would come, the prodigal daughter. She could see it now, the smug looks and knowing nods as everyone accepted that she'd had to come home, back where she belonged, and how she never should have left in the first place.

She prickled instinctively against such a notion, even as she acknowledged it wouldn't be *quite* like that. But it would be close.

"Look, we're barely a couple," she told Harriet. "We kissed this morning and that's it. I want to see how things go on before I start thinking about the future or any potential solutions."

"Fair enough," Harriet replied equably, but Rachel had the niggling sense she'd just disappointed her sister. Maybe she'd even disappointed herself.

"Would you even want me back?" she asked, and Harriet glanced at her, surprised.

"Why wouldn't I?"

"Living here, with you? It might feel a bit, I don't know…like I'm encroaching on your space. Your domain."

Harriet was silent for a moment, her gaze distant. "You're already doing that, anyway," she said at last, "and who knows what the future will bring, Rachel? We'll need to find out Dad's MRI results and go from there."

Which brought Rachel down from her dreamy post-kiss haze to a depressing and grim reality. For a little while she'd almost forgotten about her dad's potential diagnosis. "How is he this morning?" she asked.

"Irritable at feeling frail. Not ready to get out of bed." Harriet pursed her lips, her eyes becoming shadowed. "You know he's struggling when he doesn't even try to get up."

"The fall and hospital stay really took it out of him."

"Yes." But Harriet didn't sound convinced.

Rachel finished her last spoonful of porridge and then started to clear the dishes. It was half past seven and she needed to get showered and dressed and ready for work. She hadn't yet had an email from Danielle agreeing to some time off, so in the meantime she needed to put in her hours, even if both her mind and heart felt a million miles away from the investment opportunities in London.

THAT EVENING BEN headed over to the farm just as dusk was falling, shadows gathering in the nooks and corners of the farmyard.

"I thought we could go out for a curry in Pickering," he said. "Unless you'd rather stay in?" He jangled his keys in his pocket, and with a thrill of wonder Rachel realised he seemed nervous. About *her*.

"A curry sounds nice. We were only having leftovers, anyway. Let me just check with Harriet—"

"She can come, if she likes," Ben offered, not sounding entirely enthused about the idea.

"Not bloody likely, Ben Mackey," Harriet called from the hall as she came towards them, smiling and wiping her hands on a tea towel. "I have no interest in third-wheeling. I'll have leftovers with Dad and watch *EastEnders*, thanks very much."

Ben cracked an uncharacteristically wide grin as he gave Harriet a nod. "All *reyt*, then. We'll be away."

A few minutes later they were in his Land Rover, bumping down the lane and then heading east towards Pickering. Neither of them spoke, but Rachel didn't mind. She was reminded, poignantly, of how many afternoons they'd had as children, climbing a tree or lying in the long grass or sprawled on a sofa, with no need to fill the silence that stretched golden between them.

After a few minutes like this, Ben glanced at her. "How's your dad, then?"

"He seems all right." Rachel had popped up to see him

that afternoon, during a break from work. He'd been his usual grumpy self, but she'd detected a certain, hidden pleasure at having her come up and talk to him; she hadn't been in his bedroom, her *parents'* bedroom, in decades, maybe even since before her mum had left. The room hadn't changed at all, and when Rachel had sat down at the chair in the corner, she'd been jolted to see some of her mother's old clothes in her half of the wardrobe. After twelve *years*? She didn't know what it meant; if her dad had left them there as some sort of indictment, or because he missed her, or maybe because he simply couldn't be bothered to move them. She hadn't asked, hadn't even let him know she'd seen them. She hadn't had time yet to process what it meant, or at least what it could mean.

She'd had a lot of other stuff to think about, and so she'd pushed that to the back of her mind, and she did it again now. Ben gave her a sympathetic smile.

"It's hard, waiting."

"Yes." Another thing she was pushing to the back of her mind. "Let's not talk about all that now," she told him. "One day at a time, remember?"

For a second his expression stilled, and then he nodded slowly, giving that lovely little quirk of a smile. "Right. One day at a time."

They kept the chat easy and light for the rest of the short trip to Pickering, and it wasn't until they were seated at a table in Pickering's best curry house, perusing laminated menus with a hundred different options, that Rachel realised this was actually a date. Somehow, because it was Ben, it hadn't seemed like one. It had never seemed like a date with

Ben, she realised, since the day of that disco; she'd just slotted into his life, more or less, and he'd taken her along for the happy ride.

She lowered her menu and propped her elbows on the table to give him a serious yet still teasing look. "So, is this a date?" she asked. "Like, a proper one?"

Ben glanced up from his own menu, looking jolted by the question. "A date? We're not sixteen."

"We didn't go on any dates when we were sixteen," she replied. "Not that I remember. Why *did* you ask me to dance at that disco?" she asked suddenly. She'd never asked him when they were younger; she hadn't wanted to risk losing the magic that had sprung up between them. Really, she'd been woefully insecure in their whole relationship, such as it had been. She didn't want to be that way again. "Well?" she prompted.

"Why did I?" He looked surprisingly discomfited. "Because I wanted to dance with you." He made it sound obvious, but Rachel knew it wasn't.

"When you never talked to me all through school?" she asked sceptically.

"You never talked to me," he replied, his tone mild, and she let out a laugh of genuine amusement.

"Ben, no. You were the one who blanked me first, on the bus."

"Are you talking about year *seven*?"

"Yes, as a matter of fact, I am." She gave him a serious look even though she was laughing. The agony of her eleven-year-old self felt like a long time ago, thankfully. "What of it?"

He shrugged, spreading his hands. "What can I say? I was eleven, Rachel, and not a pillar of maturity."

"No, I suppose not. But after that..." She paused. "I mean, *never*. You never talked to me once all through school, over five *years*."

He cocked his head, frowning a little. "And you never talked to me once."

She shook her head, frustration warring with amusement, as well as a flicker of that old hurt. Maybe she wasn't as far removed from her eleven-year-old self as she'd thought. As she wished she could be. "Don't put this on me. This wasn't a case of simple misunderstanding, just like you said my leaving wasn't. You *ignored* me, Ben. You know you did."

He was silent for a moment, staring at her, and then he picked up his menu and began to peruse it; it was big enough to obscure his entire head. "Why are we talking about this now?" he asked, and Rachel detected a slight edge to his voice that surprised her. She hadn't meant to start an argument, but she had a feeling she had.

And yet, she realised, she wasn't quite willing to drop it.

"Is there a reason we shouldn't be?" she asked, doing her best to keep her voice light.

Ben lowered the menu. His expression was, unfortunately, inscrutable. "It's just old history," he replied, his tone as fathomless as his face. "Very old history. What's the point?"

What *was* the point, Rachel wondered as she stared at him, unable to get a read on what he was feeling at all. She supposed the point was that, for her, it was all interconnected; Ben ignoring her had led to her swamping sense of insecurity, which had led, at least in a way, to her leaving Mathering. Although, to be fair, whether he could have made her stay if he had asked after all was a question she had no sure answer for, but she knew it would have been close.

But did she really want to go into all that now? Confess how insecure she'd felt, how dazzled by and desperate for him she'd been? No, not really, not when that eleven-year-old self was still hiding somewhere inside her.

"I don't know what the point is," she answered at last. "I didn't mean to be mithering you about it, to use a Yorkshire word." He smiled faintly, and she was heartened. With determined deliberation, she picked up her menu again. "What do you fancy? Dopiaza? Vindaloo? Or are you going to be boring and go for a tikka masala?"

Ben was silent, and when she looked up again, she saw he was gazing at her with a mingled look of affection and regret. "I'm sorry," he said. "I didn't mean to get all het up about it. It's just like what you said this morning—you didn't want to look to the past or the future. I'm sure I was a reyt old wazzock back then." He smiled wryly. "I know I was. Immature and stupid. Whatever happened back then…we can be different now. Both of us."

"Yes, of course we can." She eyed him thoughtfully, because he hadn't done anything *that* bad, as far as she could remember. Blanking someone wasn't the same as bullying or even teasing them, and Ben had absolutely never done either of those things. "I certainly hope we can," she told him with a smile. "Because I definitely hope I'm not the same as I was in secondary school."

"You were brilliant in secondary school," Ben told her, so

sincerely, that Rachel laughed aloud.

"What? No. I was—well, a geek is putting it nicely."

Ben frowned and shook his head. "Rachel, you weren't. I mean—you were smart, yes. Brilliant, even. I think everyone was intimidated by you."

"Intimidated. Right." She shook her head, genuinely amused by his version of events, but Ben was serious. He reached over to put his hand on top of hers.

"You *were*. That first day on the bus? Yes, I'll talk about it now. You were so confident, swinging down the aisle. When you looked at me, I felt about two inches tall."

"What?" Now she just felt confused. "Ben, you were the one who wouldn't sit with me. And who laughed when some boy asked if I was your girlfriend."

"What was I supposed to do?" Ben asked. "I was mortified."

"You? Mortified?"

He smiled faintly. "Do you know what eleven-year-old boys are like?"

"I suppose," she said slowly, "but I thought you would have talked to me later, at least."

"You never seemed as if you wanted me to. And, I suppose, I was a bit ashamed. I knew I'd acted stupidly, but you just seemed so above it all, Rachel, and you did all through school—like you were the queen above all us yobby peasants."

She found herself flushing. "You make me sound like a *reyt* cow."

"No," he assured her, squeezing her hand, "like a gorgeous warrior queen, Boudicca or whoever. I can't remember my history, but I was always impressed with you, and I know I wasn't the only one."

Rachel let out an unsteady laugh. Once again, she was being forced to revisit her version of the past; her memories were like a kaleidoscope, one twist of the dial and all the shapes reconfigured into a wholly new and unfamiliar picture.

Of course, she knew Ben's version might not be accurate. In fact, it probably wasn't. She definitely remembered tables of girls giggling behind their hands as she'd walked past in the cafeteria, friendless. Her memories weren't that skewed, certainly.

But had Ben been dazzled by her, the way he said, the way she'd been dazzled by him? It was a strange and new thought, and she wasn't quite sure what to do with it. But maybe Ben was right, and she didn't need to do anything with it. She could just do what she'd told him she wanted to do, and live in this moment, wonderful as it was, where they were now both openly dazzled by each other.

"All right," she said, and gave his hand a squeeze in return. "I think we've sorted all that out for the moment. Now what are we having? As I recall, the only curry dish you ever get is a very boring tikka masala, or maybe a korma."

Ben gave her a slow, sure smile. "All right, then," he replied. "I'll have a vindaloo."

Rachel raised her eyebrows in speculation. Ben had never eaten anything as spicy as a vindaloo when they were younger. "Are you serious?"

"Why not? Just to show you I'm not as boring or predictable as you seem to think I am."

"You don't have to prove anything to me, you know, Ben," she replied, half-seriously. Part of his appeal, his charm, was that he *was* boring and predictable. Or really, steady and trustworthy and *solid*.

"Vindaloo it is," he said firmly, and tossed down the menu.

Fifteen minutes later, when their curries had arrived, he was coughing and sputtering, his eyes streaming from the spiciness, until Rachel took pity on him and gave him her much milder dopiaza.

"You can't teach an old dog new tricks, it seems," she said sorrowfully, shaking her head.

And Ben, his face flushed bright red, his eyes still watering, replied affably enough, "Or a Yorkshireman new curries."

Chapter Nineteen

RACHEL HAD FOUR more nearly perfect days before reality invaded. Four perfect Indian summer days, warm and blue-skied, moments that felt out of time as well as of season. On Saturday afternoon, she and Ben took off into the wilder sections of the North York Moors Park and went for a hike through rolling moorland and a picnic that ended with them happily tangled together on a blanket; on Sunday they had a roast dinner at a pub in Mathering and a walk along the river; on Monday and Tuesday he helped with the morning milking, and, to her surprise, five a.m. in the barn became her favourite part of the day.

"You're so loved up," Harriet told her without any rancour when she floated in from the barn on Tuesday morning. "It's kind of disgusting."

"Sorry," Rachel replied with a smile. "I know how irritating happy people can be."

"Only when you're unhappy yourself," Harriet answered seriously.

Rachel couldn't tell if that was a heavy-handed hint or just a statement of fact. "Are you unhappy, Hats?" she asked quietly, and her sister sighed.

"No—not *un*happy, although I certainly have been in

the past. But not completely happy, either. And I don't have a hot farmer boyfriend, so that might be something to do with it."

"Is there anyone you're interested in?"

"No," Harriet replied with a sigh. "Not even someone whom I could dredge up the energy to have a lukewarm crush on, unfortunately. There are slim pickings in Mathering, and you've just picked them."

Rachel ducked her head, repentant, except not really. "Sorry."

"Don't be sorry, although I don't actually think you are. Ben was always yours."

Hers. It was a wonderful, wonderful thought, and one she was starting to believe in…that Ben was hers, and she was his…as long as she didn't think about the future.

"Maybe someone will turn up," she said optimistically. "Isn't the old manor house on the other side of town being turned into a hotel or something?"

Harriet shrugged. "I think so, but I'm not sure what that has to do with meeting someone suitable."

"Some new blood into the area?" Rachel suggested. "Investors? Proprietor? Waiters, even?"

"I'm not that desperate," Harriet replied, wrinkling her nose. "I don't need to start sniffing around a building site, thanks very much!"

"Just trying to be helpful," Rachel replied, all solicitude, while her sister rolled her eyes.

"Thanks, but no thanks," she said firmly.

"Who were you dancing with at the ceilidh?" Rachel asked as a memory sparked, of Harriet laughing up at her dancing partner. "You seemed pretty partnered up there, and as I recall that guy was pretty cute."

To her surprise, her sister blushed. "I don't actually know. He just turned up out of the blue, asked me to dance, and then left again."

"What!" Rachel's interest sharpened. "A genuine man of mystery."

"So it seems," Harriet returned on a sigh. "He *was* handsome, but I don't think he's from around her and I'm ninety-nine per cent sure I've never going to see him again, so..."

"You never know," Rachel returned sagely, and Harriet rolled her eyes again.

"Sometimes," she replied, "you do."

A COUPLE OF hours later, the call came. Rachel took it on the landline; working in the dining room, she was closest to the phone on the table in the hall, with its old-fashioned, insistent buzz of a ring.

"I'm coming, I'm coming," she called a bit irritably, as if the phone could hear her. She'd been sitting at the dining room table for the last few hours, staring at her laptop and not feeling particularly effective. Danielle still hadn't responded to her email about taking some time off, which was most unlike her, and Rachel didn't know if she should take it as some sort of sign—although whether to keep working or stop, she didn't know.

She reached the phone on the third ring. "Hello?"

"May I speak to Peter Mowbray?"

"I'm afraid he's sleeping." Her dad had been sleeping a lot since getting back from the hospital. "Can I help?"

"I'm calling from the neurology department at James Cook. Mr Miller, a consultant in the department, would like to schedule an appointment to discuss the results of Mr Mowbray's MRI."

Rachel felt as if her stomach had dropped down to her toes. She hadn't forgotten this call was coming, of course she hadn't, not for a moment, and yet…

She sort of had. She'd let herself not think about it, at least for a little while, because it had been so utterly blissful simply to be with Ben.

Now the reality was staring at her, smacking her, in the face. "Yes, of course," she managed after what felt like an endless pause but was probably only a few seconds. "When would be convenient?"

"Tomorrow, at eleven in the morning?"

So soon? She supposed she should be relieved, since waiting lists on the NHS were notorious, but the immediacy of it, the urgency, alarmed her. "All right."

"Wonderful. See you then."

The receptionist rang off, leaving Rachel standing there in the hall, holding the phone. Harriet came in from the kitchen, where she'd been baking another batch of scones for the tea room in Pickering; they'd said they wanted a weekly order.

"Rachel?" she asked, the uncertainty as well as the knowledge there in her tone.

Slowly Rachel replaced the receiver in its cradle. She took

a deep breath and let it out slowly. "That was the hospital. Dad's MRI results have come back. They want to discuss them tomorrow."

"Did they say...?"

"No, but it's what they didn't say, isn't it?" Rachel said heavily. "They didn't say 'all clear, no worries'."

"Well, they wouldn't say anything, not over the phone," Harriet argued, a stubborn note entering her voice. "We don't *know*, Rachel."

"But we sort of do," she replied quietly.

"These things are treatable—"

"I know. They can be."

They stared at each other for a long, silent moment.

"Well, there's absolutely no point in speculating," Harriet declared as she turned back to the kitchen. Rachel stared at her retreating back for a moment before she followed her in.

"I know that," she told her as Harriet began kneading the scone dough as if her life depended on it. "I just want to be prepared. And Dad should be, too. We'll have to tell him—"

"We can tell him he has an appointment," Harriet replied, flipping the dough over and patting it out rather forcefully. "We don't have to tell him anything else, because we don't *know*."

"Right. But he might balk at the appointment, even."

Harriet shrugged. "That's his choice."

Rachel suppressed a sigh. She knew they thought a little differently about this; it was funny, she supposed, how protective Harriet was of their dad, considering how neglected she'd felt growing up. Maybe that was all part of it, somehow. Heaven knew Rachel had her own issues with both her parents, ones she was still in the process of untangling.

"All right, I'll go tell him," she said, and Harriet did not reply, focused completely on the dough in front of her.

Rachel walked slowly upstairs, each step feeling heavier than the last. In the five days since her dad had returned from hospital, she had, Rachel acknowledged guiltily, spent very little time with him. She'd been so taken up with Ben, and it felt as if for a few days she'd been in a complete, and wonderful, tailspin. She was spiralling back to earth now.

She knocked once, gently, on the door before poking her head inside. "Hey, Dad."

Her father's eyes fluttered open as he did his best to hoist himself up in bed. "Eh? Just resting my eyes…"

"I know." She leaned against the doorjamb, feeling a rush of affection for him, ornery old man that he was, or at least that he could be. "Do you want anything? Tea, coffee?"

"No, I was thinking I'd come down in a bit, head out to the barn." He didn't look at her as he said it and Rachel merely nodded, deciding it was kindest to maintain the fiction that her dad would be up for that. He had barely left his bedroom since coming back from the hospital, and in just the week at home he seemed much diminished—smaller, somehow, and certainly frailer. He hadn't shaved, and his hair stuck out about his head in white wisps. He was only seventy-three, and a few weeks ago he'd been as vibrant and competent as ever, but now he seemed much older than his years.

"The hospital called," she said after a moment, doing her best to keep her voice light yet matter-of-fact, even though her heart was aching. "They have the results from your MRI and they'd like to discuss them with you tomorrow."

"Eh?" Her father's eyes narrowed suspiciously, and with a lurch of alarm Rachel wondered if he was having one of his memory lapses.

"The MRI, Dad? Remember?"

"I remember the MRI!" he exclaimed irritably. "I'm not that daft. What do they want to talk about?"

"Just the results."

"Well, it's not going to be bloody good news, is it?" he returned. "I don't want to go all the way to Middlesbrough for that."

"We need to know what's going on, Dad," Rachel returned gently, "even if it is difficult news."

"Do we?" he replied with sudden, unexpected shrewdness. "I don't know if we do." Rachel searched for something to say to that as he glanced out the window and heaved a sigh. "Well, we'd best get on with it, then. I've got to get my house in order."

"Dad—"

He turned to face her, a tired smile lining his careworn features. "Rachel girl, you know it as well as I do."

"I don't," she replied, but her voice choked a little and her dad just shook his head and turned back to the window. Knowing there was no more to say, Rachel quietly went back downstairs.

"Well?" Harriet asked as she came back into the kitchen.

"He'll go."

"Okay."

"We can all go," Rachel suggested. "The three of us, hear what the doctor has to say. I think it can be good to have a couple of pairs of ears, you know, in case one of us misses something." Harriet did not reply, and she added, a bit stiltedly, "I think it would be good if we were both there."

Harriet nodded slowly. "Yes," she agreed. "Let's all go."

THAT NIGHT RACHEL walked over to the Mackeys' farmhouse through the gathering dusk. She and Harriet had had tea with their dad, who had ventured downstairs for the first time to eat with them. He'd even dressed and combed his hair, and Rachel wondered who he was making the effort for—them, or himself. Maybe both.

As she walked down the lane, the sun dropping behind the hill and leaving shadows in its wake, she realised she hadn't actually been to Ben's house since their relationship had changed four days ago. Only four days! Already it felt like forever, and yet no time at all.

The dogs set to their usual chorus of barking as Rachel came through the barnyard, to the kitchen door. She was expecting Ben, but it was Diana who opened the door, wreathed in smiles when she saw her.

"Oh, *Rachel*!" This was said with definite meaning, and just in case Rachel wasn't sure, Diana stepped forward and enveloped her in a warm hug. "It's so lovely to see you, darling!" she said. Rachel felt almost as if she was already an in-law, and while it was a nice feeling, it also freaked her out just a little.

"It's good to see you too, Diana," she said, as she stepped into the kitchen. "Is Ben around?"

"So, so lovely," Diana murmured, beaming at her. "And yes, Ben's just upstairs changing. He'll be down in two ticks. Will you stay for tea?"

"No, sorry, I've already had it. I just was hoping to chat to Ben for a bit." To her horror, her voice wobbled slightly, and Diana's face softened into sadness.

"Oh, my dear, is it Peter? Have you heard anything?"

"No, not yet." With heroic effort, Rachel managed to compose her face and moderate her voice into a semblance of matter-of-fact normality. Since when had she become so emotional? Oh, wait, she knew the answer to that. Since coming home. "We have an appointment tomorrow to discuss the MRI results."

"Oh, my dear." Diana shook her head slowly. "I can only hope…" she began, and then trailed off, and Rachel thought that was where they all were. They could only hope.

"Rach." Ben came in, hair damp from the shower, smelling delicious, and Rachel was suddenly, intensely glad she came.

"I wondered if you fancied a walk?" she blurted. "Maybe up the hill?"

He glanced outside at the darkness fast encroaching and then gave an easy shrug. "All right, sure."

Rachel loved him for his answer, especially when she realised she was feeling just the tiniest bit unhinged, or maybe unmoored. She hadn't been aware that was how she was feeling when she'd walked over, only that she'd wanted to see

Ben. But now, as they set out into a twilight evening, the warmth of the day long gone, she realised she was definitely feeling unhinged. Unmoored. Un-everything.

"What's going on?" Ben asked affably enough as they set up towards the hill.

"I don't know." Rachel managed a shaky laugh. "I'm just feeling…strange, I suppose."

Ben frowned, his expression barely visible in the gathering darkness. "Strange?"

"Dad's MRI results are tomorrow. The doctor's office called today, saying he wanted to discuss them. It's not going to be good news, is it?"

"No," Ben replied briefly, and Rachel was glad he hadn't prevaricated. "But that's not just it, is it, Rachel?" he asked gently. "I mean…you've known about that for a bit, that it was coming."

"No, you're right." She folded her arms, cupping her elbows with her hands, as they continued up the hill, her feet finding the way in the darkness without needing to look. "It's more than that." Ben waited for her to continue, while Rachel tried to sort through her jumbled thoughts. "Coming home has shaken me up," she finally admitted, feeling her way through the words. "I thought I knew how everything happened. I thought the way I remembered things was the right way. The only way, even."

"Well, how you remembered something might be how you experienced it," Ben pointed out, and Rachel nodded, then shook her head, then nodded again. She really was feeling confused.

"Yes, but what if I can't trust my memories? I read

somewhere that our memories are terribly faulty—we *think* we're remembering the truth, and we become more and more convinced that we are, but actually we're just remembering the last time we remembered something, and the emotions associated with *that* recollection, not the actual event." Her voice was becoming faster and faster, higher and higher. "And so," she continued, practically squeaking now, "the more we remember a particular thing, whatever it is, the more we are convinced that we're remembering it correctly, and the more inaccurately we're remembering it. How screwed up is that?"

"You lost me a little there," Ben answered after a moment, "but I think I get the gist. We can't trust our memories."

"No, we can't."

"Well, that makes a kind of sense, doesn't it? Everything is coloured by our emotions." He paused. "And this is upsetting you because—?"

"Because it makes me question everything," Rachel blurted. She'd had no idea she was going to say that—*feel* that—until the words came out of her mouth, and she knew, absolutely, that they were the right ones.

Ben stopped, turning to face her. "Everything?" he asked quietly.

"Well, mostly everything. Was my mum as unhappy as I remember her? Was my dad as distant? Were you as—as cool?"

His mouth twisted wryly. "Um, yes to the last one?" he said, and she let out a distinctly wobbly laugh.

"Was I as miserable?" she made herself continue. "Because I've painted this picture of myself, of my childhood, and I don't know if it's completely accurate anymore. At least, I'm starting to wonder, based on what Harriet's said. What you've said. What I've started to remember."

"Okay." Ben rubbed his jaw. "Well, if your childhood wasn't as miserable as you remember, surely that's a good thing?"

"Is it?" Rachel burst out. "Because I stayed away as much as I did because I thought it was." The words seemed to ring through the still night air. "It's just *strange*," she confessed, her voice a throb of emotion, "to start to question everything. And then to start to wonder if you made mistakes."

"We all make mistakes, Rach." Ben drew her into his arms, which was exactly where she wanted to be, her arms wrapped around his waist and her cheek pressed to his chest. "You can second-guess your life forever, all the decisions you made, all the feelings you felt, but it doesn't change the way things are now. Wasn't it you who said we were going to stop rehashing the past?"

"I want to," she whispered. "I just want to make sure I've remembered it right first."

"Do any of us remember anything right?" His arms tightened around her. "It's all just a matter of perception, isn't it? I remember your dad being quiet, but proud of you. Whenever you got your report card, he'd mention all the A stars."

"I'd forgotten that," she whispered shakily.

"And I remember your mum being quiet, too. Sometimes, yes, she seemed unhappy, especially later on. I came into the kitchen once, to ask if you and Harriet could play out, and she was at the table, her head in her hands."

"Yes," Rachel whispered. "I have memories like that, too."

"And I don't remember being cool," he added, a lilt of humour in his voice. "Much as I'd like to say I was. I remember sticking around with the rugby lads even though a lot of them were right mugginses because I was too scared to go it alone...or talk to you, even though that was what I wanted, most of all."

She tilted her head up to face him, blinking the tears from her eyes. "You can talk to me now."

"It was always you, you know that, Rachel?" Ben said quietly. A thrill went through her, half wonder, half terror. "Always. I didn't turn around that night in the barn—when you told me about uni—because I knew you'd see how much I wanted you to stay, and I also knew how much you wanted to go. I'd say I was being noble, but I think it was more about being proud. I didn't want to ask you to stay and have you leave, anyway." His hands came up to frame her face. "But maybe," he whispered as he kissed her, "I should have."

Rachel's eyes fluttered closed as she surrendered to the sweetness of the kiss. Yes, maybe he should have, she thought, but she was here now, and it was wonderful.

Chapter Twenty

"IT'S A GLIOBLASTOMA."

The neurology consultant, Mr Miller, gave them a straight but sympathetic look. "That is, a brain tumour that often starts at the base of the brain or on the spinal cord. It can happen at any age, but it tends to occur more often in older adults, especially men." He steepled his fingers under his chin. "As far as brain tumours go, I have to say, it's not a good one to have."

Was any brain tumour a good one to have? Rachel wondered rather wildly. There were no real surprises here, and yet she felt utterly winded. Her father, sat between her and Harriet, stared stonily at the consultant and said nothing.

"Is there…" Harriet cleared her throat. "Is there any treatment?"

"Well." Mr Miller paused, glancing down at his notes, and Rachel felt herself tense. This was where he was meant to jump in with reassuring statistics, possibilities, options. Chemotherapy, surgery, survival rates. She wanted it all, and she wanted it to be good. "Generally speaking, yes." Now he was the one clearing his throat. "Every brain tumour is different—located in a different part of the brain, with a different rate of growth. Some tumours are quite neat, as it were, and can be removed surgically without too much difficulty. Others are a bit more…enmeshed." He laced his fingers together to demonstrate in a way that made Rachel want to wince. "Growing into the healthy brain tissue in a way that makes surgery difficult, if not impossible."

"And let me guess," their dad interjected, his voice actually possessing a thread of humour. "Mine's the enmeshed kind."

Mr Miller smiled faintly and inclined his head. "I'm afraid it looks that way, Mr Mowbray, although it's difficult to say for certain without performing surgery."

"Cutting into my brain just to see."

"Well." The consultant gave a rather abashed smile. "Something like that, I suppose."

Her dad nodded slowly, accepting, unsurprised. "All right, then."

"But there must be something you can do," Rachel said. It was the first time she'd spoken since receiving the news, and her voice sounded croaky. "Some kind of treatment."

"In some cases," Mr Miller said, "I would advise surgery to remove as much of the tumour as possible, and then chemotherapy and radiation to reduce the remaining cancerous cells. There is also targeted therapy, which attacks certain chemicals in those cells, and tumour treating fields therapy, which uses an electrical field to keep those cells from multiplying."

"Okay." This was sounding better. There were options, at least. Several.

"But in this case," Mr Miller continued, his tone apologetic but also final, "I'm afraid I wouldn't recommend any of those treatments, although of course, if Mr Mowbray wishes it, we can discuss possible avenues."

"Why wouldn't he wish it?" Rachel demanded, while Harriet interjected quietly, "What possible avenues?"

"I'm too far gone," their dad stated, giving the doctor a canny look. "Aren't I?"

He sighed and then nodded. "That's the short of it, I'm afraid. The tumour looks to be fast-growing, based on its size, and it appears to be quite entangled with your healthy brain tissue. Considering its size, and how long you've had the symptoms, as well as your age in terms of how the potential treatments would affect you..." He trailed off, spreading his hands. "Well, it's a choice only you can make, Mr Mowbray. I would not recommend surgery in any case, but potentially some mild chemotherapy or radiation to extend life expectancy."

"Right, then." To Rachel's horror, her dad stood up, as if getting ready to leave.

"Dad, *Dad.*" She tugged on his arm, urging him to sit down. "Can't we at least hear about the possible treatments?"

"I don't—" her father began to bluster, and Rachel tugged on his arm again.

"Just hear," she implored quietly.

With a grumble, her father sat down again.

Mr Miller glanced between them all with some apprehension, and then began again. "As I said, a mild form of chemotherapy or radiation might help increase life expectancy, but of course any type of treatment of that nature will have certain side effects that you may find...detrimental." He looked directly at their father. "Only you can decide whether the benefits outweigh the risks."

"Surely—" Rachel began, only to fall silent at a quelling look from Harriet.

"What is the cost-benefit analysis of the treatments?" she asked quietly.

Mr Miller sighed and shook his head. "I cannot say definitively, I'm afraid, but based on what I've seen from the MRI, I don't think this particular type of tumour would respond well to treatment. Chemotherapy or radiation might extend your father's life for a few weeks."

Weeks? He was talking in *weeks*? Rachel stared at him in mute horror.

"How much time have I got, Doc?" her dad asked, even managing a small smile. "Not long by the sounds of it, hey?"

Mr Miller gave a grimace of apology. "I cannot predict with a high level of accuracy, of course, but I would say…at most…three to six months."

For the first time during the appointment, her dad looked shaken. He swallowed and then nodded a couple of times. "Right," he said, and pulled at his collar. "Right."

"I'm sorry."

Her dad nodded again, while Rachel simply stared blindly in front of her, reeling from the news. *Three to six months.* That was, at most, March, maybe Christmas. *Christmas.* She opened her mouth and then closed it again, because she had no idea what to say. She could barely think.

"If you have any questions…" Mr Miller began, only for her dad to shake his head and start to rise.

"No, I think that about covers it."

"Those possible avenues of treatment," he persevered,

only to stop as her father shook his head with firm decision.

"No, I won't be having those."

"Dad," Rachel protested, only to have him turn to her with a suddenly fierce look.

"Don't lecture me on this, my girl," he said sternly. "This is my life and tha' have nowt to say about it. I don't want to spend my last days feeling jiggered and gipping all over the place just to have another couple of weeks at most." He raised a warning finger. "Don't get the monk on or go ruering, because I won't have owt to do with these so-called treatments."

The Yorkshire really came out when her father was emotional, Rachel thought, as she tried to smile through a haze of tears. "All right," she replied quietly, pronouncing it *ah reyt* in true Yorkshire fashion. Her father smiled faintly.

"That's it, my girl," he said. "That's it."

It wasn't until they'd walked out of the consultant's office that Rachel realised he'd barely looked at Harriet once during the whole appointment.

THEY DIDN'T SPEAK much on the drive home, and then their dad stomped up to his bedroom as soon as they got back.

"Can I bring you a cuppa, Dad?" Rachel asked, and he shook his head.

"I'll have a rest."

Rachel exchanged a look with Harriet, who shrugged. "He must be tired," she said quietly, once they heard the bedroom door upstairs closing.

Rachel let out a ragged sigh as she raked her hand through her hair. "Do you think the consultant's right? Three to six months?"

"Right-ish, I suppose," Harriet replied as she headed into the kitchen. "It's only a guess, after all, but I imagine it's an educated one."

"I can't believe it." Rachel followed her into the kitchen, standing in the doorway while Harriet filled the kettle at the sink. "Three to six months. That's no time at all."

"No." Harriet plonked the kettle on top of the Rayburn. "I suppose he's been having the symptoms for a while, longer than I even suspected." Her lips trembled and she pressed them together. "I should have rung sooner." And then her face crumpled, and she put her hands up to cover it.

"Oh, Harriet," Rachel said, crossing over to hug her. "Hats, you can't blame yourself." Harriet stiffened in her embrace for a few seconds and Rachel squeezed her.

"Come on, duck, give us a proper hug, then," she said, putting on even more of a Yorkshire accent, and Harriet let out a shaky laugh as she hugged her back.

"How can you do such a dreadful accent when you're actually from Yorkshire?" she demanded, and Rachel laughed.

"It's been a long time, I suppose." For the first time she could say such a thing without recrimination, without regret. She was here now, and she was staying.

"I can't believe we're going to lose him," Harriet said as she eased back, wiping her eyes. "I thought there would be more time. Time to…"

She trailed off, shaking her head, and Rachel blurted,

"There's still time, Harriet. If you want to…talk to him. Make things better between the two of you."

Harriet let out a weary, dispirited laugh. "And how would I do that? 'You've got six months to live, Dad, do you think you could spare me some attention?'" She shook her head. "No thanks."

"When he was in hospital the other week," Rachel said, "he told me he had some regrets." Harriet turned to look at her, her brow furrowed. "I don't know what they are," Rachel continued. "And I'm afraid I didn't ask. I wasn't sure I could handle any major revelations just then. But…you could talk to him. Honestly, about how you've felt. You should."

"I don't know." Harriet shook her head slowly, her shoulders slumping. "I don't know," she said again, and then, with reluctance, "Maybe."

Rachel decided to leave it at that. It was up to Harriet whether she wanted to broach that particular subject with their dad, but *three to six months* certainly made you think about things.

The kettle boiled, and Harriet poured water into the teapot. A long, ragged sigh escaped her as she plonked the kettle back on the stove, the sound turning into something almost like a sob as she stared blankly in front of her.

"Harriet…" Rachel began, only to stop as her sister shook her head.

"Sometimes," she said, "I really hate this place." Rachel remained silent, watching her warily, having no idea what the right thing to say was. "I hate that I never left," Harriet continued, still staring into space. "I hate that I wasn't able to. I hate that no one said I should. Except you, maybe," she added, turning to Rachel with a sigh. "And I didn't want to listen to you."

"I'm sorry," Rachel said, knowing the sentiment was sincere but utterly inadequate.

"Do you know what I really hate?" Harriet continued with a nod towards the doorway. Rachel shook her head, waiting. "I hate the damned wallpaper. Every room in this house except the kitchen. It's why I spend so much time in here, I think. That wallpaper is enough to drive you mad. Maybe it drove Mum mad, like the woman in that short story we read in English."

"*The Yellow Wallpaper*?" Rachel guessed.

"Yes, that one. Maybe she walked out on us because of the wallpaper." She let out a weary sound that Rachel thought was meant to be a laugh.

"You know, I hate the wallpaper too," she said. "It's hideous and ancient. I was thinking this place needed a facelift, earlier." She paused. "We could tear it off, you know."

Harriet looked at her as if she'd been speaking a foreign language. "What?"

"Tear it off. Strip it. Get rid of it all." Rachel raised her eyebrows. "Why not?"

"Rachel," Harriet said, sounding severe, "that wallpaper is probably a hundred years old."

"At *least*. Time for it to go, don't you think?"

They stared at each other for a long, frozen moment and then, in one accord, they both bolted for the door. They got caught in the doorway, struggling like a couple of clowns emerging from a Mini, and Harriet started giggling, with

Rachel following suit. By the time they made it to the hallway, they were helpless with laughter, or perhaps hysteria.

Rachel stood on the bottom step of the staircase and, standing on her tiptoes, managed to reach the top, curling end of a strip of wallpaper. She gave a hard tug and the whole piece fell away with a shower of yellowed flakes of wallpaper paste, and a smell of dust and age.

Harriet let out a little shriek. "Oh my goodness, that looked *so* satisfying," she exclaimed.

"It was," Rachel confirmed as she tossed the long, tattered strip of wallpaper onto the floor. "It really was. You should try it."

With something like a squeal Harriet clambered onto the step and reached for another curling edge. She tugged, even harder than Rachel had, and the whole thing came away in a single, shredded piece.

"Oh, my giddy aunt," Harriet exclaimed, almost reverently, as she tossed the strip aside. "That felt amazing."

Then they were both at it, straining and lunging, reaching for the curling edges and pulling as hard as they could. Dust, dried wallpaper paste, and bits of plaster came raining down as the floor was soon covered in strips of wallpaper, and the wall of the hallway became a speckled canvas of spackled wall.

By the time they'd finished the whole wall, they were both breathless and sweating. Harriet looked down at the knee-deep pieces of wallpaper littering the floor and shook her head slowly. "What have we done?" she asked. Rachel couldn't tell if she sounded horrified or impressed.

"We made an improvement to this place," Rachel stated firmly. "Definitely."

"What will Dad think—"

"He won't even notice."

Harriet let out a huff of laughter. "Probably not, if we clean all this up." She nodded towards the floor.

"We will," Rachel replied, "but first let's get the rest of it off."

It took them another hour, but they managed to strip most of the wallpaper from the entire hallway. By the time they were finished, they were aching with tiredness and caked in dust and dried paste; Rachel could feel it, gritty on her scalp, her eyeballs. She desperately needed a bath, and she felt as if she'd gone a bit crazy, but she was glad, fiercely so, that they'd done it. It felt like a step, a big one, necessary and important.

"Right," Harriet said as they bundled the old wallpaper into bin bags and took it all outside. "Time for that cuppa."

Rachel washed her hands at the kitchen sink while Harriet boiled up another brew. She was just handing Rachel her mug when her phone, forgotten in her pocket, pinged with a text. Hoping it was from Ben, Rachel slid her phone out of her pocket, everything in her jolting in surprise when she saw it wasn't from Ben at all. It was from Danielle.

Call me. ASAP.

"Rach?" Harriet asked uncertainly, and Rachel realised she was frowning, somewhat ferociously.

"Just a work thing," she told her sister as she slid her phone back into her pocket. She hadn't heard from Danielle in days, and now she was texting her urgently? It didn't bode well—Rachel knew that much—but she also knew she didn't want to think about it right now. She didn't want to be distracted by work from the business of living.

"Should we check on Dad?" she asked Harriet.

"I'll bring him up a cuppa. He might be asleep, but..."

"Yes, you do that."

Rachel waited while her sister made their dad a cup of tea just as he liked it, and then took it upstairs. Knowing she couldn't put it off even though she longed to, Rachel swiped her phone and pressed for Danielle's number. It rang only once before her boss answered.

"Rachel?"

"Yes—"

"You need to come back to London. Immediately. That is, if you want your job. If you don't, by all means, stay where you are."

"What..." Rachel shook her head, even though of course Danielle couldn't see her. "Why—"

"There's been a shake-up. Shakedown. Whatever." Danielle blew out a breath. "The higher-ups are getting antsy about the markets, and there's going to be a shedload of redundancies coming. I've already resigned, as it happens. Decided I'd had enough, after all. I'm retiring early, might do something crazy like start a pottery studio or move to Spain."

What on earth? "Danielle, what—"

"I've recommended you for my position," her boss continued briskly, "if you want it. I don't know that you do, but I didn't want to leave you hanging, with nothing to come back to. The trouble is, as you haven't been around for a month, that suggestion was taken with several grains of salt, to put it mildly."

It hadn't been quite a month, but Rachel wasn't about to argue the point. "I…I can't come back just now," she said helplessly. "My dad was just diagnosed with a brain tumour *today*. He has three months to live."

"I'm sorry," Danielle said after a pause. "I really am. And maybe that will affect your decision—hell, if it were me, it would. At least, it *should*. But I have to tell you, that's not going to hold water at the moment with those in authority. They want boots on the ground, Rachel, faces around the table." She sighed. "I suppose this is what I was talking about before. The people we could have become. If you need to stay, stay, by all means. I really do mean that. But realise that unfortunately, in this case, it will probably cost you your job, and certainly any promotion." Her voice gentled. "I've made my decision, and only you can make yours. But you need to decide today—if you want to keep your job, you need to be at your desk by tomorrow morning."

As she ended the call, Rachel stared into space, her mind spinning. She could hardly believe things had happened so suddenly, so drastically, and yet part of her wasn't even surprised. The business world was brutal. Little things like brain tumours didn't factor into decision making at all.

And yet…how on earth could she leave?

How could she not?

Rachel slumped against the counter, closing her eyes. She'd worked at Wakeman and Wallace for nearly ten years, her entire working life. She'd poured *everything* into her job—all her time, effort, ambition, *hope*. She'd sacrificed holidays, hobbies, relationships, all to get ahead. And she might lose it all now, simply because a few nameless, faceless higher-ups needed to see her at her desk, looking busy and productive? *That* was how it worked?

As a matter of fact, yes, it was. She'd always known that. She'd always been willing to pay the price…until now.

"Rachel?" Rachel opened her eyes to see Harriet standing in the kitchen doorway, gazing at her uncertainly. "Are you okay?"

She knew she couldn't go into the whole job thing now, the worst possible moment to say she might have to leave for a little while, just to secure her future. How long would she have to be gone? A couple of days? Weeks? Time that was precious, more precious than she could ever have imagined. Did she really want to spend it in London, preserving a job she wasn't even sure she cared about anymore? And yet her job had been her *life*. If she left it, what was she saying about the choices she'd made over the last ten years? And what was she saying about the choices she was making *now*, when everything still felt fragile, especially between her and Ben? "Yes," she said, trying to smile. "I'm fine. Just tired, you know."

"Yes." Harriet nodded in sympathy. "I know."

"How was Dad?"

"He seemed…okay. Pensive. He said thank you for the tea, which was a first."

"That's something, then."

"I suppose. Baby steps." She paused, tried to smile. "I think I will talk to him. Eventually. Soon, I mean."

Rachel smiled, genuinely glad for her sister. "That's

great, Hats."

They stood in silence for a moment, while Rachel felt as if a tsunami were coming towards her, ready to swamp her with hopelessness—not just about her job, but about her dad. Everything was about to change. For five days, five measly days, she'd lived in happiness and hope. She'd lived in the present, enjoying every moment with Ben, accepting each one like a gift. But reality had now intruded in all of its grimness—her father's prognosis as well as the life she'd left behind.

What, she wondered despairingly, was she going to do?

Chapter Twenty-One

DUSK WAS FALLING as Rachel made her way over to the Mackeys' farm, her feet feeling as leaden as her heart. She was filled with grief—grief for her father, for the life she was losing, for the choices she'd made in the past. She wanted to think about the future, but right now it felt too hard. And how would Ben take it all? They'd had only five days together, which was practically no time at all. The only reason you asked somebody to take it day by day was because you didn't want to think about the future, she realised, but now the future was here, and she was afraid to talk about it, afraid to demand promises Ben might not be ready to give. Afraid to put herself out there again, and even more so, than she ever had before. Yet how else could she prove to herself, to Ben, that she really had changed?

Because she knew she had.

Rachel had spent the last few hours in a welter of indecision, all the while knowing in her gut what she had to do. What she needed and wanted to do, even if it was hard. It was right, and despite the grief and fear she still felt, a certainty had settled in her bones. She just had to tell Ben…

The light came on outside the kitchen door as she approached the farmyard, with the usual excited clamour of dogs barking starting before she'd crossed it halfway.

"Rachel!" Diana's face was furrowed with concern even as she smiled, opening the door and then standing aside to welcome her in. "How are you? How was the doctor's appointment?"

"Well, it wasn't good news." She tried to keep her tone bracing as she stepped across the threshold. "But I think we all knew it wasn't going to be."

"Oh, Rachel." Diana laid a hand on her shoulder while Rachel did her best to give a philosophical smile. She was tired of trying to hold back tears; she was already tired of having these kinds of conversations, having to tell people, and she knew it was only the beginning.

That evening, at tea, her father had come downstairs and informed her and Harriet with brisk matter-of-factness that he didn't want any 'palaver'.

"Dad," Rachel had protested instinctively. She wasn't sure what her father would classify as a palaver, but she had a feeling she'd make it, one way or another, over the next few months.

"No, I mean it," he'd cut her off. "This is actually a gift."

"A *gift*—" Rachel had spluttered.

"Yes, Rachel girl, a gift." He'd looked at her steadily. "I watched my mother die slowly, losing herself in pieces, for thirteen years. When I consider that, three to six months sounds reyt good." He'd turned to look at Harriet too, a weary smile creasing his face. "I've known something was wrong for a while. This doesn't come as a surprise. And three to six months gives me enough time, I hope, to put everything in order, the way I want it." And with that, seeming to feel the discussion was over, her dad had picked up his knife and fork and began ploughing through the chicken and dumplings Harriet had made.

"It's all right," she told Diana now, not wanting to get into the grim prognosis and all it meant. "Really. But I was wondering if I could chat with Ben…?"

"Of course, love. He's in the barn."

Of course he was in the barn, Rachel thought as she smiled her thanks to Diana and headed outside with a weary sort of inevitability. Just like last time…except this time it could be different. It *would* be.

She'd come to talk to Ben all those years ago because it had been the night before she had to decide her university choice—Exeter or Bristol—and she'd wanted to talk to him. What she'd been going to say, what she'd been hoping he would say, she hadn't completely known. She'd been excited, yes, but she'd also been rather ridiculously sure about *them*. She'd thought they would talk about options, how to make their relationship work, and in the end, they hadn't talked at all. Considering how insecure she'd been about Ben before, her certainty on that night had clearly been rather disastrously misplaced. But he'd chosen her, she'd thought back then, and they'd been so happy, and she'd believed it could all work out. She'd wanted to believe, so much.

Well, it hadn't worked out, that was for sure. And as for now? Would it work out now? She was afraid—again—but she was still going to try…in a way she never had before.

Just as before, Ben was pitching hay into a stall, his back to Rachel. He looked exactly the same—maybe a little broader in the shoulders, but otherwise unchanged from his eighteen-year-old self. And what about her? Rachel wondered. Had she changed? She hoped so. She didn't want to be that heartbroken girl again, but maybe she wouldn't be able to avoid it.

"Ben." She spoke softly, but he heard her anyway, turning around, resting his hand on top of the pitchfork.

"Rachel." His voice was warm, along with his smile, which was encouraging, but of course he had no idea what she was going to say. "How was the appointment? I would have texted, but I thought you guys might need a bit of space."

"Yeah." She stepped farther into the barn, folding her arms and hunching her shoulders. "You were right, it's a brain tumour. A glio—something. Glioblastoma."

"Ah, Rachel." He pulled her into his arms, and she came willingly, glad to be there. "I'm so sorry."

"It's okay, actually," she told him, her voice muffled against his chest. "I mean, for what it is. Dad said he'd rather go this way than some prolonged dementia affair. Which I understand."

"Yes, but that doesn't make it easier."

"No." She took a deep breath and then forced herself to take a step back, even though part of her simply wanted to stay in the shelter of Ben's embrace for—oh, another few hours. Days, maybe. "That's not what I came here to talk about, though," she said.

She saw Ben's expression turn alert and wary, like a curtain dropping down over his eyes, stilling his features. "Oh?" he said, and there was a wealth of understanding in that single syllable that made her heart sink. Already he seemed as if he were shutting down, and she hadn't even started yet.

"Yes, you see..." Rachel swallowed hard. "My boss rang me yesterday, and there's a bit of a brouhaha at my office. The higher-ups are getting anxious about the markets, that sort of thing." He gave a twitchy sort of shrug, waiting for her to continue. "If I want to keep my job, I'd have to head back tomorrow morning. Probably just for a few days, maybe weeks, but I was thinking about it, and I decided—"

"You're going back." This was said flatly, without surprise, his expression turning stony, his arms folded.

Rachel stopped, cowed by his tone. "I was thinking about it," she replied carefully. It hadn't been a snap decision, and she wanted Ben to appreciate that. "I've worked at Wallace and Wakeman for nearly ten years. It's hard to think about just throwing it all away. If I don't go back, I'll lose my job, almost certainly."

He shrugged. "Well, I'm not asking you to throw your job away, am I?"

Ouch. Considering what she'd been about to say, to *hope*, that hurt. A lot. "What, then?" Rachel demanded, her voice raw. "If you're not asking that, Ben, if you're not...what's going on here, between us?" She gestured to the few feet between them that now felt like a vast ocean. "I know it's only been five days," she added, trying to be fair, "and I said we didn't have to think about the future. But right now, it seems we do. So, what is going on here, between us?" Her voice throbbed painfully.

Ben shrugged again, his expression unyielding, obdurate. "Not much, I guess."

What? Rachel blinked, feeling winded. "Not much?" she

repeated in little more than a whisper.

"If you're heading back to London, dumping Harriet in it again, then what can I say?" His voice rose in anger. "I thought you'd changed, but clearly you haven't."

"And was I the only one who ever needed to change?" Rachel demanded, her voice rising to match his. "Was this always about me fitting in with your plans, your life?" She shook her head slowly, blinking back tears.

"Ah." Too much knowledge in that particular syllable. He said so much without saying anything at all. "So that's how you see it."

"How else am I supposed to see it?" she demanded. "Just like before, you're not even willing to have a discussion, consider possibilities, how we could make *us* work."

"What possibilities are there, Rachel?"

"Well, as it happened," she told him, her voice trembling as she brushed a tear from her eye, "I came over here to tell you I *wasn't* going to go back. That I was willing to give up my job to stay here with my family, with *you*. But I was scared, because it made me feel—well, like I was risking a lot, and I guess I was, because you certainly shut me down quick enough, didn't you?"

Ben's jaw slackened. "Rachel—"

"You say I haven't changed, Ben, but maybe you're the one who hasn't. You're willing to let me walk away even—even when I wasn't going to!"

Her voice rose on a wail of fury and hurt, and then, not trusting herself not to collapse into sobs, she turned on her heel and strode out of the barn, walking blindly across the farmyard. She was angry, yes, but more than that, she was hurt. She thought they'd both grown and changed, had moved on from who they'd been in the past, those old fears and insecurities that had dominated so many of their decisions no longer holding sway. But here they were, arguing again, without even using enough words. She'd *had* it with Yorkshire farmers and their taciturn ways! She could do with a bit more *emoting*, right about now. She could do with someone who listened and talked to her and didn't jump to his judgemental conclusions, making her feel like she did back then.

She'd been willing to give everything up for a man who seemed inclined to let her go without a fight, without a word. Why couldn't Ben come up with some solutions? Ask her how she felt? Tell her he wanted her to stay? Why couldn't he problem-solve with her, show her that she—*they*—were worth fighting for, figuring things out for? Instead, he simply stood there, silent, accepting, willing her to walk out the door.

A sudden spurt of anger jetted inside her. She was not going to let him do the same thing to her, *again*. She turned around and stalked back to the barn. Ben was standing in the same place he'd been when she'd left moments earlier, looking a little dazed.

"I can't believe you're doing this again," she declared, her hands on her hips.

Ben blinked at her. "*I* am—"

"Yes, you. Letting me walk away. Practically daring me to. Do you know, Ben Mackey," she told him, her voice shaking with fury, vibrating with hurt, "I had a crush on you for our whole childhood?" His eyes widened and she rushed on, not wanting to hear what he might have said to *that.* "I would have denied it to anyone, of course, but I did. You were my everything—sun, moon, and stars. When you ignored me that day on the bus, and yes, I *know* it was year seven—I was devastated. *Devastated.* And when you looked at me at that disco in sixth form, I felt as if the lights had come on again, after *years* of darkness. If you had asked me not to go to uni, I wouldn't have gone. Maybe that would have been a bad thing, and in any case, I'm glad I went, but you were *important* to me, Ben. You still are. And yet I feel like I'm staring at a brick wall, a blank window, when it comes to these conversations. And I can't do all the heavy lifting on my own, because frankly I've been on my own for a lot of my life." Her voice broke and another tear trickled down her cheek; she swiped it away angrily. "Why can't you say, 'Let's work this out, Rach'? Or 'I care about you, Rachel, and I know we can figure things out'. *Anything.* But, no. It's all on me. Again. *I* have to decide. I'm the one who has to walk away *because you never bloody stop me*!"

Fearing she would start to sob and never stop, she whirled around and rushed out of the barn. Again.

"Rachel—" she heard Ben call, but she kept running. He wouldn't bloody stop her, she thought, because she was too fast.

She ran all the way back to the Mowbray farm, like the proverbial bat out of hell Ben had called her before, into the house, past the tattered remnants of wallpaper hanging off the walls to her bedroom. She slammed the door behind her, breathless, and then sat on her bed, her head in her hands.

After a few seconds, Harriet tapped on the door and then

opened it.

"Rachel..." she began cautiously.

"My boss asked me to go back to London," Rachel said through her fingers. "If I want to keep my job."

"Oh—"

"I told her I wasn't going to go. That I want to stay here. And I went over to Ben to talk to him about it, and he basically told me he knew I'd always leave and to go." Or something like that. She couldn't remember exactly what he'd said, only how much it had hurt. "I wanted him to talk to me, have a reasonable discussion, maybe even offer a little comfort, but instead he just shut down." She shook her head, a sob escaping her like a hiccup. "Bloody Yorkshire farmers. I *hate* them."

"Oy." To both her and Harriet's shock, their father's voice was heard through the door. Rachel looked up in surprise, wiping her face, as their dad opened her bedroom door, giving them a cautious smile. "Is this about Ben Mackey, then?"

"Dad..." Rachel shook her head slowly. She had no idea what to say.

"Listen, my girl," he said, resting one shoulder against the doorway of her bedroom. "He's a good man, Ben Mackey is. The best. And he may not say all you want him to, or the way you want him to, but I know when a man loves a woman." He tapped his temple. "I'm not that far gone, nor too much of a bloody Yorkshire farmer, to know that full well. That man loves you. And if you want him to fight for you, well, then maybe you'd better bloody well fight for him. It's a two-way street, you know."

Rachel could only gape. Relationship advice from her dad? She never, ever would have expected it.

"Dad..." she began, still having no idea what to say.

"It's advice your mother and I should have heeded," he continued gruffly, shocking her all the more. He never talked about their mother. Ever. "God knows I made my fair share of mistakes, and then some. I know it; I've always known it. I should have told her as much, I expect, but it was a two-way street. It always is."

"Except for Coppergate in York," Harriet chimed in. "That one actually is one-way."

Their father looked startled, and then he let out a wheezy laugh, like the sound of an old lawnmower suddenly gasping to life. "You're right there, lass," he said, with a look of affection for Harriet, the likes of which Rachel hadn't seen before. "You're right there."

A sudden thundering at the front door had them all blinking wide-eyed at each other.

"Well," their dad said, pushing off from the doorway. "I wonder who that'll be." He turned to the top of the stairs. "Calm tha'self down, Ben Mackey!" he shouted. "She's coming."

Chapter Twenty-Two

RACHEL OPENED THE front door with trepidation, but also with hope. She felt as if her world had been rocked several times in the space of a few minutes, and she didn't know if she could handle any more recalibrating. But she did want to see Ben…at least, she hoped she did. The fact that he was here at all seemed like a very good sign, and yet even now she felt afraid, uncertain. They'd come so far, and yet back in the barn it had felt as if they were right back at the beginning.

"Rachel." He stood on her doorstep, looking breathless, aggrieved, and determined all at once, his hands braced on his thighs as he tried to catch his breath.

"Did you run all the way here?" she asked in surprise.

"Yes, I damned well did. The way you hurtled out of the barn—I thought you'd be halfway to the motorway by now."

"I told you, I wasn't going back to London," she told him flatly, and he nodded.

"I thought maybe you would, after all, since I was such an idiot."

For a second, she thought she hadn't heard him right. "Wha…what?"

"I'm an idiot." He shook his head, regret etched on his

features. "You came into the barn, and you had such a sad look on your face—sad but stubborn, and I thought I knew what was coming, and it made me feel—well it made me feel like I was seventeen again, and just like you, that was not a great feeling." He sighed, reaching for her hands, drawing them against his chest, next to his heart. "I reacted. Badly. I'm sorry. And if you need to go back for a few days, a few weeks, to keep your job—"

"I told you, I'm not going back," Rachel replied quietly. "I want to spend these last weeks and months with my dad, with my family. And I can find another job—maybe not in Mathering, but near here. It's not…it's not the end of my career. At least, it doesn't have to be." She shook her head slowly. "It wasn't even about whether I stayed or left, Ben. It's about *us*. Can we work these things out, can we talk about them, without it being the end of us, before we've had a beginning? I was scared to come into the barn and talk to you, even to tell you I wasn't going. Because we'd agreed not to talk about the future, and I know that was my idea, but…I didn't know if I could trust us."

"You mean trust me," Ben stated quietly.

"I don't know." She sighed. "I've got emotional baggage. I know that. I'm working through it, and I have changed, but there's more to do."

"Rach, maybe we haven't been fair to you," Ben said quietly. "You're not the only one with baggage, you know? But because you left, it was easier to blame you. But we all had our…stuff. We still do."

She nodded slowly. "I know."

"People don't have to be perfect to stay together," he told

her, and there was a little wobble in his voice that made her ache.

"No," she agreed, "but they need to be able to talk about things. They need to work things out, without worrying that every discussion might be the last one. If…if they want to think about the future. If they want to face it together."

"I know that." He squeezed her hands. "I do. And that's what I want. I love you, Rachel Mowbray. I've loved you for a long time." His expression was serious, his golden-brown gaze blazing into hers. "You want to talk about childhood crushes…"

"What?" Rachel shook her head instinctively. "No."

"Why do you think I told that yob on the bus that you weren't my girlfriend?" Ben demanded. "Because I didn't want you to say it first! I was terrified you'd reject me right there on the bus, and I couldn't bear it. It's always been you, Rachel. Always. From when we were children. For as long as I can remember."

He'd intimated as much before, yesterday, but she hadn't believed him, not entirely. Looking at his intent expression, the emotion blazing out of him, she knew she did now. "Ben…" she began. "I—" Love you too. She tried to say it, but he cut across her, determined now, on a roll.

"Look, I'll say my piece and then you can take it or leave it. You deserve that much, to know how I really feel." He gave a brisk nod, his hands planted on his hips, his expression endearingly obdurate as he continued, "I love you and I'll damned well fight for you, if that's what it takes. Yes, the farm's here, I'm here, and I'll be honest, I can't really see myself in London. There aren't many sheep there, for starters."

"No," Rachel agreed with a small smile.

"But there could be other things." He raked a hand through his hair, so clearly out of his comfort zone yet still determined to stride forward, no matter how hard it was. "I don't know what that would be, not yet, but I could turn my hand to a lot of things, if I tried, I reckon. I think I'd manage in London, if I had to. If you were there. If you needed to be, for work."

Rachel's heart felt as if it had been filled to overflowing, tipped over like a jug. "Ben," she said quietly, her voice full of tenderness, "I couldn't ask you to move to London." She knew that with a bone-deep certainty; a fish out of water wouldn't even begin to cover it. "I wouldn't do that," she told him.

"You wouldn't have to," Ben replied. "I'm volunteering."

This man, Rachel thought with a thrill of wonder, a rush of love. *This man would do that for her?* "Still," she said. "I appreciate the offer, more than you can possibly know. That you would be willing... Well." She found she had to clear her throat as she smiled at him. "But I don't want to be in London anymore. My family's here; you're here. We can find other solutions. I know we can. I just wanted you to talk about it."

"Like I said, I'm an idiot." He gave her a wry smile. "There is York not too far away, and Newcastle just a bit farther. I reckon there are some finance-type jobs in those places, if you were willing. We could even...well, I could sell up here, find another place closer to a city. If that's—"

"Sell your family farm?" Rachel couldn't keep the horror

from her voice. She'd never have suggested such a thing. "No. No way."

"I'm trying here, Rach—"

"And that's all I've ever wanted." Suddenly it seemed simple, wonderfully so, and easy. The insecurity she'd felt for so long, the hurt she'd held on to, fell away in one clean swoop, just like the old wallpaper coming away from the wall, revealing something old, and yet now made new. Her true self, loved by this man. "I just wanted you to try," she whispered. "And I'll try too, and somehow, *somehow* we'll make it work. I know we will." She took a step closer to him, and then another, and then she put her arms around him, drawing him into an embrace. It really was a two-way street. Ben put his arms around her waist into a hug as she nestled closer. "I love you, Ben," she whispered. "I always have."

"We're a sorry pair, aren't we?" He shook his head ruefully and then kissed her hair, his arms tightening around her. "All these years."

"All these years," she agreed softly. "And all the years in future." As she stood there in the shelter of his arms, she realised she had no idea what that future would bring—and that was actually okay. Would she move to Mathering, find a job in York or Newcastle, do something else entirely? Would her dad be here at Christmas, in the spring? She didn't know any of it, but she realised she was looking forward to finding out because whatever happened, whatever the future held, they would face it together, her and Ben.

"That business all sorted now?" her dad asked as he stumped into the kitchen, his grumpy tone belying the wide smile on his face.

"I think it is," Rachel replied shyly, stepping back as Ben kept one arm slung around her shoulders.

"It most certainly is," Ben interjected firmly.

"Good," her dad replied. "Then any chance of getting a cuppa?"

Rachel let out a little laugh as Harriet came into the room, shooting first her a knowing smile, and then Ben, before reaching for the kettle.

"I'll do it, Dad," Harriet said, and Rachel leaned her head against Ben's shoulder, amazed at how happy she felt. So much hadn't changed, not yet—her dad still had a terminal diagnosis, her sister could still be prickly, her mother was pretty much AWOL—and yet so much *had.* They were taking steps towards the future, and that was all that mattered.

Inside her, as well as around her, change was happening. Whatever lay ahead, they would see it through together—not just her and Ben, but her and her family. And for the first time in years—decades, even—Rachel knew she was truly home.

The End

Find out what happens with Harriet and the mysterious Quinn, as well as with the Mowbrays, in the second Mowbray Sisters story,
Christmas at Embthwaite Farm!

Acknowledgements

It takes many people to bring a book to readers, and I'd like to thank everyone on the fantastic Tule team for helping bring this new series to light—especially Sinclair, my editor; Helena, my copyeditor, and Marlene, my proofreader. I'd also like to thank Meghan, Cyndi, Nikki, and Jane, who all help bring Tule books to the most readers they can. Lastly, thank you to my readers, who have read my series and recommended them to others. Without you there would be no books!

If you enjoyed *Return to Embthwaite Farm*,
you'll love the other books in the…

The Mowbray Sisters series

Book 1: *Return to Embthwaite Farm*
View the series here!

Book 2: *Christmas at Embthwaite Farm*

Book 3: *Coming soon!*

Available now at your favorite online retailer!

More books by Kate Hewitt

Keeping Up with the Penryns series

Book 1: *A Casterglass Christmas*

Book 2: *A Casterglass Garden*

Book 3: *The Casterglass Heir*

Book 4: *The Last Casterglass*

The Return to Willoughby Close series

Book 1: *Cupcakes for Christmas*

Book 2: *Welcome Me to Willoughby Close*

Book 3: *Christmas at Willoughby Close*

Book 4: *Remember Me at Willoughby Close*

The Willoughby Close series

Book 1: *A Cotswold Christmas*

Book 2: *Meet Me at Willoughby Close*

Book 3: *Find Me at Willoughby Close*

Book 4: *Kiss Me at Willoughby Close*

Book 5: *Marry Me at Willoughby Close*

The Holley Sisters of Thornthwaite series

Book 1: *A Vicarage Christmas*

Book 2: *A Vicarage Reunion*

Book 3: *A Vicarage Wedding*

Book 4: *A Vicarage Homecoming*

Available now at your favorite online retailer!

About the Author

After spending three years as a diehard New Yorker, **Kate Hewitt** now lives in the Lake District in England with her husband, their five children, and a Golden Retriever. She enjoys such novel things as long country walks and chatting with people in the street, and her children love the freedom of village life—although she often has to ring four or five people to figure out where they've gone off to.

She writes women's fiction as well as contemporary romance under the name Kate Hewitt, and whatever the genre she enjoys delivering a compelling and intensely emotional story.

Thank you for reading

Return to Embthwaite Farm

If you enjoyed this book, you can find more from all our great authors at TulePublishing.com, or from your favorite online retailer.

Made in United States
North Haven, CT
19 August 2024

56292651R00171